JESSE'S GHOST

Also by Frank Bergon

Wild Game

The Temptations of St. Ed & Brother S

The Journals of Lewis and Clark, editor

Shoshone Mike

A Sharp Lookout: Selected Nature Essays of John Burroughs, editor

The Wilderness Reader, editor

The Western Writings of Stephen Crane, editor

Looking Far West: The Search for the American West in History, Myth, and Literature, co-editor with Zeese Papanikolas

Stephen Crane's Artistry

JESSE'S GHOST

a novel

Frank Bergon

Heyday, Berkeley, California

Heyday would like to thank the James Irvine Foundation for their support of Central Valley literature.

Library of Congress Cataloging-in-Publication Data
Bergon, Frank.
Jesse's ghost : a novel / Frank Bergon.
    p. cm.
ISBN 978-1-59714-153-6 (hardcover : alk. paper)
1. Best friends--Fiction. 2. Male friendship--Fiction. 3. Triangles (Interpersonal relations)--Fiction. 4. Murder--Fiction. 5. Loss (Psychology)--Fiction. 6. Memory--Fiction. 7. Youth--California--Central Valley (Valley)--Fiction. 8. Psychological fiction. I. Title.
PS3552.E71935J47 2011
813'.54--dc22
                                2011000051

Cover Art: *One Way of Looking* by Michael Gregory
Cover Design: Lorraine Rath
Interior Design/Typesetting: Rebecca LeGates
Printing and Binding: Thomson-Shore, Dexter, MI

Orders, inquiries, and correspondence should be addressed to:
    Heyday
    P.O. Box 9145, Berkeley, CA 94709
    (510) 549-3564, Fax (510) 549-1889
    www.heydaybooks.com

10 9 8 7 6 5 4 3 2 1

For Frank April and Joe Claassen,
valley boys and fellow begetters of this story

You been down to the bottom with a bad man, babe,
But you're back where you belong.
Go get me my pistol, babe.
Honey, I can't tell right from wrong.

—Bob Dylan, "Baby, Stop Crying"

CONTENTS

I

HARDPAN KID

The story of how I came to kill my best friend keeps pressing on my brain like a dream so bad I can feel it, but I can't remember it whole. In bed at night when I can't sleep—just about every night anymore—bits of my life buzz and clatter in my skull. "I will haunt you when I'm dead," my mother told me all the time when I was a kid, yet the person who haunts me now is the friend I loved more than my momma or my daddy or even my own brother. His name was Jesse Floyd.

I guess I became Jesse's friend one day on a California playground in the sixth grade when a tough pachuco—an eighth-grader named Ray Castaneda—said he was going to beat the crap out of me. Ray stared at me with eyes like dull aggies. Killer eyes. Behind him the spring sun turned the edges of his hair into a kind of halo. Two of his pals stood near him on the dry Bermuda grass, the tops of their shirts unbuttoned, hands in their pockets. I knew they would join Ray in pounding me. I didn't know what I'd done. I hadn't done anything. I was just a guy to beat up. They would wait until after school for the fun to start.

Jesse must've got wind of Ray's threat because after school he said, "I'll walk home with you." He didn't have to do that—we hardly knew each other—but he was good-hearted that way, always was.

Outside the schoolyard, when Ray saw us he stiffened. His buddies looked surprised, too. Jesse wasn't big then, he hadn't filled out yet. He was no taller than me, kind of scrawny, but already he was known to be picking fights with high school kids and whipping them. He was scrappy and fast.

He walked up to Ray and said, "You got a beef with Sonny?" My real name's Wade, same as my dad's, so I was called Sonny.

I knew Ray wouldn't back down all the way. "I ain't looking for trouble 'less you are," he said. "We're just going home."

Jesse's face broke into a big smile. "Broke" is the best word because it was like daybreak when Jesse smiled. Most people just smile with their mouths, but Jesse's baby blue eyes, high cheek-bones, and smooth skin took on a glow so you knew his heart was smiling, too. The girls all talked about Jesse's great smile.

"That's good," he told Ray, "'cause we are, too. Let's go, Sonny."

He touched my arm and we started to turn away. Ray's shoulders untightened, his face slackened with relief, and just then Jesse whirled around and slammed his fist square into Ray's nose. It was like the move I'd seen a sideshow magician make at the county fair when I caught him gesture into the air with one hand to draw everyone's eyes away from the other doing a quick, one-handed card switch. Ray hit the ground on his butt. He pivoted sideways onto his hands and knees to get up, but the toe of Jesse's shoe kicked him hard under the jaw. With a howl Ray flopped facedown in the dirt, his hands cradling his head. His buddies stood still as two trees.

Jesse gave me a push on the small of my back. We started to walk away, but fearing Ray and his cohorts might run up behind us, I turned to glance over my shoulder.

"Don't look back," Jesse said. "Keep walking."

That's pretty much what my wife tells me these days: *Put the past behind you. It's time to move on. Keep walking.*

If I've had another chance in this thing called life, it's because of Lynette. We've been together now sixteen years, the second marriage for us both. We each have a daughter from our first, plus one of our own named Trisha. The house can become tense on holidays if the timing's not right and I'm cooped up with four females on the rag, but I've learned to bite my tongue. In bed at night with Lynette's wide hips spreading warmth through the mattress, I think how far we've come since we were two valley kids growing up in the shamble of shacks called Little Oklahoma. We live in the foothill gold country now, up the road from the Coarsegold casino in an Indian Lakes Estates home a lot nicer than the houses of those ranchers our dads used to work for. We have a garden, two dogs, an extra-wide garage, and a fence to keep the deer out. It was Lynette's idea to move into higher country, to leave Jesse and the past down below us in the valley fog.

Lynette commutes forty-five minutes to Fresno County Hospital, where she works as a nurse, and I'm on the road a lot for the Madera Irrigation District, or I was until seven months ago. Now I'm on disability from the MID, but that will pass. Neither of us has lived anywhere for long except right here in the heart of California. I was in the army at Fort Ord and Camp Roberts and later in Folsom State Prison, yet even then I was in California.

People say there are two kinds of women: those you love and those you marry. But that's not true for me. I love Lynette and I loved Sonia.

"How can you love me if you don't know me?" That was another favorite line of my mother's when she was drunk. Maybe what she said, now that I think of it, makes a point about me

and Sonia. The problem was Sonia never stopped loving Jesse,
something I knew but didn't really know until it was too late.
Sonia was red-haired, quick, and foxy where Lynette is blonde,
curvy, and steady. We all knew each other in high school, but
Lynette didn't really run with us except for dances at Bass Lake
or in the gym. Her parents wouldn't let her, since she was a
couple years younger. They'd sent her to grammar school at St.
Joachim's to keep her away from Okie riffraff like me, though
there was plenty of riffraff there, too. Lynette's folks were as Okie
as they come; they just acted like they weren't because they were
from Texas. Same as Jesse. He was born in Texas, grew up in the
valley, pure Okie.

Some people think I became a Catholic because of Lynette,
but it was really the priest I met when doing my time. I had to
become something. I couldn't live alone with what I'd done. This
priest—Father Dan—grew up in Coalinga, where his daddy
worked in the oil fields, so we had a valley connection. His
weathered face carried that sad, tired look you see in oil-field
workers as he showed me the direct line stretching from the
Church today all the way back to when Jesus told Simon Peter,
"You are the rock upon which I will build my church." Sure,
it's full of failings, but that's the whole point. The Blood of the
Lamb doesn't just wash everything away, how other churches say.
Even Peter betrayed his best friend, denied he ever knew him in
the Garden of Agony, and did nothing to stop the Romans from
killing him. Jesus forgave him, but Peter suffered for it all the
rest of his life.

The thing that got me going thinking a lot about Jesse happened last November, when Mitch Etcheverry showed up on
a Saturday afternoon. It'd been maybe twenty years since I'd
seen him. His dad was a Basco rancher me and Jesse worked for
southwest of Madera. Mitch got sent away to boarding school in
the Bay Area, but he hung around with us some weekends and

during summers, and then for a time he was even Jesse's brother-in-law, at least legally, though nobody thought of the two of them that way. He's now a big-shot newspaperman in San Francisco and called out of the blue to say he wanted to talk to me about the old days and Jesse. He wanted to write a book, he said, but first he had to write an article to get the facts straight. There were a lot of things he didn't know.

As soon as Mitch showed up and we popped a couple of beers, Lynette looked worried. She'd known Mitch since grammar school and warned me not to get into the booze with him. A tall, gawky guy with thick black eyebrows and a long nose, he was a pretty good tennis player in school and always a joker. Jesse liked him for that. They used to tease each other. Mitch still looked in good shape for being such a lush back then. Probably still is, I thought. It's funny how after a few minutes with him the years fell away from his face and he was a kid again.

"You look good," I told him.

"That's because I took care of myself when I was young. Not like you guys."

"Tell me about it, tell me about it," I said. "Drink your ass off and chase pussy."

Lynette came out of the bedroom wearing tight black slacks and a snug turtleneck. She said she was taking Trisha shopping in Fresno. Trisha gave me a surly look. She's that age, fifteen. Blonde like Lynette, with her hair cut short around her ears and spiky in the back, she wore hip-hugger jeans so low a little tug would drop them to the floor. A short tank top showed off her bellybutton. She's going to be stacked like Lynette. Already her high, perky chest swooped up the way Lynette's did in the pink angora sweater she wore in high school that got her the nickname "Ski Jumps." Truth told, Jesse named her that. He had a way with words, Jesse did.

"Today is Sonny's birthday," Lynette told Mitch. I wouldn't have said nothing.

"That's great," Mitch said. "I'll take you down to the Basque Hotel for dinner."

"They have a good buffet here at the casino," I said. "All you can eat."

"You boys go where you want," Lynette said. "Don't wait on us."

She pecked me on the cheek, and Mitch checked her out as she went through the door. Lynette can still turn heads when she goes clicking across the floor, especially in high heels. She's put on a few pounds since we were married, but when we go into a restaurant with her wearing a low-cut dress that dips lower when she sits down, the hemline riding up her thighs as she crosses her legs, men's eyes—and women's, too—slide in our direction, and I'm a proud husband, not just because everything about her says she's luscious, which she is, but because the way she carries herself says she's got a heart that's alive and bright. That's what makes her such a good nurse. She's so naturally herself in a no-nonsense way you feel a duty to get better, to be a little more like her, healthy and at attention. It's what makes me not want to let her down, and why I'm miserable every time I do. Like the fling I had awhile back with her brother-in-law's sister. Or last week when she climbed all over me for not going to see about my job at the MID the way I said I would.

After the girls drove away, Mitch and I drank beers and swapped stories about Jesse. I could never beat Jesse in a fight. I could outbox him, I could outwrestle him, but I couldn't out-fight him—I'd tried three times. One summer night, though, after our sophomore year, I saw my chance to finally get the best of him. We were cruising around town, driving real slow looking for girls, with me riding shotgun, Mitch in the back-seat, and Jesse at the wheel. We passed around a gallon of rotgut port sweetened with a package of Kool-Aid powder so we could stomach it. While Jesse and Mitch worked to drain the jug, I waited my time, tipping up the bottle and faking it, blowing bubbles when it came my turn. You can't really fight when you're drunk—you think you can, but you can't—and I wanted to be ready. I watched the wine go way down until only about an inch was left. "Heat Wave" was playing on the radio, and Jesse started singing along, bopping his head and tapping the steering wheel as we crept down the street. *"Somethin' inside starts burnin'…fills me with desire…burnin' my heart…Heat Waaaaave,"* he yowled. Right then I slugged him hard, catching him good under the ear.

The car braked so quick I got thrown against the dashboard before I could get off another shot. Then Jesse was out the door and coming around the back under the streetlight, where I jumped to meet him. We both started swinging right there in the street. I was holding my own when all of a sudden Mitch pushed between us, shouting, "Hey, you guys are friends!" just as Jesse's fist, coming at me, caught Mitch in the throat. Mitch fell to the street, hitting his head on the bumper on the way down, and his whole body started jerking like an epileptic's. Jesse and I knelt beside him. Mitch's eyes rolled up, his jaw locked tight, and his lips pulled away from his teeth. Spit dribbled down his chin, and his legs twitched. I thought we'd killed the sorry son of a bitch. Jesse held Mitch's shaking head in his hands so it wouldn't bang on the asphalt.

"Mitch," Jesse said, "listen to me. Your momma ain't going to like you laying out here on the ground. You hear?" Pretty soon Mitch calmed down, and his eyes slid back into place. "You feeling all right?" Jesse asked. "You okay?" A line of blood wormed from Mitch's nose to his upper lip. Jesse wiped it away.

Mitch sort of smiled. "Yeah," he said, "I'm fine."

I felt his clammy face, his nose as cold as a witch's tit. We helped him into the car and drove him home.

That was the last time Jesse and I got into it. From then on I fought alongside him or watched him fight. Some guys kicked better, others punched harder, but nobody put it all together like Jesse. When it came to the art of war, he was the master. He knew how to get his mind into a fight before it started so he was ready to explode with all the force he could muster to get things over quick. Nine times out of ten he got in the first punch—or kick—and that made the difference.

One night, the three of us—Mitch, Jesse, and myself—sat at a Formica table in Mary's Café. It must've been fall or early winter because we were wearing jackets. I can't remember where we'd been—maybe a party or just dragging main—but like other Saturday nights when we didn't end up with girls, we were eating breakfast around two or three in the morning in the bright lights of the café. Those lights helped sober you up as much as the coffee.

It took me a while to catch what was going on between Jesse and this guy at the counter, I was so busy chowing down on my fried eggs (over easy), link sausages, and buttered pancakes with maple syrup poured over everything, the way I liked back then. Funny the things you remember. I cut a sausage with the edge of my fork, and grease shot like spit across the table onto Jesse's shirt, but when I looked up I saw he wasn't paying any attention. He was staring at this stranger who was halfway turned around on the faded-red, backless counter stool, glaring at Jesse. That moment gave me a lesson in eye contact like nothing I'd seen before—what the eyes can say between two guys without saying a word.

Pretty soon this guy spun around on the plastic-topped stool and walked over to our table. He didn't seem to know Jesse from anybody, just like we didn't know him. He was a good-sized guy, a little older than us—a truck driver from Stockton, we later learned—in black Frisco jeans and a leather jacket. His

hair was winged back at the sides with comb marks plastered
stiff with Dixie Peach. You could tell from his face he'd been in
some fights.

He said to Jesse, "Do you want to go out back and square this
away or what?"

Jesse just looked at him with his pretty blue eyes all wide and
replied as polite as could be, "Well, yeah, if you'd like to."

Now, to most guys itching for a fight, that sort of courtesy
is jaw-dropping, and that's what happened to this guy's jaw.
He looked like he was trying to think of something to say in
response when Jesse gave him a smile and started reciting one
of his taunting poems. Maybe he got the idea from Muhammad Ali—or Cassius Clay, as he was known back then—but I
think Jesse was making up these poems before any of us really
knew about Ali. This stranger in his worn leather jacket just
stood there with his mouth in danger of catching flies while Jesse
recited at him:

I'm big and bad
And I won't be had.
My ass is all red,
My nose is all snotty.
If you don't know
Who you're messin' with,
You better ask somebody
'Cause you ain't gonna avoid
The kid is Jesse Floyd.

The guy looked irritated as hell at Jesse speaking poetry to
him. He jerked his head in the direction of the back door, and
we followed him out by the garbage cans. Coming from the
bright café to the dark outside is always a shock, but that night
it was foggy and the lights from the street made things stand out

in a weird haze. Outside, we saw this guy was maybe six inches taller than Jesse, with legs like tree trunks. He started to take off his leather jacket and got it just halfway down his arms—about down to his elbows—when Jesse smashed him in the face with his fist, and just like that, after one punch, the fight was over.

"That guy was stupid," Mitch said.

"He wasn't from around here," I said.

"Even so. He was as dumb as they come."

Mitch actually saw Jesse fight bigger, much older guys before I did. Mitch was a country boy who went to St. Joachim's in town and had permission to take a high school bus home since the parochial school had none. He and his friends who lived on ranches and farms walked over from St. Joachim's and waited on the lawn near the Coyote Den malt shop until the buses were ready to go. He saw this thirteen-year-old boy who came to the malt shop and called down high school boys. Jesse Floyd was his name.

"The thing that impressed me about Jesse the first time I saw him fight," Mitch said, "was his balance. He was there bouncing on one foot, kicking with the other, and throwing blows with both hands at the same time. He was whipping this high school kid, a known bully and way bigger than Jesse, but you could see the guy was scared."

"Bullies always are," I said. "Not Jesse. He never shied away from a fight, and he always took on the toughest kids. He told me once to always go for the biggest guy because then if you got whipped you had an excuse. He didn't brag about the fights he won neither."

"I never heard Jesse make an achievement out of fighting," Mitch said.

Jesse grew up getting whipped by his older brother, just like me. We had that in common and was part of the reason we'd come to be friends. Our brothers both beat the hell out of us until we got to where we could whip them. Our dads—my real dad, not Dewey, my stepdad—beat the hell out of all of us, and our mommas did, too, until we got too big. "I could've strangled you when you were born," my momma told me when I acted up. She had a point.

Me and my brother usually put on the gloves, but with Jesse and his brother the rules went out the window. Their fights came close to being lethal. Jesse once grabbed a lawn sprinkler—the kind that whirls around—and whacked his brother in the head to within an inch of his life. He was making up for all those times his brother beat the shit out of him. Another time, Jesse stabbed his brother deep in the back with a sharp-pointed school compass.

One famous battle took place out at Mitch's ranch. Jesse straddled his brother on the ground and was trying to poke out his eyes, until his brother's teeth clamped down on his finger. They both got to their feet, with Jesse trying to jerk his mangled finger out of his brother's mouth, but his brother kept biting down, Jesse squealing like a pig under a gate. We pulled them apart, and Jesse ran into the house. By the time he returned with a butcher knife from the kitchen, we'd pushed his brother into a car and got him off the ranch.

Jesse lost his share of fights back when he was still learning, but the thing about him was how much he hated to lose. Even when some guy was getting the best of him, he kept coming on until the other guy finally said fuck it. It wasn't worth putting up with Jesse's stubbornness. He just had to win. That's why he wouldn't box in the annual high school Punch Bowl. The best high school boxer at Jesse's weight was Baby Gallegos, and in the ring Baby would've handed Jesse's ass to him. Like one time in the high school gym a coach put gloves on me and Jesse and told us that whoever stayed inside the big circled M on the floor would win. My stepdaddy had taught my brother and myself how to box, so I would shoot a jab and then dance to safety outside the circle before Jesse could counterpunch. Then I'd skip back into the circle and pop him again. Pretty soon I had his nose bleeding, but he wouldn't come out of the circle. He would do anything to win. He thought he was winning by staying in the circle and getting hit. Afterward, though, he told everyone I got the best of him that day. My stepdaddy said, "It don't matter who wins. Quitters are the only losers."

Mitch finished a beer and crumpled the can. "Well," he said to me, "are you getting hungry?"

It was only five o'clock, but being November it was getting dark. We took my truck down to the casino. They hadn't put in a back entrance the way they said they were going to do, so we had to drive to Highway 41 and go in the front entrance.

"Listen," I said, "let me buy dinner."

"This is on me," Mitch insisted. "How'd that song go? *'Happy, happy birthday, baby.'*"

Usually I ate at the buffet—I like to see the food first—but Mitch wanted to go into the steakhouse, where he ordered a twenty-four-ounce Porterhouse, rare. He talked to the waiter about what he meant by rare—cool red center.

"That's what you'll get, sir," the waiter said.

"They won't get it right," Mitch said when the waiter left, and sure enough when it came it was grayish pink and Mitch sent it back. "Now they'll send it out raw," he said, and they did, but Mitch said it was fine that way.

I ordered the smallest filet and a big side order of roasted vegetables. I don't eat meat much anymore. Lynette got me onto thinking about health, and every day in the morning I eat a bowl of her homemade granola with skim milk. From working in hospitals all her life, first as a nurse and now an administrator, Lynette knows about health but she also knows about life and death and what makes people tick to a degree that others don't. One of her favorite sayings is "There's no accounting for people," and that's exactly what I thought—*there's no accounting for people*—when Mitch said he didn't want another beer or wine or anything alcoholic. He ordered seltzer water with Angostura bitters.

"I pretty much quit drinking," he said. "Except for a beer now and then, I've had it."

"Now, don't tell me you quit chasing pussy, too."

"I'm done," Mitch said. "Two divorces are enough. I went to the vet and had myself castrated."

"There's no accounting for people," I said.

We looked at each other, and I wondered if he was thinking what I was. Then I said it: "If Jesse had hisself castrated, he'd be sitting with us today."

Mitch nodded. "I keep my balls in a jar of alcohol up on the mantel to remind me. Those troubles are over."

"No bad habits," I said. "It's hard to believe."

"It's true," Mitch said. "But I will take a dip of your snoose."

"I'll give you a whole can when we get home."

"I don't need a whole tin. I don't want to get started again."

"I suppose you got religion, too."

"Unfortunately, I quit believing in magic long ago."

Back at the house, Trisha and Lynette still weren't home. Over the last couple months since being off work, I was getting used to the two of them leaving me alone at nights. I opened the freezer in the garage—it's a big two-door standup against the wall—and I could tell Mitch was impressed, though he didn't let on. "This here's how an Okie makes ice," I told him, proudlike. I've got a big block in a wooden case I made. "The stuff you get over to the ice house ain't worth squat anymore. Too much air in it or something. One of my blocks will last me a week on a hunting trip." I pulled a log of Copenhagen out of the freezer and gave a tin to Mitch. "Keep the whole thing," I said. "I got plenty."

"You got a Dixie cup?"

"Ah, man," I told him, "gut it. Don't waste that nicotine."

"Can't," he said. "Not anymore." He poured his beer into a glass and used the empty beer can for a spittoon.

I use so little dip anymore I just swallow it. One tin will last me a week. I've got it down to a pinch at a time, but it's pretty much in there all day. I just can't yet move to nothing.

We went back into the house and sat at the kitchen table. I watched Mitch load up so his lip jutted out like a golf ball, the way we used to dip when we were kids on his daddy's ranch. A tin hardly lasted each of us a day back then, but they've done something to the tobacco in recent years so it doesn't have the kick anymore. Back then on those hot summer days we'd keep our tins moist with a little brandy and stay high all day. I looked at Mitch and thought of the time his father had me and Mitch and Jesse clearing hardpan from a ranch he'd just bought. That was tough work. A Cat with a ripper turned up big slabs of hardpan from the earth, and we followed behind, loading the yellow hardpan stone onto a wagon pulled by a tractor. None of us wore shirts, and our skin was brown as dirt. The July sun scorched the sky. Some of the slabs of hardpan were so heavy it took two of us, and sometimes all three of us, to lift them. I remember Jesse at one point smiling in the fierce sunshine, his gums ridged with black snuff, his sweaty face and chest so wet it turned the dirt on his skin to mud. "I just love loading this hardpan," he said. "I'm just a hardpan-loading fool." With that big grin of his, he looked genuinely happy to be working so hard. "Whooey," he said, "we're just hardpan boys. I'm the Hardpan Kid."

Mitch now put his notebook and tape recorder on the kitchen table, and I knew it was coming, what he asked next. "Tell me about how things soured between you and Jesse."

My brain seized up like an engine drained of oil. That's the only way I can describe it. I felt my mind tighten, grind down, and quit working. I didn't want to talk anymore. We were having such a good time remembering our glory days. Now I felt kind of sick. I looked at Mitch and didn't see him as a kid anymore but as someone older, with wrinkles and gray hairs, and I thought: *He's now as old as his father was back then. We both are. We aren't the same people we were.* That was all I could think, and I told Mitch, "You sure look like your daddy."

Mitch's hand jerked when he brought the beer can to his mouth, and some brown spit dribbled down his chin. He wiped it away with the back of his hand. I knew he was annoyed with me, though his voice didn't sound it when he told me, "Lynette says it's a big drag the way you keep everything bottled up."

My face felt like dead fish skin and my brain tightened up even more, the way it does when I feel ganged up on and don't want to talk. Black specks started wobbling like gnats in the air in front of Mitch's face. I remembered that I forgot to take my shot before we went to eat. "Maybe you should just talk to Lynette," I said, feeling a little heated, "since that's what you've already been doing. She knows everything."

"Don't get the wrong idea," Mitch said. "When I called—to get hold of you—she just said it would be hard to get you to talk. I've known Lynette a long time, Sonny."

They went to parochial school together. They even dated a little bit. "I guess we were all fucking each other back then," I said.

"I didn't say that. I'm just saying that people talk about these things. You jabber like a magpie about everything else. Why not Jesse? You've got to think about these things."

"I do think about things." My face felt sweaty now. "Some things. And some things I don't. I think about you a lot, Mitch. You and your daddy and the days we were all on the ranch. If your daddy hadn't sold that ranch we might all still be on it." I meant me, my brother, my momma, and my stepdad, Dewey—we all lived on the ranch when we were working for Mitch's dad.

Maybe even Jesse might be there, too, alive and working, if that ranch hadn't gone under.

Mitch looked down at his glass of beer like he was seeing something from the past. I sensed I was making my point. He didn't want to talk about his daddy losing the ranch any more than I wanted to talk about Jesse. He looked up at me and said, "Back then"—he stopped like he was looking for the words— "that last summer especially—it's true—we were like family back then."

What he said is something I've felt, too. What he didn't say is how he started out living in a nice house on a thousand acres that his granddaddy built up from scratch while we still lived on the outskirts of town in a big canvas tent with a rough-plank floor. My stepdad, Dewey, got us all moved from place to place and finally onto the ranch into a real house, and though it wasn't much when you look at how I'm living today, back then we didn't think that. When I stepped through the door of our new house onto a hard floor covered with shiny speckled linoleum, I felt rich. It was Dewey who done it—married my momma and got us all out of Oklahoma.

"I still remember the day your daddy first took me down into your basement," I told Mitch, "with that cement floor and big freezer. He made me feel I wasn't out of place being there." Mitch knew how much we all liked his daddy. I have to say it: he was the best man I ever worked for, even though I would never have what I do today if I'd stayed working for him. "When your daddy told all of us by the barn, 'Boys, I have to sell the ranch for inheritance taxes,' I was pre-irrigating that day. I set my water for the night, went to the winery, and had a new job by evening. That just ain't right, to have to lose a ranch that way. I didn't want to leave, working for your daddy, even though at the winery I had extra money and more time than I knew what to do with. Not working on weekends left me so squirrelly I took on welding jobs to fill the hours on Saturday and Sunday. I even helped Jesse pumping honey."

"That was just the reason he gave," Mitch said about his dad losing the ranch. "It wasn't the real reason." The way his voice faded out made that part of our conversation hit a dead end.

I remember how Mitch came to see me after I got out of the hole and was living alone in an apartment in Fresno. He was bitter about his daddy's boozing and getting himself in debt—well, maybe not bitter so much as hurt at his daddy selling the ranch and then blowing what little money was left, leaving him and his sister nothing. He had to feel kind of betrayed, but at the same time, he knew he didn't want to be a farmer even if he'd inherited the ranch, so I think he got himself caught between what he wasn't and what he didn't want to be. That's why I believe he took on a hangdog look, like he'd betrayed something of his own self. Sometimes it's better just to let the past be the past, especially the bad parts.

"Let's have another," I said, but when I stood up to get more beers from the fridge, I felt dizzy again from a sharp back spasm. I stood there for a minute and grabbed the edge of the table to keep my balance.

"You look in pain," Mitch said.

"I am," I said. "I hurt constantly." The spasm passed but not the ache. I shouldn't stay sitting so long. If I stand every once in a while it frustrates the spasms. "My back has been fused. I've got plastic bones in my feet and toes—they give out from walking all night on that cement floor in the winery. Wouldn't have happened on natural ground in the fields. I've learned to live with pain. Here, look." I stretched out both hands toward Mitch. "Try to bend these wrists. Try it. As hard as you can."

"I don't want to break them."

"You can't break those cocksuckers. Bend them."

Mitch grabbed my pinned right hand and tried to jerk it down, but it didn't give. "They're stiff as crowbars," he said.

"Broke both," I said. "I was carrying a split case of wine, holding it together while trying to get out of the way of a forklift, and I fell. Crushed my vertebrae on the cement with that case on my chest, then this drunk motherfucker on the forklift drove over my wrists." That was after I got out of the clink. We were drunk out there every night. The bosses knew, and also knew we helped ourselves to cases to take home. They couldn't stop it but they didn't want it to get out of hand. "We know," the foreman told us, "that workers in a candy factory snitch candy. Just don't cross the line."

"Looks like you don't have wrists," Mitch said. "Your hands are just stuck onto your forearms."

"They're locked up," I said. "Wouldn't bend in a vice grip. This one"—I showed him my right wrist—"is straight as a board." Then I held out my left hand, bent at the wrist, curving inward. "The doc cocked this one so I can wipe my ass."

Bad as these things sound, I don't see them that way. Breaking my spine and wrists got me into the hospital, where Lynette found me and turned my life around. She never would've dated me ordinarily, I don't believe, but we got to talking in the hospital and something sparked between us. She was coming off a divorce herself. Some people think she felt sorry for me and I was just someone she could nurse, but I think it's more than that. Father Dan told me grace works that way: it strikes like lightning, but you have to be ready. That's how Father Dan talked, straight to the point.

The first time my wrists got broke, nine years earlier, I wasn't ready. I was drinking back then, too, my marriage with Sonia was on the rocks, and I was heading for a showdown with Jesse. It was Saturday night in Skeeko's—same place Dewey got in his big fight because of a woman years before. I was getting it on with this red-headed flirt next to me at the bar—I'd just lit her cigarette and she laid her hand on my thigh and I started playing with her ass—when this drunk on the other side of her— he'd also been trying to make her—leaned over and said to me, "Keep your cotton-pickin' hands to yourself."

I pushed my face close to his. "You're the one who's going to be picking cotton," I told him, "right out of your cotton-pickin' asshole, you fucking cotton picker."

We both swung off our stools when the barkeep said to me, as if I was the one who started things, "Take it outside, Sonny."

In the parking lot, we squared off, when two of this guy's buddies jumped into it. Even Jesse couldn't whip three guys—not usually, anyway—though he'd had to try sometimes when his reputation got him into those scrapes. They knocked me down, drug me across the asphalt, and hooked my hands over the back bumper of a pickup. The first guy stomped his boot onto my right wrist until it broke and then stomped on my left wrist until it broke, too. They left me there with my busted wrists hanging on the bumper.

When the casts came off, I waited a month, doing wrist curls with dumbbells at the Parkwood gym and at home until I felt strong again. It took me another two months before I caught up with those fuckers. One at a time, I found them until I finally got all three, catching the last one—the guy who started it all—out at the Fresno Barn, where Merle Haggard played before he got famous, and I hooked that son of a bitch's hands onto a bumper and busted his wrists the same way he done mine. It wasn't long after that that Jesse and I got into it. No grace saved me then.

It was like my wrists had to get broke a second time in the winery to give me a second chance with Lynette. That's when I quit the heavy drinking, went to Mass every Sunday, started to eat right, had our daughter Trisha, moved to the hills, got the job with the MID, and walked the straight and narrow for the last sixteen years until this low blood pressure and diabetes knocked me out of commission. The doctor said, "I don't know how you're even walking." Father Dan wrote me a note then: "Life with no strife is no life. If you're not struggling you're dead."

I have to believe some good—some grace—will come from this hardship, too.

Mitch watched me as I gave myself a shot in the stomach. I knew he wouldn't have any truck with what I had to say about grace.

"I'm supposed to change the needle every time," I told him, "but I use the same one till it gets dull." I pulled up my shirt, pinched some stomach fat into a tube between my fingers, jabbed in the needle, and pushed down the plunger with my thumb. "I usually get three or four shots this way."

"How long have you been laid off?" Mitch wanted to know.

"I'm not laid off," I said. "I'm on disability, seven months now. I'm itching to get back to work. I went down to Home Depot to see about part-time, but I think I put myself out of a hire when I wrote down how much money I wanted to make. I never heard back. Just sitting around the house makes you feel kind of useless."

"You got plenty of time to pick up snatch," Mitch said.

"I don't chase strange stuff no more. I'm like you. Besides, for a while I couldn't even bend over to tie my shoes. Lynette had to."

"She had to fuck you, too, I'm sure."

I shook my head no. "These shots kill your sex drive. The doc gave me Viagra, but I don't use it."

"I sure as hell would use it," Mitch said.

"You said you were done with all that."

"I'm talking about if I were you. If the pills work, what difference does it make?"

"It makes a lot of difference. You got to think ahead, 'Oh, I'm going to get laid in an hour,' but you don't think it because you don't feel any urge. There's no spontaneity. It don't matter. Since Lynette had her menopause, she don't care." I realized I was talking too much and warned him, "Now, don't go telling Lynette, 'I hear you can't get it on with Sonny.' She would kill me."

"You got your share. You had all those years Jesse never had."

"Nobody gets enough, not ever. Except maybe Jesse. No way to catch up to that cunt hound."

Even when we were little kids, girls flitted around Jesse the way hummingbirds swirl around a bowl of sugar water. He had those bright eyes even then, fixed on you when talking, and that smile everyone liked to see. His shirts and pants were always ironed because that's how we were raised as kids. We didn't have good clothes, but we had clean clothes. We were like brothers in those days, and our seventh-grade teacher, Mrs. Short, said, "I don't know what I'm going to do with you two. You both cut up in class the same way, you copy each other's homework, you wear the same clothes, and you like the same girl."

I was sweet on a Mexican gal named Yolanda who kept showing off the prettiest soft thighs under her skirt, but just when I thought I was doing pretty good with her, what do I see one day out behind the backstop but her with her skirt hiked up and Jesse with his hand up between those sweet thighs. It was like seeing a car wreck. That's how I felt. And it wasn't the last time.

"He was a magnet for the girls," Mitch said, "no doubt about it."

I felt suspicious of how Mitch was talking about Jesse considering how mad he was when Jesse ran off with his sister. I wasn't sure what Mitch knew about Ana and me. I thought maybe he was just saying these things to needle me into spilling the beans, but I went along with him. "Everyone liked Jesse," I said. "Adults, colored people, girls—everyone. I liked him, too."

"We all did," Mitch said. "That's the problem: we all wanted to like him."

Jesse had friends all over town, and in the country, too, from Mex Town to Dixieland to Little Oklahoma. One buddy of his was Wilbur Flowers, the black hurdler on the track team. Another was Hank Palacios, the football player and wrestler. One day Jesse would be over at Wilbur's house eating black-eyed peas and ham hocks, the next he'd be at Hank's eating tamales.

"You know how your aunt was with Jesse," I told Mitch. "He was the kind of guy adults liked to help. He could make them laugh."

Mitch's aunt was our junior-year English teacher. We picked up words from her like "aggrieved" and "perplexed" and "disconcerted" and teased each other with them, saying things like, "I'm perplexed that you're so aggrieved, Jesse." Mitch's aunt favored Jesse. She let him off the hook when he clowned around in class and kept him after school to help him with his work. He wasn't much of a student, but he knew when to cut the joking and be serious, whether he was listening to the football coach tell us the game plan or Mitch's aunt talking about poets. Earnest, I guess you'd call it. Mitch's dad sat him down one morning before we started work, gave him a potato omelet, and tried to get him to think about not getting into so much trouble, but Jesse told him, "Sometimes I just gotta fight, boss. I don't know why, I just gotta fight."

"He held his own, he kept his word, and he always got the girl," Mitch said. "If he wasn't busting you in the face, he was fun to be with."

"That's what made him a hero," I said.

Mitch snapped back, surprising me. "Jesse was no hero. He was a punk."

I heard myself protesting, "If you want to think Jesse was a punk, you can probably find plenty of evidence, but Jesse Floyd was no punk."

"He fucked you up good, Sonny. He didn't care about you.
He crossed the line."

"He crossed the line, all right. More than once." I knew
Mitch was trying to trick me into talking, but I tricked him into
remembering the time we both saw Jesse go berserk. It happened
the second time he fought Ray Castaneda. That's when Jesse
came into his own. Up to then, he was just another tough Okie
kid, but the second fight with Ray lifted his legend in the valley.

After their first fight in grammar school over me, Ray went on
to become a good high school baseball player. He was a switch
hitter and so strong he could power a ball out of the park even
when he swung late. He was also a mean son of a bitch, not just
tough but mean as a nursing sow. I guess he was kind of like the
baseball player Ty Cobb that way. He had some fights where he
beat guys up pretty bad. Nobody wanted to mess with Ray.

The second fight between Jesse and Ray took place at night
in the parking lot of the Safeway. It was summer. Something
like fifteen of us showed up to watch. We didn't know what was
going to happen. You couldn't judge the outcome by a long-ago
elementary school fight. Jesse and I had just finished our sophomore year, but Ray had already graduated and looked more
mature, more confident than Jesse. Ray was a grownup guy, out
in the world, working, while Jesse was still just a high school kid.

As I drove into the parking lot behind the grocery store, Jesse
drummed his fingers on the dashboard. I knew his mind was
working. Ray leaned against the fender of his raked maroon
Merc coupe, waiting, along with some of his buddies. I had no
sooner parked than Jesse burst out the door and was all over
Ray like stink on shit, throwing blows from every angle you can
imagine. I don't think Ray landed a shot. Then Jesse stepped
back and looked at his arm. He stood in the dark parking lot
in a cone of light. He was wearing a white T-shirt. A slick gash
reddened his bicep. Blood smeared down his arm. Ray crouched

in front of him with a straight razor in his hand. None of us could believe that Ray had actually pulled a razor in a fistfight. Jesse looked at Ray in disbelief, then down at his bleeding arm as though trying to comprehend something beyond comprehension, then back at Ray, who showed he'd crossed a line because he just hovered there, with his arm extended, the razor aglint in the lights of the market's back lot.

What happened next took about four seconds. Jesse lunged forward, charging directly at Ray and the straight razor. Ray tried to swing the razor again, and I think if Jesse would've hesitated for a second, if he hadn't charged forward like a linebacker making a goal-line stand, Ray would've cut him to the guts, but Jesse crashed into Ray and smothered the swing by grabbing the wrist of the hand holding the razor while his fist whacked Ray's face like a piston flying through a broken crankcase. Somehow the razor got flung to the asphalt. I ran over and grabbed it. When I turned around, Ray was down, with Jesse on top walloping the hell out of him.

Usually at this point in a fight Jesse would pull back. But not this time. He was bent on getting Ray. I can say this: I never seen Jesse so ferocious in the way his fists flew. He hurt Ray pretty bad. I can still hear those thuds against Ray's head. I felt scared, looking at Ray take that beating, and I grabbed Jesse's shoulders and with some of the other guys we pulled him off. He was ready to fight us, too, but we got him hobbled up till he calmed down.

Mitch sounded a little like he was talking to himself as he changed his tune. "I guess if you take the fights out of the equation, and what he did to you, he really was the All-American Boy. He had those crystal clear blue eyes, a great smile, he was a hard worker and a loyal friend. I liked him, too, at one time."

He also drank more milk than you can imagine. He even mixed powdered milk into a glass of regular to make it thicker.

Some girl actually wrote into Jesse's high school yearbook: "To the All-American Kid, Sweet & True."

Girls knew the buzz about Jesse, but nearly none saw him fight. They saw him in school or up at Bass Lake or at parties or dragging main. It was like he lived two lives, one with the guys and one with the girls. Like I said, he wasn't a show-off or a bragger. Of course, the way guys treated him in high school, wanting him to lift his chin in their direction or smile at them in the hall like they were his buddies, showed the girls there was something dangerous about him that other guys respected—and I suppose that was sexy—but because he was always laughing and joking around he wasn't scary dangerous to the girls.

I can't think of a time when dealing with women was harder than in high school—it was damn hard—but Jesse had a knack, being no more afraid of girls than of other guys. Sure, he was good-looking, but his gift of gab got the girls laughing while the rest of us guys, even Mitch, stood there gawking with our hands in our pockets. Never would I have met the girls I did but for Jesse. Being his friend meant the girls swarmed around. He looked like a photograph I'd seen of the bank robber Johnny Dillinger when he was young. The outlaw, I learned back then, is going to get a hell of a lot more pussy than the sheriff.

"It was those snazzy cars," Mitch said. "All the girls liked his cars. I remember picking up my date in my dad's car and seeing Jesse's pink Oldsmobile parked across the street at Sonia's." He also had a remodeled candy-apple '36 Ford coupe with a rumble seat and a stick shift on the floor. Later he rode a Harley, too.

"I was driving a Plymouth Valiant back then," I said, "and he had a pink Oldsmobile."

"Remember that Model A he gave me?" Mitch asked.

"Sure enough. Girls loved that car."

What happened was that Mitch had loaned Jesse some money—quite a bit, actually, for the time—and when Jesse was sorry to say he just couldn't raise the cash to pay back Mitch he offered his Model A instead.

"That car was worth more than what he owed me," Mitch said.

"We never could flip that thing, could we?" I remembered how we raced that car around the ranch until the tires came off, and then we drove it on the rims, spinning it in quick circles, trying to flip it.

"Ana almost did," Mitch said. It came back to me how much his sister liked driving that old Ford. Sonia did, too, when she later came out to the ranch.

Up at Bass Lake, the summer after our senior year, one of Jesse's girlfriends was the daughter of a rich businessman from Oakland, but his usual hard-on was for girls with daddies in the medical profession—dentists' and doctors' daughters in the ritzy suburbs. Jesse never did live with us on the ranch but with his folks on the poor side of town in a plain brick house, where he ate a lot of corn bread, beans, Okie food. To a doctor, like Sonia's daddy, Jesse was nothing more than Spam-eating trailer trash—a ditch-bank Okie. No way a doctor would want Jesse Floyd around his daughter. I wouldn't either. Hell, I would've killed the son of a bitch if he'd come around my daughter. Still, he got to go out with a dentist's daughter when she was a fresh-man—even though her dating was restricted—because her mom liked him so much. He would go over to their house in the after-noon and talk one-on-one to the mom, who once told a friend, "Jesse's a very thoughtful boy."

I was with him once when we ran across Sonia's stepmom outside Money Back Moe's while we were buying Levi's, and Jesse said, "You look so nice today, Mrs. Maycheck." Sonia's stepmom was a sourpuss, but she smiled at Jesse like he was Gene Autry just stepped out of a movie. I wouldn't even begin to think of talking to a girl's momma that way. Even if you'd told me what to say it would've sounded like someone else, not me.

I remember learning early on what a sweet-talker he was when Sonia was in a swoon. She'd told a girlfriend who told me that Jesse had said real slow-like, with pauses and beats like poetry, "The way *I* feel…makes *me* think…I *must* be…*in love,*" and I remember thinking at the time, "That's so cool, why couldn't I have thought of that?" After we were married, Sonia told me, "I never talked to a woman who didn't like Jesse." I felt kicked in the stomach the same way I did when I saw Yolanda and him out behind the backstop.

I once asked Sonia if Jesse ever roughed her up, and she said, "I wouldn't have stayed five more minutes with him if he did. He didn't have a mean streak with women. He was affectionate." That kind of surprised me because I'd heard he wasn't one to hold back from letting a girl know who was boss. He wouldn't beat up a girl—he wasn't that way—but he wouldn't take any shit either. Or maybe that's just what he told us, like the time he made Sonia get out of the car on a country road at night after she was throwing a fit. "Walking alone down that dark road cooled her heels," he told me. Of course, he just drove up out of sight and waited for her.

Then there was the time a girl from Merced named Linda Antonelli got mad and smacked him in the jaw hard enough to give him a lump. I don't know if he slapped her right back or pushed her down, but he did something, that's for sure. That weekend at the lake I had to change a flat tire before the dance and I'd got my shirt all dirty. "Here, wear this," Jesse said, and handed me his white practice jersey with his football number, 31, on it. When I walked into the dance, I sensed what it must feel like to be him, to have people look at you and step aside. "There's Jesse Floyd," I heard someone say, and I felt like a completely different person. Then this wave of high school girls rushed me. They were Linda Antonelli's friends, all from Merced High, so they didn't know me from Jesse, except they knew his number 31. There must've been ten of them and they were all over me tearing at the jersey, all the time I'm trying to tell them I'm Sonny, not Jesse, but they scratched me up like a bunch of alley cats.

"You son of a fucking bitch," I told Jesse afterward, "you set me up, you prick."

He just laughed. "You better have your momma wash that blood out of my jersey."

Same thing happened with that rich girl—a real doll—from Oakland. "Her family was at Bass Lake for the summer," I told Mitch, "and Jesse met her at the dance, and they started going together. Her father had a fancy boat and a big lake cabin—the whole ball of wax." I'd never told Mitch this story before, and I warned him, "Now, don't let this get back to Lynette."

"You have nothing to worry about," he said.

"For some reason," I said, "Jesse broke up with her. She called me up crying about it, and I tried to make her feel better, saying how maybe it was for the best. Come summer's end she would be going back to Oakland anyway. Then she asked me to take her to the dance that weekend. All her friends would be there and she didn't want to go alone. I'm thinking what if Jesse gets pissed off? I didn't want to find myself in a situation where I get my ass whipped for being a nice guy. 'Please,' she said, 'Please take me.' I mean, this girl was gorgeous, so I said okay. I couldn't believe she was going with me. Next day, though, I told Jesse what was happening. I didn't want him hearing rumors that I'd long-cocked him. 'No big deal, Sonny,' he said. 'I'm moving on.' Well, one thing led to another, and a couple of dances later I'm out in the pines by the lake banging her—and I mean she's gorgeous, *gorgeous*—and I feel something poke me in the base of my prick like an ice pick. This goddamn pine needle got stuck up in there. Talk about hurting. Well, that ended that. I was smeared with blood, and it wasn't just mine. She'd started her period.

Then she was both laughing and crying when she told me how she'd thought she was pregnant but Jesse wouldn't marry her. 'What am I going to do?' she'd asked him, and he'd said, 'Call Sonny.'"

Mitch laughed a little harder than I would've expected. "He was trying to help you out, Sonny."

"That's exactly what he said. Some friend, shit."

"I'm not going to defend him," Mitch said, "but it's like hitting that guy with his jacket on. All's fair in love and war."

Mitch always had this way of summing things up, like after Jesse's death he told me, "Live by the sword, die by the sword." Maybe he learned those sayings in school, but they were always leaving something out.

"I have to piss like a race horse," I told Mitch.

When I came out of the bathroom, I saw he'd helped himself to another beer. I cleared away the empties, except for his spit can, sponged off the table, and popped myself another. Lynette would be coming home anytime now. In fact, she should've already been home. I didn't want her to find me and Mitch still at it just the way she warned me not to be. I didn't want her getting mad at me again. It was bad enough last week after that MID business didn't work out and she'd told me she was getting fed up. "I don't mean to give you the bum's rush," I told Mitch, "but I have to hit the hay pretty early, otherwise I get too run down."

He'd pulled a brown manila envelope out of his briefcase and emptied a bunch of photographs onto the table. "I'll go in a minute," he said. "Take a look at these." They were old photos, mostly faded Polaroids from the time we were on the ranch. Pictures of him, his dad, Jesse, me, Dewey. "Remember this one?"

He held up a small, square, black-and-white snapshot, clipped from a strip taken in a coin-operated photo booth, shadowy and cracked, of me and Jesse, facing the camera, our heads side by side. We're thirteen years old. We both have flattops. "Where did you get this?" I asked.

"You gave it to me, years ago. I don't throw away anything."

"That was in the seventh grade," I told him. Seeing that old photo was like a shot in the brain. I remembered the day we took it, as a lark. We crammed together into this new photo booth in a shoe store on Yosemite Avenue and put in a coin. Lights flashed and a strip of four photos dropped into the slot, still wet, all with the same serious look because we didn't know at the time you could get four different pictures if you changed your expression each time the lights flashed.

We'd been over at Jesse's house that afternoon—it was a Saturday—and we were playing records—those old vinyl forty-fives that needed a spindle—and dancing to them. We didn't have any dance classes back then, so that's how we learned to dance. We bopped to Bill Haley and the Comets. We slow-danced together, with Jesse being the girl and me the guy, then the other way around, practicing the box step—one, two, three, four—all the steps for hours till we knew all the dances. At parties we weren't afraid to get out there and shake it. Jesse even invented new dances. By the time he was in high school, we'd adopted one he called the Hydro, a sort of bop and stomp. Jesse could lean way back, his shoulders dipping toward the floor, limbo-style, while the girl danced in and out between his legs. Then the girl leaned way back. We all danced the Hydro.

Mitch pushed another photograph across the table, a color Polaroid, though washed out. "This was quite a day," he said. In the picture we're all sitting outside on benches and eating at long wooden tables under the eucalyptus trees at Mitch's ranch—me, Mitch, his daddy, Dewey, Hank Palacios, some cowboys from the ranch, and a lot of other people. Sonia and Ana are there, too, at the big barbecue we had at the end of the summer, just before Mitch left for college. I remember Sonia singing "Under the Boardwalk," one of her and Jesse's special songs, she later told me, along with "Unchained Melody," another favorite of theirs.

I looked at Ana, sitting at the other end of the table from me, tan and smiling with her black curly hair spilling around her petite face. "How's your sister doing?" I asked. "I don't see her," Mitch replied. "She lives down south in Santa Barbara. She's put on weight."

I knew Ana was remarried and had two kids with this new guy, plus the two she'd had with Jesse, who were pretty grown up now. I wondered again if she ever told Mitch about me and her, but I doubted it. One of the things that bothered me all these years—and troubled me at night along with my feelings about Jesse—was how I'd never talked to Mitch about his sister, just carried around this secret from him that kept weighing me down. There were times when I almost brought it up, but every time I didn't it felt encased in another layer of stone that made it all the harder to break out of. It got so I felt to be carrying around in my chest a big boulder.

"Mitch," I said, "I have to tell you something. I was in love with your sister and wanted to marry her."

Mitch's face didn't change more than if I was talking to a fence post. All he said, matter-of-factly, was, "Better you than Jesse."

I didn't believe what he said any more than he did, but I appreciated him trying to make me feel better. "I even asked your daddy permission to marry her," I told him. Mitch could see that I was nervous, just as I was that day I talked to his dad out by the barn. "It was nuts, I know, but Ana and I were crazy about each other. She was fifteen. I was seventeen and one scared Okie, let me tell you, talking to your daddy. He told me to forget about the whole thing. He was nice the way he said no, but he still said no."

"What did Ana say when you told her?"

"Her? You can probably guess. She wanted to run off. I told her, 'Run off where? Uh-uh. Oh no. I wasn't raised that way. My family—your family—is here,' I said. 'I don't have a job anywhere but here. There's nowhere to run to.'"

She did finally run away with Jesse, but years later, after she'd graduated from high school and finished a year at the commercial college.

"I guess you ended up doing her two favors," Mitch said. "You didn't marry her and then you killed the two-timing son of a bitch who did."

"For Christ's sake!"

"What made you shoot him, Sonny? I mean, you and Jesse had always been friends. You and Sonia were divorced."

"We were split, not divorced."

"You were getting a divorce. It was over. Jesse and Sonia were getting back together. Those things happen every day. I can understand how you'd feel hurt and mad and all the rest, but not enough to kill someone."

He had me in a corner now, and I said the same thing I told the court: the truth. "I don't know what got into me. It was like it wasn't me that night. When I think about it now it's like I really didn't do it."

"I guess you had to depersonalize yourself as much as you did Jesse," Mitch said.

I'd heard that one before, from a prison counselor, and I still don't know what it means. "Everything was off-kilter," I said. "It wouldn't never have happened if it was anyone but Jesse."

Mitch started jamming the photographs back into the envelope with an irritated look that told me he was giving up on me and fixing to leave.

"Why do you want to know this stuff now?" I asked him. "Jesse's been dead a long time."

"Not long enough." Mitch stared down at the package of photos in his hands. "His ghost is still around."

"I thought you didn't believe in that magic."

He gazed down at the envelope. "Everything that happened keeps haunting me, and I want to understand it. I tried writing this damn thing once before, when I talked to you right after your release. You weren't much help then either."

I didn't want things to end with a bad feeling between us. Here he was the one who'd tried to get me thinking about the past and he was the one doing it more than me. I sensed the ghosts he was thinking about. Behind all his joking about cutting off his balls and whatnot was everything he'd lost: the ranch, his sister, two wives, both folks dead. I stood up and told him, "Finish your beer. I have to feed the dogs."

He watched me open the fridge and get out a pot of cooked rice. I spooned the cold rice into two plastic bowls, softened it with warm water from the tap, sprinkled in some kibbles, topped it with yogurt, and stirred everything up. Jasmine is the only rice the dogs liked. They wouldn't touch basmati, and even though they managed to spit out every speck of dog food, I still added it, thinking maybe some would get eaten by mistake. The dogs were newborn littermates the year Lynette and I were married. They'd been with us the whole time—sixteen years—and I thought often how much they'd changed since the time they were pups and ate only dry kibbles.

Mitch walked with me out into the fenced yard by the horseshoe pits. A deck light had burned out, and Buddy and Lily looked shadowy as they crept out of the doghouse where they slept together. They were black Lab mixed with Australian shepherd—mutts, like me—and even in the light their dull coats looked mottled, like they were once pale dogs that'd rolled in wet newspapers. A crescent moon and stars behind wispy clouds made the sky look milky. Down the dark hillside on the road to the casino came the sound of an unseen car with a chattering muffler.

Buddy limped over to his bowl. He could hardly walk and barely hear. Lily stood stiff-legged by the house, staring off into the night. Their personalities weren't their own anymore. Being almost blind made Lily anxious about everything, while Buddy was sad and sullen. That's the way we die, I think, not in one big blow but in bits and pieces over the years. The boy with my name in Mitch's photos was already long dead. Everyone thinks it happened because of Jesse—Father Dan told me, "You can't kill somebody without killing part of yourself"—but it's more day-by-day than that. All stove-up, with my eyes growing dimmer, my ears shutting down, my fingers numb, little by little I feel a darkness creeping into my brain.

Mitch said, "I'll send you a draft of this article before I publish it. Maybe it'll jog your memory and we can talk again. I'll call you."

"I pretty much told you all I know. He's your brother-in-law you're writing about."

"Was," Mitch said. "They weren't married in the Church. Ana could've had the marriage annulled."

I know how people like Mitch think. They can erase the past, but they don't want me to. He can chalk up Ana's marrying Jesse as a fling by the family's black sheep that doesn't count after she's legitimately married. "I think we're done," I told Mitch.

"I need to know your take on one more thing," he said. I was expecting a zinger but Mitch lobbed me a soft one. "What made Jesse fight?"

The same thing as me, I could tell him. "His brother," I said. "His mother and father—they were both alcoholics. He had to fight his daddy, he had to fight his momma, he had to fight his brother. What Okie kid didn't fight? He fought to survive. He had to fight for everything he got. But he wanted something more."

Mitch didn't seem too thrilled with what I told him. "I guess it always comes down to family. No one succeeds in life without at least one good parent."

"Ain't that the truth," I said, though I'd never before heard such an idea. "He sometimes even fought for a friend," I added. "He cold-cocked Ray Castaneda that time for threatening me after school."

"I know," Mitch said. "You pissed off Ray when you were playing dodgeball."

"What?" I had no memory of what Mitch was saying.

"You hit Ray in the nuts with the ball. Jesse told me that story himself."

I tried to think back to that day but nothing came except Ray saying he was going to beat the crap out of me and then Jesse knocking the crap out of him, and me remembering how scared I was, then how happy to see the tables turned on Ray. Right then it dawned on me what Mitch really needed to know. "Jesse just loved to fight," I told him. "You can't ignore the pleasure of it. There's no better feeling than kicking the shit out of somebody."

Lynette's voice came from behind us. She'd driven up to the front of the house and come through the garage door without us able to hear her out in the backyard. She stood in the lighted opening of the sliding glass door between the deck and the house. I could see the outline of her legs in tight pants. She'd heard what I'd just told Mitch, which I wouldn't have said in front of her. "None?" she asked. "None in the world?"

From her voice I knew Lynette wasn't liking what she saw, Mitch still there and some half-empty beer cans on the table. Mitch got her drift, too, and went inside to gather up his photographs and briefcase. On his way out the front door, he gave Lynette a kiss, which she returned in a pretty friendly way—right on the mouth—showing that if she was mad it wasn't at him.

After he left, Lynette clicked around the table, scooping up two beer cans and accidentally knocking over Mitch's spit can. Gunk spread onto the table.

"I'll get it," I said and went to the sink for some paper towels.

"Son of a bitch," Lynette said. "Look what comes of months of sitting around doing nothing." She flipped a half-full can from her fingers onto the table and it skittered onto the tile floor, spilling beer.

"What's with you?" I asked. "What the hell have you been drinking?"

Well, she hadn't been drinking. She was just getting herself worked up to try to tell me something, which I found out one week later—seven days to the Saturday after Mitch's visit—when she came back from Fresno early without Trisha. This time she was wearing a tight turquoise skirt. I must be stupid or dumb, one.

"Where's Trisha?" I asked in the kitchen.

Lynette snatched up the beer can I'd left on the table. "She's staying the night at her friend Lacey's."

I hadn't seen Trisha go out with any change of clothes. "What about school?"

"Tomorrow's Sunday. Don't you notice anything?"

I did notice the skirt hugging her ass, with a small grease stain on her butt like she'd sat on a pat of butter. Trisha must've put her clothes in the car before I saw them leave.

Lynette said, "Sit down, Sonny, I need to tell you something." I stayed standing, my back hurting. "Okay, keep standing." Her eyes looked unfocused and her face puffy, like when she used to get her period. All the glossy lipstick she'd put on in the afternoon was rubbed off. "I'm leaving you, Sonny. I'm sorry to tell you this way, but I don't know any other way."

Don't let the screen door bang you in the ass is what I'd told Sonia when she said she was leaving, but I didn't have the urge to smart-mouth Lynette. "Who is it?" I asked.

"Someone at the hospital. But that's not the reason. You mustn't think someone else is the reason. It's us, Sonny. I'm telling you this hard and fast because I don't want you to blame anyone but me. I don't want you to beat up on yourself either."

"How long has this been going on?"

"Since the Fourth." I counted up. It'd been four months. They'd had a big Fourth of July party at the hospital. "You don't need to know any more," she said. "I don't want to hurt you."

I don't want to hurt you. That's a good one. I almost told her she sounded like someone on *Days of Our Lives,* but I checked my tongue so as not to let on what I was doing when she was at work. "I don't want you to leave," I said, thinking how Father Dan used to say a divorce can't happen unless both people want it.

"Well, I am," she said. "It's for the best, Sonny, for both of us."

The top of my scalp burned the way it does when people start telling me what's good for me. "We don't have to let this one thing wreck everything," I said. "We can work it out. We don't have to throw away sixteen years."

"They were a mistake," Lynette said, "my mistake. I'm entirely to blame here, Sonny."

My brain clouded up, sudden-like. I could expect her to get on me for laying around doing nothing and lying about it—at least then I could argue back—but she was blaming herself. The pressure in my head blocked out any idea of what I was thinking to say next. I just felt a hurt swell up, the same as when I realized that Sonia felt the way Lynette did now—that marrying me was a mistake, that I wasn't good enough for them but they married me anyway and all the time they knew they'd made a mistake until they could leave me for someone better. *Fuck you and the horse you rode in on* is what I'd told Sonia, but I didn't say it now because I knew I'd regret it, just as I did after Sonia left and I wanted her back. I saw Lynette's face grow tense from trying not to cry, and I said, "Let's settle down here and talk about this in the morning."

Lynette shook her head. "I'm not staying the night. It's over, Sonny."

I walked back outside and sat in a deck chair so as not to hear her getting things from the bedroom. I hoped she'd at least come out and say goodbye, maybe kiss me on the top of the head the way she sometimes did when making up after a spat. I looked at my watch. I got up and walked into the house. She was gone.

I cracked a beer, loaded up my lip the way Mitch did, and went back onto the deck. I whistled. Buddy and Lily didn't come, that's how deaf they were. I rapped my knuckles on the roof of their house until first Buddy, then Lily poked their muzzles through the doorway. I helped them to climb next to my chair, grabbing the hips of one, then the other, to push them up the four redwood steps from the lawn to the deck. Trisha complained that I never let the dogs into the house, even when they got old, the way other people did, but I wouldn't do it, especially when they couldn't hold their pee anymore. I think my stepdad, Dewey, would've had a stroke if he saw a dog in the house. It would be like letting the chickens and the goats and the pigs in the house, too.

Buddy and Lily stretched out on either side of my chair, and I reached down and cupped their chests with my hands. I could feel their hearts. I wondered how many beats they had left, how many I had left. I looked up. The hazy clouds now moving across the sky made the stars look like pinpricks coming in and out of view. A star would sparkle one second, then vanish the next. Behind them, I knew, was just the void. If there was a God out there, I couldn't know His way of thinking any more than Buddy and Lily could know mine. The difference I saw between my mind and the dogs' kept me believing in a bigger mind than my own that I couldn't understand.

Buddy groaned. I patted his side. "It's okay, boy," I said loud enough to be sure he heard. Lily thumped the deck with her tail, and I patted her side, too.

The wooden fence at the edge of the yard blended into the oaks to look like a high black wall, cutting off the outside world. A dim halo hovered above the casino down the hill. The rest was darkness. I sensed myself imprisoned again, fenced in. I stared into the darkness.

The ache in my chest swelled up into my throat until it seemed about to choke me, and my heart was pounding so I thought it was about to bust, and I wished it would break, right there and then, and get it over with. *I've never felt this sad,* I thought, but just as quick I remembered thinking and feeling the same thing when Ana and I broke up, so many years ago. The feeling was so familiar I felt like I'd been whisked away in some sort of time machine and I was the kid in Mitch's photographs. How much was due to the coincidence of Mitch getting me thinking about the past in the same week that Lynette blindsided me I didn't know, but it'd been years since I'd felt so much myself again.

Mitch said Ana had gotten fat, but I was sure she was the same Ana, comfortable to be with. I was her first love. No one forgets their first love. Ana loved me, and I loved her. Sonia loved Jesse but married me. Ana married Jesse, but he loved Sonia. We were all hooked up in a crisscrossed love that never got straight.

That's what I should've told Mitch when he asked me why I shot Jesse. I didn't hate Jesse, the way people think. I loved him—or hated him because I loved him. I didn't want the same thing to happen now with Lynette, to have all that love—sixteen years—turn to rage and hate, the way it did with Sonia and me. Back then, on some level, I knew it was coming. I both knew and didn't know that Sonia and Jesse were fooling around, until

I thought I knew, and then a rage swelled up in me, changing
me. I bought the pistol from a friend of mine, a former cop. I
had the pistol, but I didn't think I was going to kill anyone with
it, but the rage kept swelling until Sonia admitted she was seeing
Jesse and I couldn't think straight. Now the same damn thing
was happening with Lynette. She'd met some doctor, probably,
someone with education and class, or maybe just another nurse
now that half of them are men, or an anesthesiologist or an
orderly or a psychologist—the goddamn hospital was full of men
for her picking. Full of beds, too. No telling who she ended up
with. Last time I was there hardly no one spoke English.

Maybe this guy wasn't the first. I should've pushed her on
it. I had to hand it to her for the way she kept me in the dark.
I trusted her. That made it easy for her. I was never suspicious.
All these years I thought there was trust between us, and I kept
myself blind. I know I strayed early on, but once our marriage
found its groove I stayed faithful to her. Since Trisha was about
six, I didn't stray but one more time. Still, after Lynette found
out about me and her brother-in-law's sister, I cut it off completely and promised it would never happen again, and it didn't.
I kept my word. I thought she'd forgiven me, but maybe she
hadn't. Maybe she couldn't. Maybe I deserved it, given what I'd
done in my life. I once told Father Dan that if I wasn't in prison
for killing Jesse I should've been there for the other things I've
done. "Like what?" he asked. I didn't cuss usually in front of
Father Dan, but I got carried away making a point. "Like fucking another man's wife while he was watching television in the
same fucking house."

"You can change," Father Dan said. "It's what you do from
now on that matters."

And for the last sixteen years I did my best to change. When
I was a little kid and my momma was drunk and whipping me
with a belt right across the back where my daddy—my real

daddy, not Dewey—had left scars, I turned on her and took away that belt and said, "You ain't going to whip me no more. No one is." And she didn't. That was the last time.

I stood up and threw the empty beer can across the yard. It flew into the night until I heard it chunk against the fence. I shouldn't have let Lynette walk over me. I should've jumped in the pickup and followed her into Madera or Fresno or wherever she went. It was too late now. She was already in another house, probably in the suburbs, with someone else. I could've driven behind her and parked at the end of the block and watched her walk up to the house, still in that tight turquoise skirt, to push her finger on the doorbell. I would've seen the guy then, when the porch light came on and he opened the door and she went into the house and the door closed and the light went out. I saw myself standing in front of the dark door, ringing the bell. He would either open that door or I would kick it open.

It came back to me then like a movie in my head. I was watching myself kick open the bedroom door, thinking, *She's my wife you're with. I have a right to kill you.* It was like a movie, all in Technicolor, one that I used to see over and over because that's what the counselors said I was supposed to do until Father Dan told me to stop it—I was only making things worse, making that movie permanent by constantly rerunning it.

Now it was back. I saw my foot hit the wood above the doorknob. The latch snapped, the door swung open. The guy with Lynette would look shocked and step back. That night, when it really happened, no one stepped back. That's what I could've told Mitch. *Depersonalize,* hell. No one depersonalized anyone. I knew who stood in the doorway, his eyes wild and his fists clenched. Jesse Floyd came through the open door, and he was coming at me.

II

THAT SUMMER

Here's how it started. That summer Mitch's daddy called me out by the barn and said, "I want you boys to keep your noses clean this summer. I need you to stay out of trouble and take responsibility for the Tomato Piece." He'd planted eighty acres, the biggest field of tomatoes ever in that part of the San Joaquin Valley. Jesse and I talked about when the pickers arrived and the field would fill up with more pussy than you could shake a stick at, eighty acres of it.

The whole summer stretched ahead of us. We were out of high school, graduated, free. Me and Jesse were best friends. We had jobs together on the ranch. Never again would I sit in a cramped desk in a cooped-up classroom. From sunup to sundown we worked under the open sky, and at night we tomcatted around until morning, when we were back in the fields.

The red sun coming up behind the Sierras that morning I was talking with Mitch's daddy sparked the air with the day's coming heat. Those were dawns when you could still see the silvery mountains shining at the edge of the valley. I wore rubber irrigation boots, Levi's, and a white T-shirt. My bare arms tingled with goose bumps from the morning coolness, while my forehead heated up from the sun's rays that by noon would blast the valley like a blowtorch.

I need you boys to stay out of trouble, Sam Etcheverry had said. *Stay away from my daughter,* he might've said.

Ana had just come home from boarding school. I saw her crossing the yard one morning, walking past the eucalyptus trees in white shorts and a pink top, and I felt a thump in my stomach. I hadn't seen her for months. She still had her senior year of high school left. When we were getting it on she was only a freshman, but since then she'd grown from a little girl into a young woman. That's what it was like back then: the difference between a freshman and a senior was like seeing a foal grow into a filly.

Later that morning when she came out to the barn to talk to us, Jesse gave her a little smack on the ass of those tight white shorts with his open hand and said, "Must be jelly 'cause jam don't shimmy like that." He was bold that way, Jesse was, with that old-time saying, and damned if Ana didn't seem to like it, the way she grinned, though she told Jesse, "You'll never find out."

She and I looked at each other, and I could tell from her eyes—darker than ever because the sun was behind her—and in the way she tilted her head, so her black curly hair, grown out since the time we were sneaking around, dropped over one eye, that not all feeling for me had gone, though we both knew her daddy wouldn't stand for us getting together again. He could've run my ass off the ranch. Course, he never probably would've found out about us if I hadn't asked to marry her.

It started between me and Ana when I found her by herself at sundown out by the pond in the middle of the ranch. Ana was just fourteen, going on fifteen. She had short, sturdy legs, plump around the thighs, good to crack walnuts with, as the saying goes. She'd pedaled away from her house on her bike because her momma was having one of her fits. I'd just finished setting the siphon pipes for the night along the ditch that ran out of the pond when I saw Ana sitting on the dock. The pond, dug out with a bulldozer into a square half-acre of water with high banks, was surrounded by cattails and full of carp and bullfrogs. Ana wasn't so much sad as mad.

"I'm not going to stay around that goddamn house anymore," she said.

"Your momma's a nice lady," I told her. "She's just crazy."

"Daddy says it's menopause."

"I didn't know menopause came in a bottle."

"That's what I told Daddy. She's a drunk, but he says it's hot flashes."

"She's your momma. Your daddy loves her. He loves you, too."

"Then why doesn't he do something about her? She's up all night screaming."

"My momma was the same way," I said. "She's more quiet now since both her and Dewey quit drinking."

"He thinks he solves the problem by sending me and Mitch away to school, like it's our fault or something."

Ana's momma was a good looker, a snappy dresser, full of spunk, a fiery Basco lady until she started having what Sam called her "spells," and we believed him for a while because her whole personality changed during them. She even looked different, like a whole other face—fleshier, sour, and older—replaced the pretty, younger one. When my momma got drunk she got loud and warlike, but she was still my momma, only drunk. Ana's momma was like two different people. She didn't beat on Ana the way mine done me, but she made that house a screaming hell. I don't know why Ana's daddy put up with it except that when Ana's momma was sober she wasn't the same woman who'd been tearing up the pea patch and you would just feel bad blaming her.

"I know it's tough on you," I told Ana and put my arm around her. She leaned her head on my shoulder, and we sat there for maybe fifteen minutes, saying nothing, just looking out over the pond toward the sunset and listening to the bullfrogs croak. Fifteen minutes is a long time when you're not talking.

I saw her there by the pond off and on for the next couple of weeks until late one afternoon I drove over and didn't find her but a folded note stuck between slats on the dock. It didn't say my name but only "Meet me tonight at 11. Ana." I was excited and kind of afraid because I just knew something was going to happen between us, but at the same time I feared she was careless. What if Jesse or Mitch or even her daddy found the note instead of me? I even thought she was careless enough to misspell her own name—it was the first time I saw it written out and thought it should be "Anna"—until I learned that "Ana" was the Basco spelling.

That night she showed up on her bike at eleven just like she said, and I parked the pickup on the west side of the pond so it was hid behind the cattails because I knew her daddy slept like a hound—with one eye open—and he might come out to check on Jesse, who was baling hay that night.

"Maybe you shouldn't leave notes like that out in the open," I said.

"I saw you coming on the road," she said. "I knew you'd find it."

She was only fourteen, but she was doing what it took me another twenty years to figure out: when I think I'm the one romancing a woman, she's the one calling the shots. It was the same with Sonia, then Lynette, and even in grade school with Yolanda. Ana made out with me that night for a long time, but she wouldn't let me do more than feel around so I had a bad case of blue balls the next morning. We squirmed around in the cab of the pickup and stretched out as best we could, me with my back cramped against the steering wheel. I reached over and

switched on the key to play the radio—just for a while so as
not to run down the battery—and in the dash lights Ana's face
and soft brown eyes looked so different from during the day.
I wouldn't say she looked possessed because that sounds bad,
but her face had a calm look of concentration, like someone
in church praying, an expression I came to get used to when
she was turned on. I noticed then in the glow of the dashboard
that she had two different-sized pupils—one was dilated but
the other was as small as a dot. That's how they were even in
daylight, I just hadn't noticed before. Then I started seeing how
many other expressions she had, like nobody else I'd seen, and I
called her in my mind "the girl with the thousand faces."

"I have to be getting back pretty soon," she said. "You're a
sweet kisser."

"How many boys have you kissed?" I asked.

"Just you," she said. "This way."

She'd climbed out of her bedroom window to meet me, and
she kept climbing out of it that summer until the next summer
I was climbing into it, too. I don't know how her daddy or
momma didn't catch us. That hound's eye of her daddy's got
tired and droopy, I guess.

Maybe, now that I think of it, it wasn't that many times she
crawled out the first summer, though when she came back from
school the next summer she was fifteen and we were regular
lovers. Jesse knew about it, of course, but otherwise we snuck
around. At first we did it because she was so young, then we did
it because she didn't want her brother to know. I didn't want
Mitch to know either. I worked with him during the day, and it
would've been awkward to have him hear that I was balling his
sister, though he did owe me for setting him up with his first
piece of ass, which was with my cousin.

Ana started going out on dates with other boys, and I was
seeing other girls—that's just the way it was—and we would

even do things out in the open together in town, at parties or
dances, or up at the lake, as long as other people were around,
including her brother.

One evening after work the four of us—Ana, Mitch, Jesse, and
myself—drove around the ranch shooting rabbits from the open-
topped Jeep we used for irrigating. It was the best time of day,
just before sundown when the air started to cool and all the fields
turned dark green. We had a couple six-packs of cold Olys. Jesse
drove with one hand on the wheel and a can of beer in the other.
Mitch rode shotgun—with a real shotgun, a two-triggered,
double-barreled twenty-gauge that we passed back and forth
when we jumped a rabbit or spotted one down a cotton row.

Ana lunged against me in the backseat when Jesse pulled
the gray Jeep up onto the steep bank of the pond. A new Jeep
would've flipped over, but that ranch Jeep was the old-style
wide-axle Army issue—a Willys—that we could race up and
down canal banks. A jackrabbit bounded from a clump of
Johnson grass but zigged out of sight into an alfalfa field just as
Mitch shot and missed. He was the best shot of us because he
had the most practice hunting doves, quail, pheasants, chukars,
and ducks in the fall. When we were growing up, Jesse and I had
done most of our shooting at other guys with Red Ryder BB
Guns and later at tin cans with .22s. We were both okay shots,
nothing to brag about. I thought Ana was just tagging along,
until she told her brother, "It's my turn. Let me shoot."

Mitch handed the twenty-gauge back to her and told us, "Put
your heads down, boys."

"Screw you," Ana said. "If I wanted to shoot you, I wouldn't
miss your dumb heads, even if you sat on them."

The gun had actually been her momma's, a hell of a shot
herself during dove season back before she took to the bottle.
Mitch's daddy was a good shot, too. Jesse and I once saw him
knock a gopher through the head with the pistol he carried in the

glove box of his pickup, not an easy thing to do since the gopher was way down a young corn row and a pistol is hard to aim.

"There you go," Jesse said. He jerked the steering wheel so the Jeep spun sideways and came to a skidding stop, giving Ana a clear shot at a gray jackrabbit sitting up on its haunches at the edge of the cotton field that would be the Tomato Piece the following summer. The rabbit sat at attention like a prairie dog, with its long ears straight up in the air, a bit too far away to hit with a shotgun. I imagined sighting it through the scope of a .22, with the rabbit's oblong head in the crosshairs and its pink ears looking almost transparent against the setting sun.

"Too far," I said, just as the jackrabbit bounded away and Ana pulled the two triggers, firing both barrels one after the other, *boom, boom.* The jack somersaulted in the dust and tumbled flat.

"How the hell did you hit that?" I asked.

"I aimed high," Ana said, "above the ears. Daddy taught me."

Someone farted, and we knew it was Jesse because the smell almost drove us out of the Jeep even though it had no top and we were sitting in the open air. Maybe it was all those beans he ate, but I think there was something wrong with his stomach all his life, not surprising given all the craziness at his house. My own stomach knotted up every time I went over there. Someone was always yelling, or Jesse's brother was chasing him around the table, or the other way around, and his father would say, "Ah, quit that shit. Sit down and eat." That's why I think Jesse drank so much milk, like I told Mitch, even thickening it up with Star-Lac powder the way he did. He wasn't like Hank Palacios, who could fart melodies at will—"Yankee Doodle" was his favorite— sounding like an oboe in the school band. Jesse couldn't help it. He cut the most wicked farts. Once we were double dating at the drive-in when the girls threw open the doors to escape. "Stay here. Breathe deep," Jesse told them. "Help me suck it up." Before you knew it the girls nearly bust a gut laughing.

We had four rabbits by suppertime, when we dropped off Ana and Mitch at their house. Jesse and I parked by the barn near my house and finished the Olys while skinning the rabbits. We hooked the back legs of the carcasses on nails hammered into the barn wall. "Why don't you take Ana out on a proper date?" Jesse asked. He sounded like Mitch's aunt, our English teacher, the way he mouthed the word "proper."

"You know why," I said. "Don't act ignorant."

"Last summer she was too young, I can see that. But she's dating now. Mitch has to accept that." He reached into his wallet and handed me a five-buck bill, not a small amount back then. "Here, you can take her to the Big Top for a cherry lime rickey. You can use my car."

Jesse was that way. He'd loan you dough for a date or even let you use his car, though, of course, he expected you to return the favor. He knew I was strapped at the time because I was saving up to buy a Valiant. A few bucks helped.

I looked out over the alfalfa field. My fingers were sticky with blood and rabbit fur. "You bet," I said.

That night I waited by the eucalyptus trees near Ana's house in Jesse's '36 candy-apple-red coupe until she climbed out her window and walked up the road like we'd planned. When she saw the shiny car, she stopped and turned away. I hadn't told her I'd have Jesse's car. I jumped out and ran up the road to fetch her, not wanting to shout for fear of her daddy hearing, and waited until I got close enough to call her name without yelling. "Ana. It's me, Sonny. I have Jesse's car."

We drove into Madera past the dark orchards and vineyards into the glare of the Big Top Drive In. Jesse stood on the asphalt under the lights with his arm around a guy while he bent over talking to a cop in a police car. I learned later that this guy and Jesse had just started to get into it when the cop pulled up and Jesse grabbed the guy around the shoulder and told the cop,

"Hey, me and my buddy here were just talking. There's no problem, officer." Jesse was a quick thinker that way. After the cop left, he and the guy duked it out.

The carhop brought us cherry Cokes, and we nodded, waved, and talked to other kids. "Maybe we can go to the drive-in movies this weekend," I said to Ana.

She sipped on the straw and then rattled the ice in her paper cup. "People will see us," she said.

"What do you think they're doing now?" I said.

She snuggled up close to me and put her hand on my leg.

Afterward, we parked by a canal levee near the west road into the ranch. We had to keep the windows rolled up because of the late-summer mosquitoes. A few whined inside the car and I felt around in the dark to smash them against the windshield. It was so dark I couldn't even see Ana's different-sized pupils. I felt the wetness on her cheeks, though, when I pressed my face against hers. Her momma had really gone berserk that night, she told me, throwing plates in the kitchen. She'd driven home drunk and scraped the side of her Buick on one of the metal poles holding up the carport by the side of the house. It wasn't the first time. Three of the carport poles were already bent like crimped straws.

"I can't stand it anymore," Ana said.

"Your daddy should take that car away from her."

"He's afraid of her," Ana said. "When she gets sober, we're not supposed to say a word. We're supposed to act like nothing happened. If me and Mitch say anything, she gets mad at us."

"You'll be going back to school soon," I said. Once summer ended, Ana would be sent back to boarding school on the coast.

"I still come home," she said. "It'll be more of the same."

I didn't know at that time what it was with these country women—like Ana's momma and Jesse's and mine—all going crazy with booze. I knew the saying "The West is hard on horses and women," or was it that Texas is hard on them? Same difference.

Nobody used the word "alcoholic" much in those days because it was too shameful. Women problems were just the way things were. When my momma started to rant and rave I would scream at her, "Shut the hell up," and she would scream back, "I will not shut up until I am dead! I will not shut up until I am dead! I will not shut up until I am dead!" over and over, until I went running out of the house. I figured my stepdaddy put up with it because it gave him an excuse to go catting around to the bars. Dewey would fuck a woodpile if he thought there was a snake in it. I don't think Ana's daddy was that way, but he was out of the house often enough, attending California Farm Bureau meetings or giving speeches at the Western Cotton Growers Association while Ana and Mitch stayed home to take shit from their momma.

"You'll be gone soon," I said again to console her but also to try to tell her that I would miss her.

"I don't want to go back to that damn school," she said.

"What the hell are you going to do?" I asked. "You don't want to stay home, and you don't want to go to school."

"We could get married," she said.

The next morning, I stood by the barn in Sam's yard, my hands shaking, and asked his permission to marry Ana. "I'm in love with your daughter, Sam, and I want to marry her."

Sam reached up, pushed back the brim of his hat, and then with the same hand scratched his scalp through his thick hair the way he always did before talking about something tricky. I put my own hands in my pockets to keep them from shaking. I thought about the .38 Special in his pickup.

"Now that's fine, Sonny," he said. "You're a hard worker, but no matter how hard you work you couldn't make enough to be married now. You just can't afford it."

I should've said what I was thinking: *Well, you can give me a raise.*

"You have to understand something about Ana," he went on. "Ana's spoiled. She's used to certain things. No matter how hard you work you won't be able to support those needs. She's too spoiled." I thought then Sam was going to tell me to get the hell off the ranch. Instead, he said, "Let's act like we never had this conversation."

Ana wanted us to run off, like I told Mitch, but I knew there was nowhere to run to. I told her I wasn't raised that way. "I got money," she said, showing me a few twenty-dollar bills. That's when I knew what her daddy was talking about.

I thought for sure the next day or the next week Sam would see some fuckup of mine, either irrigating or driving tractor, to give him an excuse to boot me off the ranch. He'd need a reason to tell my stepdad. They liked each other, Sam and Dewey did, and they talked together about what should or shouldn't be done ranching. Dewey would go right along with Sam in firing me if he heard I didn't do some work like I was supposed to. That way Sam could get rid of me and pretend it wasn't about Ana.

But Sam did nothing and never said anything more about it. He kept his word and acted like we never had that conversation, until the next summer when Ana showed up on the ranch in those white shorts and pink top. When he said for me to keep my nose clean, I thought he was telling me to keep away from her, but maybe that was my own mind guessing at what he might be thinking when he was simply saying what he meant—*I want you boys to stay out of trouble*—but damned if that very weekend we did exactly what he said not to.

FLAG DAY

It was June 14, and Sam Etcheverry had the stars and stripes waving from a slanted pole on the front eave of his house. That evening, me and Jesse went into town to hear him talk

at the Elks ceremony on the lawn in front of the stone courthouse. Sam gave a nice talk, sending bumps down my spine at
one point when he talked about all the wars the flag had gone
through to keep us free. Sam pointed to the concrete war memo-
rial on the courthouse lawn with the chiseled names of the boys
killed in the First World War, the Second World War, and the
Korean War, but not yet the Vietnam War. My mind wandered
off, and I got to thinking how quick time had flitted by since
our graduation. Already it was Flag Day, with half of June gone.
Soon it would be the Fourth of July—half the summer gone—
then Labor Day, with Mitch going off to college, and the summer would be over and we'd be disking up the fields for the coming year. All those boys dead, I thought, never having the chance
I had.

The next evening, Saturday, Jesse and I set our water for the
night and went to Alpha Grocery for some chile peppers and
Monterey Jack cheese, which we liked to eat while drinking
beer at the end of the day. With the grub and two six-packs, we
pulled up to the ranch feedlot, where some cowboys were roping
steers. Yellow dust swirled up from the corral as a cowboy on
horseback headed a steer and another swung a loop downward
toward its back heels. They weren't working, just practicing for
the rodeo. Sam rented out the feedlot since he was no longer in
the cattle business.

"Let's get some of their wine," Jesse said.

"We better not get tanked up early," I said, thinking of Sam's
warning.

"It's Saturday," Jesse said.

We had an open invite to help ourselves to the vat of
homemade wine inside the feedlot shed. The shed, with high
walls of corrugated sheet metal, was cavernous as a church,
only with sacks of minerals and salt instead of pews on the
cement floor. Here the hay came through from the outside to

get mixed up with barley, oats, and ground-up corn, then spiced with minerals and sweetened with molasses before it went back outside and down the conveyor belt to fatten up those spoiled cattle. Late-afternoon sunlight full of dust shined through the open door and fell right on the big wine vat. Jesse pulled the tiny nail from the bottom of the vat to fill up two Bell canning jars, then we went back outside to watch the cowboys rope.

The wine had a dark, rich color. "It tastes kind of moldy," I said.

"The best wines have that kind of undertaste," Jesse said. "People pay a lot of money for that taste."

Though he rented his feedlot to one of the cowboys who was partnering with a cattleman, Sam didn't have much use for cowboys. He liked running an efficient, up-to-date ranch, and to him cowboys were always doing things the hard way just to be old-fashioned, like roping steers to brand them when it was easier and faster to run them through the branding chute, right there in the feedlot. "Those cowboys," Sam muttered to me once, "they won't even get off a horse to shut a gate. You can always find a cowboy, but you can't always find a good irrigator. If I had my way, I'd make them walk. Sheepherders walk."

The cowboys were always trying to get Jesse, me, and Mitch to sign up for bullriding in the rodeo, but we never took the bait. They constantly pulled tricks on each other, or on us, wanting to bet on anything. Like as not, a cowboy would bet the sun wouldn't come up in the morning, not caring he'd lose so long as he got you riled up with some kind of bluff. That's what I think Jesse liked about them, how far they'd go to play a joke on someone. Not that he hung out with them, though we did gamble with them at parties and barbecues, shooting craps or dealing gin rummy—that's what they played, not poker like you'd think. The way Jesse would study them made me know something fascinated him, maybe the way they didn't care about anything except being cowboys.

One of the cowboys named Duane, sporting a reddish-blond mustache, rode over to the fence where we were watching them from. He wore chaps and a straw hat, like he always did in the summer until Mitch's daddy sold the ranch and Duane moved to Wyoming, where the Marlboro people found him and got him started appearing in commercials. Then he wore felt Stetsons all the time, even in summer.

He asked Jesse, "How's that wine going down today, Jessica?" Those cowboys rarely called anybody by their real names, always trying to get your goat. "Tastes better with a dip." He held out an open can of Copenhagen toward us, but we knew better than to take any. You might find rabbit droppings pressed against your gums.

"We got our own." Jesse patted the hip pocket of his Levi's.

Duane offered us a cigarette, but neither of us had started smoking yet. Not till the end of the summer did it dawn on us that we wouldn't be playing football anymore and I wouldn't be wrestling, so we no longer needed to lay off. Though his lip was already loaded with snoose, Duane lit up a Pall Mall, the brand all those cowboys smoked. They wouldn't turn down a Marlboro Red if you gave it to them, though they'd tear the filters off before lighting up.

"Save some of those chiles for us," Duane said in his deep-voiced drawl. "We'll join you after we put up the horses." Duane was from Oklahoma and grew up in California just like us, but he didn't talk like us. He sounded like a record on slow play.

The chiles were especially hot, and Jesse and I stuffed our mouths with cheese to cut the heat, then washed everything down with wine, which went down real smooth, so smooth that by the third Bell jar I was feeling loopy when I went back into the dusty shed for more. The cowboys never showed up for their chiles, so we ate all of them. The wine was still tasting funny to me, and on an impulse I hoisted up the wooden top of the smelly oak cask. I looked down to see the wine layered with what looked like white pus.

"Hey, Jesse," I said. "This wine is covered with maggots."

Jesse laughed. Imitating Duane's slow drawl, he said, "Sonny, you can't taste the maggots. Draw me that wine from the bottom. Maggots are good protein." Damned if he didn't drink more, though I quit.

But not soon enough. I blame what happened that night on the damn wine. Jesse said he had a date in Firebaugh—some rancher's daughter he'd met at the lake—so after showering and changing my clothes I headed alone over to Jap Corner. Lots of cars and pickups were already parked in front of the Ranchers' Round-Up, kitty-corner from Mr. Yamaguchi's store and home, where his family and other Japanese returned after they got out of the detention camps. We don't say that name no more, but that's what it was back then: Jap Corner.

Mitch was doing one of his magic shows in the bar that night. He'd done magic back in grammar school and performed for the church variety show in the eighth grade, with Ana, wearing a kimono, playing the magician's assistant and kicking off his act with a Chinese parasol dance. Last summer, he dug out his old magic tricks for a barbecue that Sam threw for all the cowboys and farmhands on the ranch, and Duane had loved the show and arranged for Mitch to do magic tricks for his kids at a Christmas party and in cowboy bars during the summer. Duane was Mitch's biggest fan. He was in the Ranchers' Round-Up that night with all his cowboy buddies to cheer Mitch on and especially to try to get him drunk before he performed.

Nobody had to try to get me drunk. That maggoty wine had got me started and I switched to brandy and water, same as all the grape growers at the bar were drinking, figuring I might as well stick with the fruit of the vine. Hazel, the hefty lady who ran the bar after her husband, Virgil, died, started loading me with pickled eggs and pigs' feet without charging, so I wouldn't get sloshed on an empty stomach, but the drinks kept going down faster than the food, especially after I saw Ana walk in with a school friend of Mitch's. I thought about Jesse smacking her on the butt of her white shorts a couple of weeks earlier. She smiled at me, but we didn't talk, the bar being so crowded, and I was at one end and her at the other. Then Sam came in, and I would've said "holy shit" if I'd been a little more sober, but since I was feeling no pain I thought everything was fine and rolled Liar's Dice with the bartender, double or nothing, for a round of drinks for Mitch, Sam, Duane, Ana, and her boyfriend. I lost, then flopped the dice again, and lost again.

So much damn noise and smoke in the room, and people walking around, made it hard to follow Mitch when he started doing his magic tricks at the far end of the bar behind a little black magician's table with a silk top hat on it. He wore a green madras jacket and a necktie and waved a wand in the air. After I had my senior yearbook picture taken I vowed never to wear a necktie again.

Mitch asked some stacked babe from the crowd to come up and help him with a trick. He tied two silk handkerchiefs together, one blue and one red, and stuffed the knotted ends between the front snaps of her cowgirl shirt, pushing his fingers and handkerchiefs between her two big knockers. The air around her was thickening up with blue cigarette smoke. The girl giggled and squirmed like she was embarrassed, but you could tell she was loving all the attention. Two guys from the bar crowd came up to help. Each guy grabbed one end of the handkerchiefs hanging in front of the girl's chest and jerked them out of her shirt. A pink bra dangled between the red and blue handkerchiefs. Duane whooped and clapped. So did everyone else.

Mitch flubbed his next "illusion," as he called it, because his fingers weren't working. We could all see him palming a coin, but nobody cared, just like nobody cared that a rope was dangling from his coat when it was supposed to be hidden.

I missed part of the next trick—Mitch announced it as "The World's Greatest Card Trick"—because I got to talking with someone at the bar, but apparently Mitch said he was not only going to name three cards picked out by people but he'd also make them fly invisibly from one envelope to another that two gals in the crowd held in their hands. A cowboy shouted, "A hundred bucks says he can't," and Duane yelled back, "A hundred says he can," and then they stopped the show to collect the money and get someone to hold the pot, which Duane won, though for a moment it seemed nip and tuck whether he would.

The cowboys kept giving Mitch drinks between tricks. I saw his daddy leave just before he finished up his show by making the rice in two Chinese bowls multiply so that it spilled all over the floor. Then, damned if he didn't put one bowl on top of the other, say some magic words, *"Andra moi ennepe, mousa, polutropon, hos mala polla planchthê,"* and the rice changed to water, which he poured from one bowl to the other as it multiplied and spilled onto the floor. I don't know if the mess he made was part of the trick or if he was just drunk or what, but everyone loved it. Hazel said, "I heard he was good, but I didn't know he was that good."

I should've switched to beer instead of sticking to the brandy because next thing I knew I felt people helping me up from the floor by the bar stool. I guess I'd lost my balance when swiveling off the stool to go to the john. When I returned, Hazel put a plate of cold fried chicken in front of me. Hazel was in her fifties with curly black hair and big, brown, caring, motherly eyes. You wouldn't know it from her name, but her folks—or maybe her grandfolks—had come from Italy. Either way, Hazel was a great cook. Her husband, Virgil, was always squabbling with his brothers over the properties they owned, and I once asked him,

"Why are you Italians always fighting amongst yourselves?" and he said, "You Okies don't have nothing to fight for." He was such a miserable bastard, Virgil was, he was probably even miserable when he was dead. But not Hazel, once she was shut of him. Though you had to pay for lunchtime meals, she dished out free food at night to keep people from getting sloshed, but the drinks never stopped coming. Back in those days, you never cut anyone off, except real drunks.

Music from the bright neon jukebox at the far end of the bar blared through a haze of smoke. The crowd thinned out, and some guys and gals started dancing. Ana leaned over the glowing jukebox display of song titles, next to her boyfriend, her ass facing me in a tight one-piece striped dress that I saw had buttons down the front when she turned around and pressed those buttons against the chest of the guy she started dancing with, cheek to cheek. You couldn't have shoved one of Mitch's playing cards between them. The jukebox wailed with the Crests singing "Sixteen Candles." That made me kind of mad. That was our song—me and Ana's! *"Sixteen candles,"* the Crests crooned, *"make a lovely light, but not as bright as your eyes tonight."* The guy had his hand spread right on Ana's tailbone above her ass that had filled out over the school year. I thought of her soft, plump thighs. I got to thinking about how me and Jesse were out in the cotton field, years ago, and I commented how this Mexican gal was pretty hot-looking except for her little chest, and Jesse got outraged at me: "You never judge a woman by her tits. You judge her by her ass." I was only thirteen then, but I never forgot that lesson.

I felt so bad seeing Ana dancing with that guy I wanted another drink but was told it was time to go home. Somebody unplugged the jukebox. Flickering fluorescent lights brightened the room. I glanced around. Duane and all the cowboys had gone, and other people were streaming out the front door. I looked for Ana, but she'd gone, too, and I saw Hazel talking to

these guys where Ana had been dancing, telling them the bar
was closing, and then I saw her spread out flat on the floor. I
jumped off the stool and went at those guys, who I thought had
knocked her down, three Mexicans.

"You sorry sons of bitches," I said, and then Mitch, drunker
than hell, was by my side ready to take them on with me.

"Let's go outside, you cocksuckers," Mitch said, but Hazel
got up and stepped between us and those cholos, saying, "No,
Sonny, no, Mitch, I slipped on the rice." I couldn't quite take in
what she was saying, or how to take it, whether she was telling
the truth or just trying to prevent a fight. I didn't care. I was
ready to fight. Those Mexicans—a tall, skinny kid between an
older guy with a scar on his lip and another kid who was kind
of fat—just stared at me and Mitch, real mean-like, not raising
their hands but not stepping back either. All I can say is that it's
a good thing Jesse wasn't there because the fur would've been
flying, but that's how me and him were different. I hesitated,
listening to what Hazel was saying, and by then her bartender
and some other guys turned me and Mitch around and seated us
at the bar while other guys hustled the Mexicans outside and on
their way home.

The next morning, I felt like hell when I went to work—
worse than hell. I didn't remember driving home at all. The
last thing I remembered was seeing those Mexicans hustled out
of the bar, and then it was like my mind went blank. After I
changed my water, I drove over to the boss's house to see what
had come of Mitch, whether he'd made it home all right. I knew
I would be in even bigger trouble than I already was if I'd let
Mitch, as drunk as he was, end up in a ditch. But Mitch was
okay, standing by the barn with my stepdad, Dewey, talking to
Jesse, who looked like he'd been run over by an eighteen-wheeler.
Both of Jesse's eyes were black, and his lip was puffed up, with
an ugly red split in it.

"I got into it with this dumb-assed Firebaugh cowboy," Jesse was saying, "when his buddies jumped in. I scrambled under a truck to get away from them, but they drug me out and worked me over. One of them had a goddamn two-by-four. They like to kill me—a bunch of redneck Okies in cowboy hats."

Just about then Duane came driving up in his pickup with two cowdogs in back. Sam came out of the house, all dressed up in his Sunday threads and string tie to take the missus to church. Duane was looking pretty hungover his own self, his eyes shot with red lines, but I saw that he had an open beer can in the pickup cab—the hair of the dog that bit him. I ached for one myself but didn't dare while Sam was there. I thought of the song my momma liked to play on the record by the singer Okie Paul.

> *Drink a little beer in a honky-tonk.*
> *Stomp the boards hard Saturday night.*
> *Go to church on Sunday.*
> *That makes everything all right.*

I hardly knew one church from the next back then, except some were for well-heeled people and others for those not so heeled.

Duane looked at me and grinned. His bushy mustache shone orange in the morning sunlight. "Jap Corner was buzzing," Duane said, adding my name, "Sonny," to show he knew who the buzzing was about. He usually would've called me by the nickname "Suzy," but today he was being formal. He should've said "Mitch," too, but I guess I was getting all the blame. "I just come from having huevos rancheros there," he continued, "and I can tell you Jap Corner was buzzing this morning."

"What's the buzzing about?" Jesse asked.

"I can't tell you their names," Duane said, "but their initials are 'Sonny' and 'Mitch.'"

I felt relieved to be sharing the blame, even though I knew if anyone was going to get fired it was going to be me. But it was like Sam didn't want to hear any of it. He just turned to Mitch and said, "You'd be better off doing your magic tricks in an opium den than at the Round-Up." He looked out across the alfalfa field at the quivering red sun rising above a dim outline of the Sierras and said, "It's going to be a scorcher today," something he often said as a signal that we'd better get cracking. Then he walked away to take the missus to church, and I realized that my earlier hunch was right: when he told me to stay out of trouble he really *was* talking about me and Ana, and as far as fighting went, as long as Jesse, me, and his son stayed out of jail and showed up for work, he didn't care. I mean, he cared—he'd tried to talk to Jesse once about not getting into fights—but he wouldn't fire our asses as long as we were there in the morning to work. I felt so grateful I wanted to get right into the field.

My relief didn't last long, though, because after Jesse finished up his story of the fight in Firebaugh and Mitch told about the Mexicans, Duane said he heard this morning that those cholos were going to take care of me and Mitch. Of a sudden, the tingly hot air I was breathing turned frosty. The only reason they didn't fight us last night, Duane said, is that one of them had just gotten out of Soledad and they were in the bar celebrating. That must've been the older cholo, I thought, with the scar on his lip. He would've been shipped right back to prison if he'd violated his parole by getting into a bar fight. That's why they held back, Duane said, but they'd soon find us. Right then I saw them again, in my mind, coming at us, only this time they had knives or guns. Mitch looked concerned and said he'd have a shotgun ready for them if they came around.

"Let's go find them," Jesse said. Like always, if a buddy of his got jumped, he was ready to go after the guys.

"We *already* found them," I said. I'd sobered up enough to know not to go looking for trouble. I didn't want nothing more to do with them. "Go find those suckers who got *you*. You look like a horse stomped on your face."

I thought he was about to swing at me, he looked so steamed. He had a snap mind, Jesse did. Where I hesitated, Jesse snapped. And once his mind snapped, it was all over. You'd better get out of the way.

"I am going to get them," he said, mad as hell. Whether it meant jail time and getting fired, he could care less because when his mind snapped he acted drunk even when he was sober.

My stepdad, Dewey, had been leaning against the barn, sharpening his pocketknife. Dewey's like a snake—he acts like he can't hear but he can—and all morning he'd just been listening and taking stock of the situation. Hard living had stripped extra flesh off Dewey, leaving him lean and leathery with washed-out blue eyes, the color of faded denim, almost white under the down-turned brim of a yellow straw hat. The skin on his face looked paler than it ought, given how he'd worked outside all his life, till you realized it had been as sun-bleached and dried as the underside of an old cowhide. Tight wrinkles sprayed out from the corners of his eyes like cracks in the hide. He wore overalls and a blue shirt and stood upright as a post, though he was in his sixties.

"The only way to do those kinds of sons of bitches," Dewey told us, "is to cut their heads plumb off."

Dewey knew what he was talking about. Once in Skeeko's he got into an argument with a guy over a dame he was flirting with at the bar—"Hell," Dewey told us, "how was I to know it was his wife?"—and her husband went outside and then came back into the bar with an axle driveshaft from his truck and laid it across the back of Dewey's head, knocking him off that stool like a sack of potatoes. Everyone who saw it thought Dewey was out cold if he wasn't dead, but he come up off the floor with his knife open and slashed the guy across his belly, cutting out his guts right there in the bar. Dewey tried to cut the guy's head off but the knife blade was so sharp it caught deep in the collarbone. Dewey couldn't get the blade unstuck and around the guy's neck before he was pulled off. The guy lived but he was crippled. Years later, I used to see him walking around town, hunched over.

Right after the knifing, Dewey hightailed it back to Oklahoma. That man knew how to survive. He made his own moonshine and ran it in Oklahoma. He loved to shoot dice. I seen him spread a cotton sack out smooth on the ground and make more money shooting dice than picking cotton. And he loved to fight. In Oklahoma, him and his brothers went into town on Saturday night to drink and fight until somebody hauled them home in a wagon and dumped them out on the front porch. But he always showed up for work. How that man knew to survive! After he married my momma, he told my brother, his sons, and me, "Boys, don't never say you can't find a job, because if you're looking for a job you can find a job."

He learned us how to work. I know that ain't proper English, but it's the right word. Teachers in school might've *taught* us, but Dewey *learned* us. He told us, "Don't do something unless you're going to do it right." I learned to drive tractor from him. The first time I tried laying down furrows with a tractor I looked back to see a banana cut in the field. "Concentrate," Dewey told me. He showed me how to gaze at the white sacks at the end of the field while keeping my mind on what I was doing. "Show a fucking example," Dewey told me. I got to where I could lay down furrows in a field with a tractor that most people thought only a Cat could cut so straight.

I remember how good I felt the day Sam was bragging on me about how I drove tractor one spring. "You don't see any dog-legged furrows out there," he said. He pointed to me and told one of his other workers, "If this Okie kid can drive a tractor this good, why the hell can't you?" I felt a prideful flush come into my face.

Dewey also taught us boys how to fight with boxing gloves. That's why later I could outbox Jesse, though, like I said before, I couldn't outfight him. Sometimes Dewey would put on just one glove and knock me and my brother silly, even though we were boxing him together with both our hands. People could look down their noses at us, but Dewey taught us how to bust those noses.

Excepting those boxing matches, Dewey didn't otherwise hit us unless he had to, though he never laid a hand on my kid sister. He spoiled her completely. She used to smart-mouth the school bus driver and if he said something back to her, she'd get off the bus and swish her ass at him while flipping him off. She needed a good ass-whipping is what she needed, but one day she told Dewey that the bus driver said he wasn't going to pick her up no more—she was just a little Okie tramp—and the next day Dewey waited for the bus and dragged that driver out and beat him into the dirt.

He did the same thing to the Russian potato farmer he worked for on the West Side. Us kids used to help out loading potato sacks, but the farmer didn't want to pay us, not until Dewey went into his house and held him down by his beard behind his own couch while clobbering him with the other hand, saying, "You will pay those boys," and he did, though that was the end of Dewey's working for him. When the elementary school vice principal spanked my brother, Dewey went to the school and knocked the living shit out of him, too. "Nobody spanks my boys except me," Dewey said. Anymore he would be in jail for what he done to that vice principal and bus driver. Course, he did do jail time for drinking and fighting, but that was before he married Momma. He was hell on wheels, Dewey was. After he was made, the good Lord busted the mold.

Jesse found out about Dewey's fists one day when we came home from school and saw Dewey, drunk as a skunk, disking in the vineyard on an old stand-up Moline. That's when we worked southeast of town. Jesse told me and my brother we had to get Dewey off that tractor because if he fell back into those disk blades he would be dead. We watched him come to the end of the row, standing up in that old Moline and swaying like a tree in the wind. I saw he was smiling and whistling, but I couldn't hear him. He was always whistling, though you couldn't make out any tune. He was like a bird in that way; if you listen close to birds they don't really whistle real tunes, not even meadowlarks. They whistle notes without melodies. Dewey could sure whistle that way, all day long.

At the end of the row we no sooner pulled him off the tractor than he flattened all three of us, breaking my nose and leaving Jesse sitting in the dirt. He tried to reach in his pocket for his knife but it wasn't there. Every night he laid out his work clothes so they would be ready in the morning, but the night before, he came home drunk and forgot his pocketknife in his other pants. Save for that, the three of us would be dead, or cut up bad. He kept that knife razor sharp. You could shave with it. Make him mad and he'd kill you.

That morning by the barn after Jesse got clobbered by the Firebaugh cowboys, Dewey asked him, "How many jumped you?"

"Three," Jesse said.

Dewey said nothing, just started whistling as he walked off, like Jesse should've been able to take better care of himself, though I could've reminded Dewey that when he fought the three of us—and broke my nose—we were just kids, not cowboys in a bar.

"Trouble comes in threes," I said to Jesse, trying to make him feel better.

"That's not what the saying means," Mitch said. "'Trouble coming in threes' means they come one after the other sequentially." Mitch knew all the sayings, even back then.

"That's how I'm going to get those bastards," Jesse said. "Sequentially." And he would, too, just like I did years later with those guys who broke my wrists.

"We've only had two troubles so far," Mitch said, trying to clarify the situation for us. "Two last night. We got one more to go."

"Like those cholos coming back for us," I said.

"Or Jesse's fight with Lloyd," Mitch said.

Jesse looked a little uneasy at Mitch, like his mentioning the upcoming fight in this way was a bad omen. I'd forgotten all about it because weeks had passed since the fight had been set up. Lloyd was a tough North Fork Indian—and I mean he was a big Indian—who had a bad reputation in the mountains. I guess you could say that if Jesse was King of the Valley when it came to fistfighting, Lloyd was King of the Mountains. That summer, right after we graduated, arrangements got made for a showdown at Bass Lake between Jesse and Lloyd—the King of the Valley versus the King of the Mountains.

"When the hell is that fight?" I asked.

Jesse looked more annoyed than ever. His anger made his busted-up lip and black eyes look worse than they had all morning, and I saw how beat up he really was. "Next Saturday, you stupid hick," he said, like I was ignorant to be asking something he thought I should have clearly in mind.

"Why should I remember that, you asshole? I'm not fighting him, you are, if you can be ready."

"Hey, hey," Mitch said when it looked like Jesse and I were about to go at it. As he spoke, Mitch stepped back, not between us the way he did once before when he got clocked. "We better get to work."

"This guy's got shit for brains," Jesse said about me.

"Well, fuck you," I said. "At least I got brains enough not to get the shit knocked out of 'em."

I drove off with Mitch in a battered black ranch pickup while Jesse took the swather to cut hay. I was glad to get away from him when he was in that kind of mood. We were already running late with changing the cotton sprinklers in North America next to the Tomato Piece. All the fields and ranches had names—South America, North America, the Bank Ranch, the Big Ranch, the Cottonwood Creek Piece, the Camp Ranch, the Pond Piece. The Tomato Piece made such a big impression on those eighty acres, its name stuck for years, even when no tomatoes were on it anymore.

Duane went off to feed his cows and then head home for the rest of the day. Cowboys never did do much on Sunday except nurse their Saturday-night hangovers and eat ice cream in the heat of the afternoon. Dewey had probably gone off home to rest, too—and even take a nap—until setting his night water in the Big Ranch alfalfa. Mitch's daddy didn't care how he did it, and as long as Dewey got everything irrigated without building up tail water he gave him a long leash.

When we were growing, Dewey was fun to be with when he was hanging around the house. He stretched out on the floor on his back and had us kids try to lift him up by his ears, which we couldn't do no matter if two of us pulled on them at once. He laid there laughing in a high, wheezy way till he cried with his eyes half shut while we tugged and pulled, getting to laughing ourselves as much as Dewey.

He liked to play tricks, Dewey did, that got us to learn how to take care of ourselves. I remember him stretching his big hand across the spark plugs of a car he was working on while the engine was running, telling Jesse to grab his other hand. I knew better because he done that to me before. Jesse no sooner touched Dewey's free hand than the electricity from those spark plugs run through Dewey's body, down his arm to his hand, and knocked Jesse to the ground. Tears squeezed out of Dewey's eyes he was laughing so hard. "You want to try that again, son?" he asked Jesse.

Jesse, learning quick, said, "No, sir."

Dewey teased us but he didn't belittle us, and he didn't put up with anyone doing so either. The time I remember most was when I was fixing up this old Pontiac as a kid and couldn't get the timing set. The engine kept missing. I changed the plugs and the points and the wires, and it was still missing. Dewey's smart-ass nephew was watching me one day—he was a guy Dewey never much liked—and I told him what I'd done and he said, "You stupid son of a bitch—" but he didn't get to finish telling me that I hadn't changed the condenser because his nose was flat against his face. Dewey hit him so hard up against the windshield his head cracked it. When he got to his feet, Dewey knocked him through the yard fence, not over it but through the wooden slats. Dewey reached into the car and broke off the stick shift and near beat that guy to death. "You don't call this boy's momma a bitch," Dewey said. Afterward, Dewey told him he could come around the house but not to be calling nobody's momma a bitch. Them's killing words.

Dewey stuck up for us that way, not like my true daddy. My true daddy was a real mean person. He was half Scot-Irish and the other half was Indian. He carried a rawhide whip that he used on both mules and us kids. My brother and me got scars on our backs and legs to prove it. Once I accidentally banged a window closed and he said I almost broke the pane, though it didn't crack at all, and to teach me a lesson he held my hand down on the windowsill and banged my fingers with a ball-peen hammer, breaking a knuckle.

He was one who belittled people. Everyone but him was stupid. When he got himself a beefsteak for supper, we ate a bowl of beans or a plate of fried potatoes. When he had slab bacon and eggs for breakfast, we had biscuits and gravy. Dewey wasn't that way. If he ate a chicken-fried steak, we all did. If we ate hot dogs, he did, too. My real daddy never left Oklahoma except only one time when he was sick and my brother went back there and took him to Arkansas. I didn't even go back to his funeral when he died.

Mitch was lucky to have the daddy he did, I was thinking as I drove slow down the dirt road with him so as not to spread dust out into the cotton for mites like red spider to build on. It was going to be a scorcher, Mitch's daddy said, and so would the summer days to come. We would soon be driving a water truck up and down the roads to keep down the dust, which now swirled inside the cab of the high-whiny, straining pickup, so junky it was hard to drive. When I tried to shift into third, the gears ground, and I tried to double-clutch, though the floor shift was still grinding.

"I can't find the hole," I said.

"Put a little hair around it," Mitch said, like I knew he would.

On the cardboard roof of the cab, with chalk we used for marking lug boxes, Mitch had scrawled the Greek alphabet he'd learned in school so he could teach it to me. It stretched out in a long row: α β γ δ ε ζ η θ ι κ λ μ ν ξ ο π ρ σ τ υ φ χ ψ ω.

Mitch had taught me how to say the letters—"psi," "omikron," "zeta," and "upsilon"—and I sometimes liked practicing them as we drove along, though now the after-effects of the booze banging on my brain and the bouncing truck made my head hurt while looking at them. The Greek letters reminded me of Mitch spouting his magic words in the bar and me drinking brandy and water when I should've known how I was going to feel in the sizzling morning sun.

As I got out of the pickup, put on my rubber irrigation boots, and sank into the mud of the cotton field to change sprinklers, I closed my eyes and saw lights popping inside my eyelids. Even though the long sprinkler pipes were aluminum, they were full of water and heavy when you first tilted them to drain before carrying them to the next setting and coupling them together until they formed one long line of unbroken pipe down a row of cotton. I took pleasure in stepping on the fucking cotton plants as I walked. As hard as changing sprinklers was, it was nothing compared to the work I'd done as a kid and would never do again: cutting grapes, digging potatoes, rolling trays, chopping cotton, picking cotton—by hand, I mean. Nobody did that anymore now that we had mechanical pickers.

"Take a flying fuck at the moon," Mitch yelled to a bunch of weeder geese in his way. Sam was always experimenting with new ways to farm—that summer instead of rows we tried irrigating cotton fields with contour levees, which were always breaking because the surveyor fucked up—and the dumb-ass weeder geese were another one of his experiments. As far as I could see they did nothing but make our job nastier by fouling the mud with green goose shit. You wouldn't think birds that only ate weeds could shit so much. Goose squat everywhere. Sam paid two dollars a goose and got a dollar back for each one returned at the end of the season, but the way they were dying of thirst in the heat, he wasn't going to get nothing in return. When a goose gave up the ghost, it died with its long neck stretched over its back. They were funny that way.

I watched a fat, white-feathered goose, so thirsty its gray tongue hung out of its orange bill, stagger down a dry cotton row like a drunk trying to walk a police line, until it dropped in the dust, too dumb to step into the next row full of water. I picked it up by its wings and tossed it to where it could get a drink. With my mouth all cottony and my head splitting, I was as dumb in my own way as the goose, only there weren't nobody there to help me out. I should've vowed not to drink on work nights, but I knew I would.

When I told Mitch how I thought humans were as dumb as geese, he said, "Don't get too philosophical about it."

It was mid-morning and we were driving to Etcheverria's little grocery store after getting the pipes changed and the pump turned back on. Alpha Grocery, where we usually stopped, was closed on Sunday, so we had to drive all the way to Etchy's market. Mitch might've had the same last name as Etcheverria if some ancestor hadn't changed his awhile back to make it more American. I bought a quart of buttermilk and some Ding Dongs, and Mitch got a quart of regular milk and a plastic package of cinnamon rolls. Jesse would've bought two quarts of milk and drunk both before we'd finished one. At the little market, Etchy was talking in Basco to a sheepherder from Nevada named Patxi Etxebarria Auertenetxea. That was the real Basque spelling, Mitch told me.

"Why don't you use Basco words instead of Greek ones for your magic tricks?" I asked him.

"I don't know any Basque," he said. "My folks know some, but it's too late for me to learn. They say the Devil tried to learn Basque by listening outside a farmhouse, but after seven years he could only say two words: 'Yes, ma'am.'"

"You sure that weren't an Okie house?" I said.

That afternoon, we had to V-out an irrigation ditch and change the sprinklers again. When we finished our work for the day, we went to watch the sundown from the shack where Mitch slept that summer. The shack was an old migrant workers' wooden cabin, moved near the ranch pond and the tomato patch. In the fall, Mitch's daddy and his friends used it as a hunting shack, but Mitch had moved into it for the summer so he didn't have to sleep at home. It was a nice place for him to get laid, before his girlfriend had dumped him and Ana saw her riding in a car with one of Mitch's buddies, sitting real close. "It looked like one driver with two heads," Ana told Mitch. I knew he was hurting. Finding out that way from his sister made the hurt worse.

Inside the one-room cabin, Mitch propped the loaded double-barrel, twenty-gauge shotgun against the wall at the head of his bed in case those Mexicans came after him at night. He probably only meant to scare them; he wasn't going to mess around fighting them the way Jesse and me would've felt we had to. No Okie, I do believe, ever ran from a fight. I was floored when Mitch told me he never saw a fistfight at his boarding school. At our high school someone was duking it out every afternoon.

Course, Mitch didn't grow up the way we did, with teachers making fun of how we talked or other kids shaming us for having poor shoes or carrying lard-can lunch buckets or eating powder biscuits filled with cold beans. Maybe we didn't have two nickels to rub together, but we had our fists. Mitch was an Eagle Scout with a sash full of merit badges. Jesse and me, our fights were our merit badges, and nobody could take those away from us.

On the pasteboard cabin wall, Mitch had pinned up magazine photographs of the sexy, gorgeous model Suzy Parker, with her flame-red hair, and half-naked in bathing suits of different kinds. Under one picture in capital letters was something Suzy Parker said: *"MARRIAGE KILLS ROMANCE."*

The cabin didn't have much in it, only a refrigerator, a hot plate on a table, a single bed, a couple of hard chairs, and maybe thirty or forty books on shelves pressed along one wall. Two books in a cardboard case had the title *Remembrance of Things Past*. An old record player with adjustable speeds sat near the bed. Mitch turned it on and set down the needle onto a thirty-three-and-a-third vinyl record already on the turntable. It was classical music. "'Jupiter,'" Mitch said. "When I woke up this morning I was still drunk, but when I put this on I thought I'd died and gone to heaven." Though the record was scratchy and the music wasn't normally what I listened to, lots of strings and horns cranked into a happiness that made me understand how he must have felt. Sometimes you wake up feeling your life is about to leave you, and you're just grateful to realize you've got another day ahead of you.

We fetched some frozen glass mugs from the freezer and filled them with cold beer and Snap-E-Tom. We carried the red beer outside and sat on the ground with our backs against the cabin to watch the sun go down over the tomato field. The cold beer with the spicy tomato juice cut through the ache of the day and the blur of last night with a clean, zingy taste and feeling. Then Ana came into my inner eye, dancing in the bar with Mitch's friend.

"Did Ana make it home last night?" I asked.

"How the hell do I know?" he said, real testy. "I was out here." I knew he and his sister were tight, and he'd been at the house that morning when I drove up, so he should know.

"How long's she had that new boyfriend?"

"That's not her boyfriend, just a buddy who goes to school with me. He came down from Modesto to visit. What do you care anyway?"

"Just asking," I said. "I don't give a rat's ass." I changed the subject quick. "Jesse is nervous about this fight coming up."

"He could get his ass handed to him. That Lloyd is one strong son of a bitch."

"I know. I seen him lift up the back end of a car."

"Bullshit."

"I seen it. A Falcon."

"Well, okay, a Falcon I can understand. Lloyd's licked a lot of guys. He knows how to fight."

"It could happen," I said.

"Jesse's hurting from last night, too. He's got to be sore."

"He usually figures out a way to win."

"He didn't figure it out last night. I've been thinking," Mitch said, "I wonder if we should've let him go after those cholos from the bar."

"Oh, Christ, Mitch, forget them. That's over."

"You heard what Duane said. I hate waiting around to see if they're going to show up."

"He also said that one just got out of prison. He's not going to be looking for trouble."

"There's the other two."

"Let it rest. We'll get them in our own good time."

As the sun dropped, a little breeze picked up and I could feel the heat of the day lifting off my skin. The air turned bronze. Sunlight lay across the tomato field like the plants had been spread with thick butter, the color of melted gold, I thought. In the distant horizon the Coast Range turned lavender.

Mitch said, "This is the best time of day."

"You were reading my mind," I said.

Mitch drained the last of the red beer from his mug. "Now we just need some pussy."

I knew Mitch was broken up and miserable inside from losing his girlfriend, especially having her run off with one of his buddies, and I was missing Ana more than I ever expected, hurting in my heart from seeing the way she pressed up to another guy while dancing last night, and hurting more because I had to keep it all bottled up from her brother.

"I know what you're saying," I said, feeling lousier by the second for betraying Mitch with his sister and never talking about it.

"Still," Mitch said, "someday we're probably going to look back on this as the best time of our life."

I didn't know what to say. Here we were without pussy, busted up from hangovers, smeared with mud and goose shit,

threatened by three thugs who said they were coming to get us—
and probably would if somebody didn't cut their heads plumb
off like Dewey advised—and my heart's hurting from betraying
my friend sitting next to me, and Mitch is saying it's the best
time of our lives. I hated to think what would be the worst.

The next Saturday, I rode up to Bass Lake with Mitch. Jesse
had been squirrelly all week and I stayed away from him. Now
that the night of the big fight was here, he'd be like a firecracker
already lit—all the more reason to keep my distance. Mitch
borrowed his daddy's Buick for the drive. We were dragging
main from the Big Top to the Sno-White when Jesse pulled up
alongside us in his red coupe full of guys. He revved the engine a
couple times, challenging us to race.

"Drop this sucker into low," I told Mitch, "and slam that
pedal to the floor." He did, spinning rubber until the tires
grabbed traction and we tore down Yosemite Avenue, side
by side with Jesse's car, racing out of town, pushing that
speedometer past a hundred, shaking it at a hundred and ten,
then a hundred and twenty until we hit the two-lane road and
Jesse had to drop behind us to keep from crashing into a car
coming at him head-on. I kept expecting to see the interior
dashboard of the Buick brighten with flashing lights from a cop
car behind us, but nothing happened. We were on our way.

We cracked open a six-pack and drove up into the mountains,
drinking beer and changing seats by sliding past each other while
still keeping up speed on those mountain curves. I drove for a
while and then handed things back to Mitch as he slid over me,
grabbing the wheel with his left hand and letting his foot take
the place of mine on the gas pedal. It was fun.

At the lake, before we even went into the dance bar called The
Falls, where I could hear the band playing, Jesse came up to me
in the parking lot. "I want you to come with me, Sonny." He
said it real friendly, with surprising calm.

"I never knowed you to need help," I said. To my knowledge, Jesse never asked for help in a fight and never expected it neither. "What about the guys that come with you?" I added. I wanted to get onto the dance floor and see about finding someone to help me forget Ana.

"I need you." His words sparked me with a good feeling. I was ready to stand by his side no matter what.

Side by side, me and Jesse walked out by the falls, with Mitch and some others from Madera following, to where a crowd of guys waited. It was almost dark but not quite, with that eerie summer half-light that hangs around after sundown. Lloyd stepped out of the crowd and—I tell no lie—he was the most enormous, fearsome-looking Indian you could imagine, wearing a purple plaid short-sleeved shirt that showed off his arms like a couple of hams. I believed he could lift a Cadillac. His face was full of flesh, bigger than any normal human's, and he didn't look happy.

I turned to Mitch and he looked scared, just like all the other guys behind Jesse. I think we were all afraid Jesse could be killed tonight.

I've lived long enough to know that it isn't how things turn out that shows if someone is brave or not. It takes a lifetime to know a guy—or even a woman—with real courage. Some people who seem to be acting brave are really cowards or fools. I thought of this night years later when I was watching a movie on TV about Muhammad Ali going out into the middle of the African night to fight George Foreman, who was the most feared fighter in the world at that time. The guys with Ali looked scared and glum as they walked to the van in the darkness. They were like us in that they thought Ali might get killed. No one thought he would win. Ali turned to his hangdog crew and said, "Hey, what's the matter with you people? It's just another fight."

That night at the lake, as we walked up together toward Lloyd, who stood solid as a war monument waiting for us, I turned to see Jesse's face break into that big smile of his. It wasn't forced like you would expect in that situation; he looked like he couldn't have been genuinely happier than to be where he was, even though he might soon be down in his own blood. No way in the world could he know for sure what would happen in the coming moments, and he still loved it.

He wore shin-high combat boots, ready for kicking, white Levi's, and a snow-white sweatshirt that he took off and handed to me. He needed me, I come to know, to keep his sweatshirt from getting tossed in the dirt. I stood by his shoulder, the way a second would hold a fighter's robe in the boxing ring.

Jesse bounced a little on the balls of his feet, still grinning, and began to chant.

Hey, Lloyd, Lloyd,
Start singing to your Lord,
'Cause I'm Jesse Floyd
And you're gonna get floored.

Poetry always pisses guys off, but Lloyd got enraged beyond being pissed. He swung at Jesse without sparring or feeling him out, just a big roundhouse swing with his giant fist, and Jesse casually leaned back, almost amused, as Lloyd's fist whizzed past his chin, missing him. The next thing I knew, I was looking up into the sky. I felt wetness on my cheeks and I knew it was my blood. My nose was broken, I knew it was, just the way Dewey had broken it. Both Jesse's and Lloyd's blurry faces looked down on me as they knelt over me, their heads almost touching. My feet went numb.

Jesse lifted my head and rested it on his knee. "Are you okay?" he asked, like when he'd knocked out Mitch by accident.

I stared up at him and Lloyd. Unlike Mitch, I hadn't passed out, except maybe between the time Lloyd slugged me and I hit the ground. I didn't remember falling. I tried to say something but just grunted.

"His nose broke," Lloyd said.

"Here," Jesse said. He pulled a handkerchief and laid it across my nose. "Squeeze it tight. It'll stop bleeding. Hold it. It's clean."

It was a red paisley bandanna. I sounded congested when I talked with it pressed to my nose, saying, "You summabitch."

My cussing seemed enough sign to Jesse that I was all right for both him and Lloyd to stand up. I laid there looking up at them grinning at one another. They said something to each other. They shook hands, still smiling, like they were the two best friends in the world.

Jesse helped me into the backseat of Mitch's car and I laid there for a while with my head tilted back until the bleeding stopped. It felt like a big rock sat on my nose, causing a fierce pressure behind my eyeballs. I knew both my eyes would be black in the morning, just like they were after Dewey whacked me. I thought about hot-wiring Mitch's car and heading out of there. Someone would give Mitch a ride home, but since it was really his daddy's car I dropped that idea.

After a while, I crawled out of the backseat and walked across the dark mountain road toward The Falls and the music. My legs turned shaky. I stopped and held the rough bark of a tree to get my balance. I looked up at the darkening sky and the stars between the tips of two pines, swaying back and forth without making a sound.

From where I stood I could see guys and girls spilled onto the balcony over the lake, and when I reached the doorway and looked inside at everyone dancing, the room was so crowded I couldn't make out individuals at first, only the bobbing heads and shuffling feet of a big dark human mass all melted together. Eddie and the Rebels wailed away on their guitars at the end of the room, playing "Lucille." Eddie screamed into the microphone, mimicking Little Richard. *"Oh, Lucille, please come back where you belong."* The racket hurt my head. *"I been good to you, baby, please, don't leave me alone."*

Then I saw Jesse in his shin-high combat boots and white sweatshirt dancing up a storm with Linda Antonelli, the girl from Merced whose girlfriends scratched me to pieces when I was wearing Jesse's football jersey. My eyes started to water from the pain swelling up through my nose. Jesse stomped his feet, leaned back, doing the Hydro, and Linda in her tight skirt danced up between the legs of his white Levi's, splattered with my blood. Her bouncing tits made my nose ache just from thinking how I'd feel if I tried hopping up and down that way. Then she leaned back and Jesse danced up close to her, both of them smiling at each other. I could only stand there with my nose pounding while Jesse wiggled his fingers above his head, stamped his feet, and howled along with the band, like he'd just won the biggest fight of his life and was King of the Mountains.

THE FOURTH OF JULY

The skin under my eyes turned raw and purple, then greenish yellow like the inside of a Santa Rosa plum. Dewey fixed my nose by clasping it between his palms and snapping it into place. That made it a little straighter. Then the skin around my eyes puffed up and turned black.

One morning later that week when I tried to open my eyes, I thought it was still night. The roar of an airplane shook the walls, sounding about to crash through the roof. I was supposed to be up flagging a crop duster, but I overslept. Crop dusters start spraying just before dawn, when the air is stillest. Old Lonnie Simmons was dive-bombing the house to wake me up.

Dewey busted into my bedroom, a shadowy blur, but through my squinting eyes I could make out the gray nightshirt that hung to his hips, his long, bare pecker nearly knocking against his knees. Nobody cusses worse than a man on a cold morning trying to start a chainsaw, but Dewey came close. "Get your fucking lazy ass out of that bed so that cocksucking son of a bitch leaves us the fuck alone. Your momma's trying to fucking sleep."

Only one time did I smart-mouth Dewey when I didn't want to get up and go to work. It was right after he'd married Momma, and I was a little kid. I was supposed to chop cotton. "Fuck you," I said. "I ain't going to work." That was the first and last time I said "fuck you" to Dewey. That day I got my up-and-comin', as the old-time Okies called it, though I call it the down-and-goin'. Another time I was in the eighth grade and I called Jesse's daddy by his front name—Orville—and Dewey whopped me good. We weren't to show disrespect. It was always "Mr." and "Mrs." and "Yes, sir" and "No, ma'am."

When Dewey got through with me he wore my ass out. I don't mean he spanked me with an open hand, neither. That man had the biggest fucking fists. And he was worse if he got something in his hand, a stick shift maybe, like that time with his nephew, or the time he done in a sow that was coming at my momma. Momma loved raising hogs, and at one point we had three hundred head. When it came time to castrate a boar, Dewey hooked a cable through its nose so it would strain back on that cable, trying to pull away, while he got behind it with his Case knife, sliced open the sack, and scraped out the nuts. You don't cut off the nuts, the way some people think, but scrape them out to avoid infection, then throw on some pink salve to keep the flies off. Three months later we would have pork.

One day, Dewey was castrating a boar when a sow left the litter she was nursing and charged at Momma. Nothing in the world is meaner than a nursing sow with a litter. Quicker than I knew what was happening Dewey picked up a metal pipe and leveled that sow with one blow to the head. Afterward, we had to raise her pigs on a bottle because that sow was dead.

So I knew better than to smart-mouth Dewey when he told me to get the hell out of bed that morning, especially since he attached it to leaving Momma to sleep in peace. I threw on my pants and ran out of the house, carrying my T-shirt and waving my arms at the crop duster, but he'd already banked and was diving back down at the house. The roaring engine shook the ground it was so loud.

Old Lonnie Simmons, I believe, never drew a sober breath in his life, and I knew he just loved an excuse to stir up the household, certain that Dewey would rip my ass for the rest of the week. I hopped into the pickup, with my T-shirt and work shoes on the seat next to me, and drove toward the cotton field. Without rubber pads the metal clutch and brake cut into my bare feet. Wind and dust roiled up through cracks in the floorboard, and I was thinking, *That's it for me. I'm getting the hell out of that house.*

The sky in the east was just lighting up, but it was still night in the west, with a few stars and a silvery moon slice, fading quick. I stood at the end of the cotton row and held up the hoe with the white flag tied to the end of it. The big biplane roared down behind me, coming over my head, its wheels a few feet above the cotton plants, gray pesticide pluming down the row and onto my hair and shirt. I don't know how those old boxy First World War–style crates still flew. I walked along the edge of the field, counting eleven rows, stopped and raised the hoe again so that Old Lonnie could see the white flag from the far end of the field after he'd pulled up, just clearing the electric lines and banking to the left, then looping to the right in the pale sky until he was coming back at me, like a huge, angry, double-winged dragonfly, dropping over the power line, hugging the top of the cotton, the nose and swirling propeller of the plane buzzing straight at me, trailing a cloud of spray, until the plane pulled up, cutting the spray, but not before I felt its wetness drift down on me. I wore a handkerchief over my mouth, but I still tasted the bitter Kelthane. My T-shirt was sticky with spray.

I went home to take a shower and change my clothes. I washed out my eyes with milk the way Dewey told me to earlier in the summer after we first sprayed the cotton with sulfur. On the way to work, I passed the shack of a Mexican hand nicknamed Nellie, who waved me down and wanted me to take him to the store for groceries. I said I would take him later because now I had to go to work. I smelled the wine on Nellie and I thought, *Here's what I could be if I don't soon quit fucking up.*

Mitch's daddy was in the ranch yard by the butane tank where we serviced the rigs. One of the workers was fueling up a tractor to spray a field with Malathion. The tractor got down closer to the plants and was cheaper than an airplane. That field was infested bad with red spider.

Sam called me over to his pickup and pulled a flashlight from his glove box, where he kept his .38 Special. "Shine this light in my eyes, will you, Sonny?"

"You bet," I said. I turned on the beam and pointed it at one eye, then the other.

"What do you see?" he asked.

"Your eyes," I said. I could've said that his brown eyes reminded me of his daughter's.

"Are they contracting with the light on them?"

I shined the flashlight close to one pupil, then the other, but they didn't shrink down the way they should. Both dark pupils stayed expanded. "No," I told Sam.

"I thought so," he said. "I'm poisoned."

I didn't ask him to check my eyes because I didn't want him focusing on the bruises and, anyway, poison doesn't act that fast. Sam had been helping the men spray for the past couple of days. He was worried about his workers getting poisoned and was emptying the Malathion into the sprayer himself. He made sure the tractor driver wore a gas mask. That's how he went and got polluted his own self.

As for me getting sprayed that morning, it wasn't that Sam didn't care about me, it's just that back in those days we didn't think much about a flagger getting a little bug spray or yellow sulfur dust on him. He even let his own son flag those planes and go home covered. That stuff sure had a funny tacky feel on your skin.

I knew he had me check his eyes because he'd probably been throwing up.

"You going to see a doctor?" I said.

"I'll go in the morning," he said. "We have to get done spraying today."

The tractor driver finished fueling up. He shut down both valves and uncoupled the nozzle from the tractor tank. Just the way a garden hose would be full of water if you turned off both the nozzle at the tip and then the faucet at the base, the fuel hose was full of butane. The driver sprayed it into the weeds to clear the hose. A cloud of freezing butane turned the weeds instantly silver, like in a heavy frost. Jesse and I usually held a match in front of the nozzle when we released the butane to create a temporary flame-thrower, with fire shooting out twenty feet or more, but we didn't do it when Sam was around.

"Do you want me to drive you to the doctor?" I asked Sam, thinking it might be hard for him to see since his eyes weren't working. I sometimes drove him when he went into town to the bank to get money for field crews. I'd sit in the pickup while he strapped on his shoulder holster with the pistol in it and went into the bank for a sack of money.

"It's a wonder you can see yourself," Sam said, "with those eyes of yours."

"I can see fine," I said.

"Dewey and I were talking," Sam went on, "and it's about time you started settling down. I'm all for partying, but the way you're headed you're apt to get hurt or hurt somebody else. I tried talking to Jesse, but you've got more sense."

Where the hell does Dewey get off? I thought. Dewey never stopped drinking and fighting until he was an old man. Given the direction Sam was going, I saw my chance to tell him, "I've been thinking the same thing. I want to get my own place."

Sam answered like he was ready for me. "I don't have a place for you on the ranch here," he said, "but find yourself a house, Sonny, and I'll pay your rent, electric, propane, and all the rest. Since you'll be driving your own car back and forth to work, you can fill it up with gas here."

One minute I'm thinking he's about to throw me off the ranch and the next minute he's fixing to help me settle down permanent. He'd done the same thing for my older brother—paid his rent, electric, and all the rest—then made him ranch foreman, moving him into the house next to Dewey's, until my brother left for a ranch manager's job on the West Side. Sam hadn't yet found a new foreman. That's why he was giving all the orders that summer, and it was wearing on him. The new foreman sure as hell wouldn't be me or Jesse, not yet anyway, but it looked like Sam might think that way down the line, if I kept my nose clean and settled down. Getting my own place was the first step.

Out in the yard, a decrepit old Mexican who'd worked for Sam's daddy—we called him Old Antiguo—was raking damp eucalyptus leaves. The old man was Nellie's uncle. He wore a high-crowned straw hat and overalls and was bent like a fishhook while he raked. Where there weren't any leaves on the ground, he just stroked the dirt in a slow, steady motion all day long, after he'd dampened it down with a garden hose. He lived in a shack next to the barn at Sam's house. Nobody asked him to work, he just wanted to. Sam took care of him, like he cared for another old Mexican named Pablo who'd worked almost forty years for Sam's daddy. I was thinking that I didn't want to end up this way, all by myself as an old man with nothing to do but wet down the yard and rake leaves, depending on Sam. Or like his nephew Nellie, drunked up and bumming rides to the store. I was glad to be finding my own place, and I'd soon have enough down to get me a new car.

I couldn't go looking for a new place right off, though, or a new car neither, because the day after Sam and I had our little conversation, the tomato pickers arrived and we were busy as hell loading those tomatoes onto trucks and out of the field. Jesse and I were swampers. Jesse swung the boxes of tomatoes up to me, and I stacked them on the big truck bed. Jesse liked to swing a box up as high as he could with one hand as a way to exercise. His bicep bulged out from the sleeve of his T-shirt as he flung the box up. Over the days, I watched his muscles grow.

The field filled up with tomato pickers all right, but not the pussy we'd expected. Most of the pickers were Mexican men— "braceros," they called them—though some were women and a few were locals, but not many because you couldn't find more than a handful of locals who wanted to pick tomatoes. Hell, I wouldn't. Stooped under that hot sun, filling a big bucket with rock-hard green tomatoes, then dumping the heavy bucket into lug boxes that were stacked up in the field like high bee boxes for me, Jesse, and Mitch to load onto trucks. You had to go down into Mexico to get pickers to do that shitty work.

The fine thing for us about having these braceros in the field was that the government required them to get good hot lunches.

Me and Jesse—and even Mitch—ate with them at noontime.
No more cold bologna sandwiches on Rainbo bread for me.
Stainless steel pots as big as washtubs and filled with sweet-
smelling beans and some kind of carne adovada or pork chile
verde sat on folding tables under canvas awnings. A barbecue pit
held grape stumps burned down to hot coals to heat the tortillas.
Porta-potties were even set up at the edge of the field, something
that ranch had never seen before or since.

Eating those hot burritos was when we had a chance to check
out the chicks as they got paper plates and ladled the steaming
meat and beans onto the tortillas, but there were so few of them,
the burritos interested us more than the pussy.

Except for one, old Pablo's granddaughter, who wore a straw
hat with a white scarf over the crown and tied under her chin,
a loose long-sleeved shirt that hid her boobs, though both Jesse
and I knew what those melons looked and tasted like, and
khaki pants that hugged her ass in a nice way when she walked.
Under the shade of the hat brim, her big, dark eyes seemed to
smile along with her mouth and her beautiful white teeth, but I
couldn't tell if she was smiling at Jesse or me.

"Oh, man," Jesse said, "there's a tomato for you. She's calling
me. We need some tall corn around here."

"Go ahead," I said. "I guess it's your turn."

"My turn, hell. You ain't never gonna have a turn."

"I did," I said.

"When would that be?" Jesse asked.

"Wednesday." It was Friday, and I knew Jesse was with her on
Wednesday night, but *after* me, because I drove up to his pickup
with my lights out and saw he was in the cab pouring the coals
to her when he was supposed to be baling hay. He looked at me
funny-like, knowing he'd been with her Wednesday. "I hope you
liked the way she kissed," I told him, "'cause she just finished
sucking my dick."

Jesse knew I had him. "Fuck you," he said.

"Fuck you, too," I said, though I was the one grinning.

I never would've said nothing if Jesse hadn't set himself up for it. It's a good thing I waited my time, otherwise I wouldn't have had no comeback. There's no point to some things if you can't brag about them, but timing is everything.

Then that girl—Pablo's granddaughter, her name was Rosie—did a sweet thing that lunchtime. The tomatoes we were shipping back east in refrigerated train cars were so green that if you threw one hard enough you could shatter a windshield on a truck. A lot of pressure lay on us to get this first picking—the one that made the most money—out of the field before the tomatoes ripened too much. Here and there scattered in the field you could see balls reddening up, but the pickers left them behind along with the smaller green ones. Each picker had a metal ring to make sure a tomato was big enough to pluck, but nobody needed to use those rings. They knew the right size and hardness by the look and feel.

It slayed me that people back east had to pay prime money for hard, green tomatoes. Well, they were edible by the time they got back east and had reddened up a little in the refrigerated railroad cars, but they didn't have the flavor of the vine-ripened ones we plucked for nothing. Every night we went home with four or five big tomatoes that had to be as good as any you could find in the world. You can imagine how in eighty acres you were bound to turn up some beauties. We kept our eyes out for them while we worked. "Whooey!" Jesse yelled when he spotted one. "Look what I found. What a beaut." Then it was my turn to find one better.

When you sliced open those tomatoes, they were deep red all the way through without any yellow gelatin, and you couldn't hardly see any seeds they were so embedded in the meat. You wouldn't chill them because you wanted that warm field taste. A little salt and pepper was all you needed to be in heaven.

At lunchtime that day, Rosie showed up with a tomato the size of a small cantaloupe, so perfect and ripe you could imagine a blue ribbon dangling from it. She handed it to me. Now we knew who she'd been smiling at. She pulled off her straw hat and let her hair fall down around her face. I'm sure a tomato must've been the forbidden fruit in the Garden of Eden. A juicy tomato, heavy in your hand and warm off the vine, sends a zing all the way into your balls.

I pulled out my pocketknife—I carried a Tree Brand and kept it sharp, but not so sharp as Dewey's Case brand—and cut the tomato three ways—for me, Jesse, and Rosie. Jesse didn't carry a pocketknife. He didn't want anyone able to accuse him of using a knife in a fight, or even of having a knife in his pocket that he could use.

Jesse looked like he didn't give a hoot who Rosie gave the tomato to, he was just happy to have his share to bite into. He closed his eyes. Slick juice glistened on the sides of his mouth and down his chin. "Oh my," he said. "Better'n pussy and almost as good as milk."

Rosie smiled with her eyes sparkling like she thought Jesse's saying was cute. She walked away from us, swishing her ass, a cute tomato herself.

That afternoon, after we got the last of the trucks loaded for the day, I was driving the pickup to check on the water in a cornfield, and then go look at a house to rent, when a rifle cracked in the distance and a bullet hummed over the cab of the truck. I jammed on the brakes, put it in reverse, spun around, and headed for where the rifle shot had come from. I knew who the hell it was and what the deal was before I even drove up to see Nellie, all sweaty and drunk as a skunk under his pith helmet, standing by an irrigation ditch with a lever-action .30-30 in his hands. Nellie had a body like a dwarf and a big head like a burl on a tree, and his black eyes, crooked nose, and

droopy mouth looked carved into tree bark. In the ground was
a deep hole where he was digging for Joaquín Murieta's buried
treasure. A suitcase-style box with dials for locating treasure sat
by the hole.

"What in hell are you doing shooting at me, Nellie?"

"I shot over you."

"I could've kept going."

"I could've aimed lower."

I knew he was pissed because I hadn't showed up after I'd told
him I would come by to drive him to the store for groceries,
though it was mainly booze he would be wanting. Sam had taken
away his truck keys until he sobered up, and the cowboys had put
a padlock on the feedlot shed where they kept their wine. Sam
said he didn't want Nellie irrigating while he was drunk, so Nellie
started digging for the gold, which he knew would irritate Sam,
who would make him cover up the hole once he found it because
a worker or some animal could fall into it.

"You know Sam doesn't want you digging up these holes,
especially with all the pickers coming back and forth." A year
ago I probably would've just slugged Nellie and driven off, but
now I knew I was talking like Dewey, helping Sam out.

"I cover them," Nellie said. He meant that he put boards and
dirt over the hole when he wasn't digging, which was actually
worse because someone could drive up without seeing the hole
and the boards would cave in under a truck or a car. Nellie never
dug in the same spot, either, because he claimed the treasure
mysteriously moved through the ground to different places on
the ranch, so Sam never knew where he might find a new hole.
The two of them always went through the same dance: Sam
ordered Nellie to fill in the hole, and Nellie cried and said that
now he wouldn't give Sam part of the treasure when he found it.
He also always claimed that the gold was near at hand when Sam
made him stop digging.

Nellie would sober up and go to work for a few weeks until his next binge. He lived by himself in the middle of the ranch in a one-room shack cluttered with books, a little TV, a wood cook stove, a sagging, narrow cot, magazines, including a lot of nudist ones, and eight-millimeter porno films that he ordered out of magazines. It was fun when he got in a new batch to set up his little projector in the feedlot shed with the cowboys and watch them while drinking wine after work. You could hardly call them porn—flicks about farmers' daughters and horny maids who liked to be spanked, that sort of thing.

Nellie also had an expensive telescope to check out the stars. I looked through it one night and saw the rings of Saturn, which knocked me for a loop. I had no idea that what looked to be a little dot up in the sky was actually this strange planet that could be seen. To be standing there in the middle of the San Joaquin Valley and see those mysterious rings in the sky, like they were only a few miles away, made me know that maybe Nellie's other claims might not be so far-fetched, especially about ghosts and the old Mexican bandit's buried treasure.

Nellie wasn't stupid. He'd been a cook in the army. I know that because I seen his discharge papers. Before he left for the service, he'd worked for Sam's daddy. His real name was Tiburcio, but they called him Nello in the army—don't ask me why—and then Cowboy Duane nicknamed him Nellie, and it stuck. For a while Nellie was married to an eighteen-year-old West Virginia gal, then afterward he moved to Illinois, where he worked on a farm. One day a few years ago he showed up to see his uncle, Old Antiguo, and said he wanted to work on the ranch again. Mitch told me that though they were Mexicans their last name was Basque—Arriaga—from their ancestors. Fat lot of good it did them. Nellie arrived on the ranch with thirty-two cartons of belongings and two suitcase-style pieces of equipment with meters and dials for locating buried treasure.

Nellie said he'd given up booze, got religion, and had walked the straight and narrow for years. That situation held out for a few months until some workers took him to the county fair to see the strippers and he come back drunk.

"Whew!" Nellie said in a big dramatic way. "It's sure hot. I could use a cold beer."

"You don't need no more booze," I said. "You better sober up." I don't know why Sam didn't run him off the ranch. It was kindness, I guess. Nellie had nowhere to go, and the only relative he had in the world, Old Antiguo, lived here on the ranch. If he left he sure wasn't going to sober up. No one else in the valley would hire him. At least here he had a home, and he wasn't always drunk.

"Just drive me to Alpha," Nellie said.

"I ain't going that way," I said.

He swung the .30-30 around and pointed it right at me with his finger on the trigger, giving me a hard-ass look. "You better take me," he said.

The muzzle of the gun wasn't pointed at me more than half a second before I swung my hand around, grabbed the barrel, and jerked the rifle away from him. I wanted to whack him upside the face with it, and almost did, but knew that a stiff blow to the temple would've probably killed him, like a rabbit.

"You son of a bitch," I said.

Nellie started to cry. "Don't take my rifle." He lunged toward me and fell to his hands and knees, almost tumbling into the stupid hole he'd dug.

On his hands and knees, he glanced up from under his pith helmet that had somehow stayed on his head, and his eyes looked so pitiful and his mouth spread out so sad-like that I said, "Okay. Keep your goddamn fucking gun, but I'm taking the bullets." I jerked the lever back and forth until all the cartridges were ejected into the dirt. I put them in my pocket and tossed the rifle to the ground. "Pull the trigger all you want."

Nellie must've banged his face into the dirt when he fell because now when he stood up the sweat on his face had turned the dirt into muddy streaks down the sides of his big nose. I climbed into the pickup, my fingers shimmying as I cranked up the engine. I looked in the side mirror and saw Nellie standing with the rifle in his hands like a little kid with a play gun. I thought of his old uncle raking leaves under the eucalyptus trees and Nellie dreaming of finding gold but always having the boss stop him from getting rich. Maybe he had a point. I backed up the pickup next to him and said, "Get your ass in here. I'll take you to the store, but just for groceries."

On the way to Alpha Grocery, he told me how he'd come to know where to dig a few nights earlier by following the ghost of the Sikh, who'd died on the ranch years ago. The Sikh's ghost carried a lantern from the blacksmith shop to the spot where the light shone into the ground. That was always the sign of where Joaquín Murieta's gold had migrated. A column of light penetrated right into the ground. Nellie was the only one who saw the Sikh. The ghost still wore the same big turban as when he'd irrigated for Sam's daddy, long ago, after Nellie had come to the ranch with his uncle as a young man. The Sikh hovered around the ranch, crossed the yard at night in his own ghostly glow, and disappeared into the blacksmith shop. When he appeared with a lantern, though, it was time for Nellie to follow him to the site of Joaquín Murieta's treasure.

I didn't disbelieve him when he was talking because I was pretty sure Nellie saw the ghost, whether it was real or not. Who really knows about these things? After he picked out his groceries, I decided to let him buy a little beer, though not a case, the way he wanted. He bought a six-pack of Lucky Lager with the double XX on the label that reminded Mexicans of Dos Equis, and he bought another six-pack for me for taking him to the store. I stopped him from buying ammunition, and that made him mad all over. Then I drove him home and fetched the rest of the cartridges out of his house, which made him even madder.

"You shoot at me again," I told him, "and I'll kill your ass." I didn't want to end up dying because some crazy asshole was out on a drunken rampage. Now that I'd made up my mind to get out of Dewey and my momma's house, I thought I might just start thinking about finding another job and getting off this nuthouse of a ranch altogether before I ended up dying around here and haunting it like the Sikh.

I left Nellie standing on his stoop yelling at me and drove to check the corn water, which was running fine. I'd set enough siphon pipes to keep the ditch level for the night. Then I drove through the main ranch yard toward the front gate, intending to scope out a house for rent. I don't know what it was about that day—maybe it was the hot wind—but I no sooner got into the yard than Mitch's daddy waved me down.

"Give me a hand, Sonny," he said. He pointed down the country road just outside the ranch, where two black workers were getting into a fight. He climbed into my pickup while still strapping on his shoulder holster. "I just paid them," he said, "a couple of minutes ago."

I could see from where their faded red Studebaker was pulled to the side of the road that the two men had turned out of the ranch yard, drove about a fifth of a mile, and stopped sudden, leaving the car parked cockeyed on the roadside with both doors flung open. Rackenback swung a short-handled hoe at Sid, who was swinging back at him with a hatchet.

That morning, when we were all by the home ranch barn, Sam had told Rackenback and Sid that he wanted them to grind hay for the feedlot because Jesse and me were busy with the tomatoes. A big cone of ground-up hay that Sam had sold to the cowboys, as high as a two-story house, stood next to the feedlot.

It wasn't much fun to pull hay onto the conveyor belt, especially on a hot day. After it was ground and shot up a metal chute onto the big cone, the fine hay drifted down and stuck to your sweaty skin, itchy as hell. It sifted down your neck and clogged up your nose. If it was windy, it was like pitching sawdust in a sandstorm.

"We got to finish up them weeds in the big cotton piece before the water gets on them," Rackenback told Sam. He and Sid were digging out goatheads and Johnson grass in a field just ahead of where me and Jesse were irrigating, and if the irrigation water caught up with them, it would be too muddy for them to chop weeds.

Sam took off his hat and scratched his head. That man could sure scratch his head. "I need to get this hay done today," Sam told them. "I got some other guys weeding."

If it was me, I'd rather grind hay than weed cotton any day, but Rackenback thought different. As he walked away, he snatched up some dirt from the ground and flung it into the air, watching it blow sideways, to show Sam it was too windy to be grinding hay.

"He's mad," Jesse said.

"Come on, old man," Sid told Rackenback. "I'll pitch the hay. You don't do no work nohow."

That's what got them fighting, we learned later. After they got paid, they started arguing about who worked harder and then stopped the car to fight about it.

"I'll get Rackenback," Sam told me as we drove up to where they were fighting. "You grab Sid."

Sam unsnapped the leather guard on his shoulder holster. The crossed-up expression on his face—somewhere between being annoyed and in pain—made me see this fight the same way he must've seen the fights me and Jesse got into. *How fucking stupid!*

I thought. Sid with his hatchet and Rackenback with his sharp
hoe crouched and circled each other with murder in their eyes.

Sam and I winged open the doors and jumped out of the
pickup. Rackenback was heavier than Sid but older and with
graying hair. Sid was tall and lean with a bald head. He had long
arms and legs, but I pressed up behind him the way I would in
a wrestling match and locked his arms up against his back so
he couldn't swing the hatchet. When Rackenback saw that Sid
was tied up, he threw down the hoe as Sam grabbed his arms.
I guess maybe he saw that pistol hugging Sam's shoulder. The
hoe wasn't a regular short-handled one, like I thought it would
be. Rather, Rackenback had broke a regular-handled one so he
could swing it better. You would have to put your money on Sid
in this fight because he was younger and stronger, but even as
we drove up I could tell from the way Rackenback was swinging
the hoe that he'd had a lot of experience. The edge of that hoe
glinted from being filed sharp. Sid was cut on the arm through
his yellow shirtsleeve, and Rackenback had an ugly gash across
his forehead. Blood smeared down over his face in a scary mask.
In the sunlight on his black skin the blood looked almost black,
too. That's how I remember it.

Sam looked at the cut on Sid's arm, which wasn't too bad,
and told him to take the car and get out of there. I had his blood
all over my T-shirt. We drove Rackenback to the ranch house,
where Ana's momma pressed a dishtowel against his bleeding
forehead and walked him to the back bathroom. Sam told me
to go with them to make sure there wasn't any trouble. In the
bathroom, Ana's momma took a little key and unlocked a drawer
that was full of all kinds of medicine and tape and drugs that
she got from when she worked as a nurse. She'd recently gone
back to working at the county hospital, but then her drinking
got in the way. She was sober and good-looking right then—I
could see a lot of Ana in her face—as she sewed up the cut on

Rackenback's forehead while he sat on the closed toilet seat. It gave me the creeps to see that needle poke through his skin, but it didn't faze her. She was always sewing up one of her kids or someone on the ranch.

"You tell Sid to let me look at his arm tomorrow," she said. "I don't want him getting an infection."

"Yes, ma'am," Rackenback said in a voice that sounded strange. I'd known Rackenback for a couple of years but hadn't ever heard him talking to a woman before. It was like he was saying someone else's words in someone else's voice. He grinned the whole time Ana's momma put in the stitches. She knotted the thread and trimmed it with blunt-tipped scissors. She didn't wear gloves, and her fingers were sticky with blood.

"It's a shame, you boys fighting like this," she said, "especially you and Sir Sid, friends that you are." She'd dubbed Sid as "Sir Sid" because she thought he was so royally handsome when she was drunk, Ana had told me, but she still apparently thought of him that way when she was sober, too.

"Yes, ma'am," Rackenback said. "When us colored folks gets to fighting, Mrs. Etcheverry, there's no stopping us. If someone yells, 'Fried chicken,' and someone else yells, 'Fight,' we're going to the fight." I'd never heard him say things like that neither.

"You've got fourteen stitches," Ana's momma told Rackenback. "You're going to have a headache."

Hunched over in the bathroom with his graying hair, Rackenback looked a lot like an old black neighbor I knew when I was a kid. That old guy couldn't quite talk right because a mule kicked him when he was a little boy, but I could understand him, and he took a liking to me. "If anybody do something to you, boy," he told me, "I going to hurt them." He was a milker with powerful fingers from squeezing cow tits most of his life. Shake his hand and he could make you sink down on your knees. He often had me into his home to give me something to eat, but he would never come into my house, though I tried my damndest to get him to. He wouldn't go into any white person's home. That was a true black person back then.

On the way out of the house, as Rackenback walked toward the pickup, Ana's momma clutched me by the elbow in the laundry room, stopping me, and said, "I hear Sam's going to be paying for you to get your own house, Sonny."

"That's right, ma'am," I said, "just as soon the nuts on this ranch stop fighting or shooting at me so I can locate a place."

"You'll probably be getting married," she said, "now that you're through with school and out on your own."

I scrutinized her dark Basco eyes for some I-know-about-you-and-Ana kind of look, but nothing tricky or sly flickered on her sad, pretty face. She was talking only about me. I told her I had no plans for marrying, but I supposed I would. "Once I meet the right gal," I added, trying to show I took the issue with a seriousness equal to what I heard in her voice.

"Marry someone younger," she said, "otherwise when you're still young she'll be an old lady."

I wished I had Jesse's way with words because sweat slipped down my neck slick as spit and I couldn't find anything to say as I thought how she must be talking about herself. Sober and beautiful and kind in that moment, she appeared no older than Sam, who I knew was one year younger than her. What I wanted to say was "I would've married someone younger if your lunkhead husband had let me."

I could see why Ana thought of her momma as an entirely different person when she was loaded. She was known for her earthy bluntness that won guys over. And she was pretty.

"I sure will," I said, recalling something Jesse once spoke to send the words popping from my brain onto my tongue, "if she could be someone like you." I wasn't blowing fog.

Ana's momma smiled and patted my bare arm, mother-like, before opening the screen door for me to go out. "Just be nice to her, Sonny, and she'll do anything for you."

With Rackenback all taped up, I drove him to his house, where Sid sat shirtless on the porch, his long legs stretched out, drinking a beer, a bandage tied around his bare arm. The bandage looked like Sid made it himself out of a torn sheet. I saw Rackenback grinning again.

"I got that nigger good," he said. Seemed to me he was the one who got it good.

Him and Sid started talking like nothing had happened. Maybe they were like me and Jesse when we used to fight. Nothing personal.

I drove back toward the ranch, thinking about what Ana's momma told me. Her last words at the screen door were "You're a good boy, Sonny," which left me glad for what I'd told her because you could see she was the kind of loving wildcat a man might want, except, of course, when she was on the bottle and only a wildcat. They say if you want to know what your wife will be like, look at her mother. I couldn't see a lot of Ana in her momma, though she was close enough. I knew what I'd missed. I would have to do the best I could, but first I had to see about that house for rent.

I drove through the ranch yard, heading home to change out of my bloody shirt and grab a quick bite before looking at the house, when Sam waved me down again. *Fuck a duck,* I thought. *What's going on today?* I was never going to get that house rented.

"Nellie is drunk up at the pond," Sam said. "Ana and Jesse found him in the water almost drowning. He said you bought him beer." Sam didn't say it like he was mad, just matter-of-fact. "You can't be buying him beer, Sonny. He's crazy enough without it."

That double-crossing little squirt, I thought, snitching on me.

"I didn't buy him beer," I said, which was true. "I took him to the store, but only for just one six-pack. He bought it hisself."

"When you see he's drunk, don't add to it. He's not like his uncle. He doesn't know when to quit."

Nellie's uncle used to go on a drunk maybe once a year, and after a week or so of staying drunk Sam would wean him off the booze by taking him a little wine or beer every day, less and less each time, until Old Antiguo was sober. A couple of years ago, the old man had himself a woman in his shack when he was drunk. I don't know how he found her, as old as he was. Maybe one of the ranch hands set it up and Old Antiguo paid her, but things didn't work out too good. He was just too old. Old Antiguo told me, "I pushed and pushed and pushed it in with my fingers, but it fell out the bottom." Since that time, he didn't get drunk no more and he sure didn't try to have a woman again. He just raked leaves.

Pissed at Nellie for getting me on Sam's bad side, I drove up to the pond and saw Jesse and Mitch sitting with Ana on the dock, drinking beer, while Nellie waded in his clothes through the cattails, trying to catch frogs with his hands. Everyone was having a good time except me. Jesse and Ana sat close to each other, laughing and talking, and Nellie lunged for a frog and flopped facedown in the water. He came to his feet standing waist-deep in the black water with a young frog in his hands, the damn pith helmet still on his head, his face streaked with stringy moss and muck. He had a big smile.

"You little shit," I told him. "I'm never taking you for groceries or wine or beer again. You told on me. That's it. Finito. Comprendo?"

He ignored me and waded back into the cattails after more frogs, happy as a kid.

"Hey, why are you so hot and bothered?" Jesse said. "Come and have a drink and cool down." He raised up a tall Hamm's.

I didn't like Hamm's. I thought about cracking open one of the Luckys Nellie bought me, but they were too hot. Jesse wiggled the can. "From the land of sky-blue waters," he said with a big grin. Ana giggled. I didn't like them sitting together that way. I wanted to punch him. Instead, I took the Hamm's.

I sat on the dock with them, the same dock where I'd met Ana two summers before. Jesse handed me a church key. I popped the can and took a slug. "They should've left it in the horse," I said.

"You have a hair across your ass or something?" Jesse asked. "Sam told us what a good job you did with Sid."

Surprised as I was at Sam bragging on me, I was more surprised at how good it made me feel. I took another slug of beer. It wasn't as bad as I'd thought—kind of syrupy but cold and fizzy. After a few cans we were all laughing at Nellie, flopping around in the muddy water, half in and out of the tules and cattails, trying to catch frogs. I took off my bloody T-shirt and let the last rays of the sun warm up my chest.

That day felt like a turning point in the summer for me. Things started to come together. Two days later, I found a little house, not the place I intended to rent but a much nicer one Jesse heard about, owned by an Armenian grape grower, ten miles from the ranch, surrounded by vineyard. The same day I signed the lease, I bought the new Valiant—a powder-blue job. The first call I got on my new house phone was from a rich girl up at the lake Jesse had broken up with, and she wanted me to take her to the dance that weekend. Her name was Adelaide. Her daddy had a business in the Bay Area, fancy cars up the kazoo, a cabin on the lake, a big motorboat, the whole deal. I couldn't figure why Jesse cut it off with her. As I told Mitch, she was gorgeous, with a set of knockers that made your eyes pop out. I couldn't believe she'd called.

"How'd you get my number?" I said.

"From Jesse," she said.

That should've made me suspicious, but it didn't. Next day in the tomato field, I put it straight to Jesse about her calling and wanting me to take her to the dance.

"That's fine, Sonny," Jesse said, like he could care less. "I'm moving on."

I knew he was going out with different girls that summer. There was Linda Antonelli and Adelaide and Sonia Maycheck, though he'd broken up with Sonia right after graduation. I was going out with different girls, too, ones I knew from high school or met at the lake, sometimes two in one night, like after one date when I sneaked off in the field with Pablo's granddaughter, but nothing really clicked how it had with Ana. Truth be told, we were working so hard I oftentimes couldn't hardly get home quick enough, happy just to crawl into bed alone. I wasn't tied down and didn't want to be. I remembered last February when I gave my senior ring to Jolene Autry, and she wrapped it with gold thread to fit her finger, then lacquered the thread with clear nail polish till it was hard as plastic and looked to be part of the ring. I was stuck. I was going steady. After we broke up, I never did get that ring back, and I didn't care. I had no intention of giving a ring to anyone else till I was fixing to get married.

When I drove up to the lake that Saturday, I half-expected not to find Adelaide, thinking it was all too unreal for such a doll to want to be with me, but there she was waiting at the end of the driveway to her family's vacation house. We danced all night and made out a little bit afterward and talked about getting together at the next dance. I thought this must be a dream.

At the ranch, we finished shipping out the first picking of tomatoes, and we were all so damn happy about it, Mitch, Jesse, and I went to the Basque Hotel in Fresno and got tanked up on picons at the bar before chowing down at the boarders' table on shrimp potato salad and everything else they threw at us—all you could eat—beef tongue and short ribs, I think they were, and roasted peppers and fried chicken. But of everything, I loved the shrimp potato salad best. When you're happy, everything makes you happier, even potato salad.

Mitch's daddy was happy, too, to be done with the picking. As I said, having these tomatoes on the ranch was a first for him, and every now and then he showed up to take movies with his sixteen-millimeter camera, starting with the planting, the irrigating, the spraying, the picking, the swamping, and the shipping. He took movies of us eating lunch with the braceros under the canvas awning and of pickers in the field, including Pablo's good-looking granddaughter, stooped over in the hot rows throwing green tomatoes into the buckets, then dumping the buckets into the boxes that got stacked up until we came along, me and Jesse and Mitch, to toss them onto the trucks.

"I bought tickets for all of us to go up and see the Giants," Sam told us. He didn't say outright "You boys did a good job with those tomatoes," but that's what he meant.

We headed out the next morning, after having coffee with Sam in his big kitchen. Where my rented house had pasteboard walls and a linoleum floor, Sam's had fancy tile— tile everywhere, even on the wall above the built-in stove where maroon tile spelled out the capital letter "E" of his family name. The missus didn't show that morning, but Ana wandered out in a red robe just as we all were leaving. She didn't say nothing to me—I followed Mitch and Sam out the screen door—but she spoke to Jesse, who hung back, and I thought of them sitting together up on the dock of the pond and wondered if something was going on between them. But he never mentioned it—and he usually wouldn't be shy to if something was going on—so I put it out of my mind, except when I recalled I hadn't said anything to Mitch about me and Ana when we were together.

Outside, when I looked across the sparkling alfalfa at the sun coming up above the Sierras I felt in a new country. Not having to go to work—just knowing that I wouldn't be in a sweltering field covered with sweat—made my bones go light. A breeze smelled of eucalyptus leaves and Mrs. Etcheverry's flowers. Even the blazing sun bounced as it popped up fresh from the Nevada desert behind the mountains. The whole ranch shined full of light, something familiar but strange, too, like in a movie. The skin on my stomach and legs tingled inside my blue short-sleeved shirt and fresh-washed Levi's, as if I'd gone to the coast, free for the whole day, looking out over the ocean.

We took turns driving Sam's big Buick, but Jesse drove first, all the way to Los Banos, zipping past sweet-scented alfalfa fields and over big canals of water with the air full of trilling meadowlarks.

"Hey, lead-foot," Sam told Jesse. "Ease up. You don't want to end up like Billy V." A lot of good racecar drivers came out of the valley, but none like Billy Vukovich, up until he crashed. "I want to get this crate home in one piece," Sam added. Jesse grinned and eased up.

Sam was one of these guys who liked to give directions to drivers in other cars, too. In Gilroy, we waited behind a pickup at a traffic light. After the red light changed, the truck ahead of us didn't move, and Sam said in a loud voice, as if the driver could actually hear, "It's not going to get any greener, bub. Step on it."

We got to the stadium out on Candlestick Point in plenty of time. Cottony clouds slid overhead and disappeared, leaving the sky clear blue. Despite the June sun, a cold wind whipped in across the water through the open outfield, and I was glad I brought a jacket. We sat looking down at first base, good seats so you could see from home plate to the cyclone fence in the outfield in one sweep. Jesse and I really didn't know squat about baseball, though Mitch did because his daddy was always listening to games, especially when he was cutting his lawn of crabgrass around the house with his push-mower, the radio blaring from a bedroom window. Mitch followed the Pacific Coast League and owned a whole set of baseball cards of San Francisco Seals players from when he was a kid. He didn't know much about any major league teams except during World Series time, at least up until the Giants moved to San Francisco, but by then he was too old to collect cards.

Sam bought himself a beer and us Cokes and bags of peanuts. When we were kids, Jesse and I used to shake up Planters salted peanuts in bottles of Pepsi. Jesse once got to laughing so hard Pepsi sprayed out his nose and a peanut caught in his sinuses and he had to go to Dr. Maycheck to fish it out. Today we had paper cups, not bottles, and peanuts in shells, so we just cracked them open one at a time, envying Sam his beer but knowing he wasn't about to buy us none. Pretty soon Jesse went to take a piss, and when he come back he had three fresh Coke cups for him, me, and Mitch. "Sorry they wouldn't let me buy you a beer, Sam," Jesse said.

"That's okay," Sam said. "Here comes a vendor."

I tasted my Coke and it was beer. I don't know how Jesse did it, but all three of our Coke cups had beer in them. Sam sure as hell saw the foam on our upper lips, but he was a good sport and didn't say anything. The game started, and I felt light and dizzy, like a kid on a swing.

Mitch's favorite player was the pitcher Juan Marichal, and Sam's was Willie McCovey. "If they'd pitch to Willie," Sam said, "he'd knock the ball out of the park every time." Fans tumbled out of the low bleachers in the outfield and pressed against the cyclone fence when McCovey came up. They did the same thing when Willie Mays batted, but Sam wasn't as fond of him—"He's a New Yorker," Sam said—but Jesse got fascinated with the way Willie Mays always stepped on first base when coming into the dugout from the outfield, and then on second base when he ran to the outfield for the next inning. He always stepped on a bag, never the line.

The first time Willie Mays came up, the pitcher threw the ball at his head, but Willie flopped backward on the ground so quick the ball whizzed over him. Mitch told us that Willie said they could throw at him as much as they wanted but he wouldn't be there. Jesse liked that about him, too—"He never gets hit," Mitch said—and the way he did basket catches like a grammar school kid, breaking all the rules of the big league players and getting away with it. But more special was his stepping on the same bases when he was going in and out of the outfield—nine times on second base when he ran to center field and nine times on first when he come back to the dugout—like there was some magic in those regular steps that made him great. The Giants' dugout stretched directly below us, and when Mays jogged in from the outfield, Jesse shouted, "Say hey, Willie"—the way other fans did—and it almost looked as if the "Say Hey Kid," as he was called, glanced up at Jesse like he recognized him.

On the way home we pulled off Highway 101 in San Jose near Mitch's boarding school to eat at the Wagon Wheel Chuckwagon—an all-you-can-eat joint with a buffet of salad stuff and big copper pots mounded with golden fried chicken and mashed potatoes and pink hams and sparkling vegetables, all under bright lights. At the end stood a guy in a tall chef's hat who cut slabs of prime rib cooked any way you liked. We kept going back for the red prime rib and juicy chicken. I never saw anything like that in the valley.

Sam had a drink called an "old fashioned," then some wine. What with all the beer he downed at the game, he got a little loopy in a way I'd never seen. He wasn't drunk, but he was feeling good. "Pass me your bones, Mitch," he said.

Mitch scraped his chicken bones, not the big prime rib bones, onto an empty salad plate, and passed them to his dad, who gnawed them until there wasn't a lick of meat or gristle left. Then Jesse and I passed him ours. I thought I'd cleaned mine off pretty good, but when Sam was done those bones glistened.

"When I was a kid," he said, "my family and all the workers on the ranch ate together at a big table. Those Sikhs who irrigated for my pop used to watch me when I ate, and Pop said if I didn't clean every speck of meat off my chicken bones the Sikhs would eat me."

"I guess that's one of the Sikhs' ghosts who Nellie says he's been seeing," I said.

"That's the one," Sam said. "He was a great irrigator. Only a Sikh can make water run uphill."

I drove from the Chuckwagon to Gilroy on 101. At a red light, we waited to cross the railroad tracks and take the shortcut to 152. As soon as the light changed, Sam told the driver in the unmoving car in front of us, "That's the only shade of green, buddy."

I drove through the hills up into Pacheco Pass, where the steering wheel commenced to vibrate and the front tire started thumping. I hadn't hit anything that I noticed, but when I pulled off the road we saw how the right front tire was blown out, squashed flat to the hub.

Jesse told Mitch where to put the jack while he cracked the lug nuts loose, then ordered me to jack up the car while he got out the spare. In no time at all, Jesse was spinning the spare on the hub, tightening the nuts with the lug wrench, throwing the jack and the flat into the trunk, and we were on our way again, almost like we'd just been Billy V.'s speedy pit crew at the Indianapolis 500.

"Nice job, boys," Sam said, and I felt good, until he added, "Take it easy, lead-foot," just like he told Jesse. "Watch out for Holsteins."

Sam fell asleep with his head resting against the door window. The inside of the car darkened fast as we dropped down the east slope of the hills into the valley at the same time the sun fell behind the Coast Range. In the rearview I could see shadowy reflections of Jesse and Mitch in the backseat, slumped against each other, their heads tilted back, sound asleep. "Earth Angel" played on the radio. I turned it low so as not to bother the guys. It reminded me of when Jesse and I were back in grade school, teaching each other to dance.

Out in the flat, dark valley, distant lights from the farms looked like signals from ships at sea. In the quiet car, except for the hum of the engine, the radio, and Sam's soft snore, I felt like I was navigating through a black ocean, not quite able to see where I was going except to the edge of the headlights that kept pushing against the night. The fight between Sid and Rackenback came to mind, and I thought how it was a blessing for me. It delayed me so that I came up with a nicer house than otherwise. Goes to show how what seems bad luck at first might be good. With Sam as my boss, and Jesse and Mitch as my friends, I thought how lucky I was. I had my own house, years before Dewey ever did, steady work, and steady pay. I wasn't picking cotton the way Dewey was when he was my age. I had a nice car all my own while back in Oklahoma Dewey had nothing but a jalopy shared with his brothers. Best of all, I had a new girl I wanted to be with—a girl named Adelaide, waiting for me up at the lake.

When I slowed down and pulled off the road into Sam's yard, the tires crunching on the dirt driveway, the guys woke up. A large limb had crashed down into the yard from a eucalyptus tree, the way they sometimes did, they were so old and heavy.

It looked like it must have hit the roof of Sam's house, bounced up, and flopped near the front porch, where it sprawled as big as a small tree itself, leaving eucalyptus leaves scattered across the ground like miniature sickle blades. Old Antiguo would have a lot of raking to do once we got the limb cut up and carried off. Sam had hired an outfit to trim the trees just a year ago because so many limbs kept falling. The trimmer was actually on a limb up in a tree when the trunk split on him and knocked him to the ground with blood running out of his ears. That man was the first I ever saw killed outright.

I drove around the eucalyptus limb and pulled into the carport with the crimped metal poles. The house windows lit up and the back door opened to show Ana's momma in a bare nightgown that you could almost see through, but I didn't want to look too close. Her hair was a mess and her face looked all twisted. The air was thick with the smell of eucalyptus oil from the leaves crushed under the big limb. I could see again what Ana meant when she said her mother drunk wasn't her real mother. She sure wasn't the same woman I saw sewing up Rackenback or talking to me in the laundry room.

"Where's Ana?" she shouted from the back door. "She's not home."

We all scrambled out of the car and headed for our own vehicles to get the hell out of the yard, except Sam, of course, who said, "See you boys first thing in the morning," and headed toward his wife. Who the hell would want to come home to that? I hopped in my new Valiant and spun out of the ranch yard, glad to know that no one like her would be waiting for me. I wondered what Willie Mays's wife was like when he came home. A guy like that had to be lucky. Players got lots on the side, too, they were on the road so much.

As I drove home, I thought how the Fourth of July was coming up. We all looked forward to a big blowout at the lake, and I was hot to see Adelaide again up there. She hadn't let me into her pants yet, but I was getting close.

In the middle of the week before the Fourth, a bunch of us guys stood around the cars on the asphalt at the Big Top Drive In. Jesse leaned back against his new pink Oldsmobile, telling stories the way he did, getting us all laughing at some pretty raunchy talk, as he did when the girls weren't within earshot. Under the lights of the drive-in hamburger joint, wearing a loose short-sleeved shirt in the warm summer night, I felt the valley air against my skin and I got turned on just standing out there and knowing the girls were looking at us from their cars. Engines revved with the mufflers rumbling, chugging out more heat over the asphalt, along with the heady smell of exhaust fumes. The asphalt under my feet vibrated, and my legs, too, when a hot car cranked up. Music from the car radios faded in and out—slow songs, rock songs, all mixed up in the air. I could make out Buddy Holly's voice singing "That'll Be the Day."

Jesse leaned against the fender of his Olds, wearing blue Levi's and a white shirt buttoned tight across his pecs, with the short sleeves rolled up even shorter onto his biceps, swelled from swamping tomatoes all summer. He got us all laughing with his tall talk about the organization he'd invented called the 4Cs. Now, some of the guys after graduating from high school went to 4Cs in Fresno, which was short for the Central California Commercial College, a two-year college that Ana would also go to after high school. Jesse had come up with his idea for his club called the 4Cs—short for the Central California Crotch Cannibals—and he said we all could join.

As founder and president, he had a lot of responsibility. "I was practicing the other night," he said, "and got so carried away that my sticky eyes got gummed up and when I got home they'd glued completely shut, and I had to wake my momma to heat up the teakettle on the stove to steam them open."

I shouldn't have been too happy, but I couldn't help laughing when he started telling why he'd broken up with Adelaide at the lake. "I had my head up there and found a necktie," he said, "and then somebody's sunglasses. This was too much for me, so I told her, 'Call Sonny.'"

When the guys started to laugh and razz me, I saw Jesse's eyes dart my way, and he backed off and said, "Actually, this son of a bitch"—meaning me—"got her away from me," and the guys quit laughing because they couldn't tell if Jesse was putting them on or he was going to pop me for horning in on his snatch. What was typical of him is he wouldn't shame you, at least not out in public. He'd fight you but not embarrass you. So he backed off, though he no sooner let me off the hook and built me up in front of these guys than he made clear how he was still the number one rooster in the henhouse: "Yeah, after Adelaide started going out with Sonny, I only dipped my wick about two more times." The guys started laughing again, looking relieved that they were able to.

Just about then, a highway patrolman we knew pulled into the Big Top and eased his Holstein right up to us. He stuck his face out his rolled-down window and told us, "A lot of Hell's Angels are coming up to the lake for the Fourth. I don't want to see you boys up there this weekend. If I see you on the road, I'm pulling you over."

"Thanks for warning us ahead of time, officer," Jesse said, real polite.

"It's not just me," the cop said. "The sheriff doesn't want to see you there either."

And sure enough, here comes a deputy sheriff in his car to tell us the same damn thing. The deputy, Hank Palacios's uncle, was a little more blunt. "We're going to have our hands full with these bikers, and I don't want to see your fucking asses anywhere near them. You hear what I'm saying, Jesse?" Jesse nodded, but

I could tell by the way he pressed his lips he was madder than a
wet hen.

After they left, Jesse said, "Who the hell are they to tell us
what to do? Whose lake is it anyway?"

It just riled him in a way that registered on me, too, how a
bunch of bikers could come in from the outside and dictate
that Bass Lake was off-limits to us. We went there almost every
weekend. Like he said, whose lake was it?

"Those fuckers," Jesse said about the bikers, "are *not* going to
take over the lake."

Jesse was so steamed he got everyone worked up to where
more guys than ever headed up to the lake on the Fourth. Jesse
said we all had to meet at the Big Top that evening before we
took off so we could drive up in a convoy. We couldn't just go
up there piecemeal, he told us, because the Angels would be in
gangs. "The highway patrol can't do a thing," he said. "They're
just blowing hot air. We've got a right to those roads." And to
the lake, he might've added. I realized then how insulting he
found the cops' failure to recognize that if there was a King of
the Lake, it was him.

I set my water in the corn that morning, but I had the rest of
the day off because Nellie—he was sober now—said he would
change it in the evening. Even though he'd been in the army,
he didn't care about the Fourth, but for the rest of us—Jesse,
Dewey, myself, and others—no way we weren't going to take off
for the day. The rest can have Christmas or Easter, but if there's
an Okie holiday, it's the Fourth of July.

When I went out into the field that morning, I thought
about the old-time claim that corn needs to be knee-high by the
Fourth of July. Where the hell did that saying come from? I held
my shovel by the tip of the handle straight up over my head. The
shovel blade still didn't reach the top tassels of the corn, that's
how high it was. Maybe elsewhere, like in Kansas, that saying

held true, but it wasn't worth a damn in the San Joaquin Valley. Here even cotton was knee-high by now.

Walking into the corn to check if the rows were out was like plunging into a stifling jungle, it was so closed in and hot. Not so much in the early morning, but in the late afternoon you could hardly breathe. I came out of those rows with razor slits on my arms and neck from the sharp-edged corn leaves. It always made me think of being in India for some reason, maybe from a book we read in grammar school about the steamy heat there in the jungles and the flooded fields.

I was supposed to meet Adelaide at the dance that night and the next day go waterskiing with her. I was checking my irrigation water in the steamy cornfield when it hit me like a sledgehammer on a cow skull what must have happened between her and Jesse. When I was a kid, my brother bought a fourteen-foot glass ski boat and taught me to waterski. I was lucky that way. One day, after we started high school, we took Jesse with us up to Millerton Lake, where me, my brother, and even my little brother showed off, first on single skis, then on a disk. Jesse wanted to give it a try. We put him on a set of doubles, but every time he pulled himself up and almost got to standing he fell back. Over and over, he plopped into the water, and we kept spinning the boat around to get him. "Goddamn it, Jesse," I told him, "just make like you're sitting down in a chair and then stand up."

"I'm going to give it my all," he said. "Just keep going. Don't stop the boat."

I revved up the Johnson outboard and roared across the lake. Jesse's arms strained as he pulled himself up, his eyes big as chicken eggs, his legs bent and shaking. Then he squatted back down, bumped the water with his butt, and started to pull himself up again. I did what he told me and didn't stop. Like they say, it ain't over till the fat lady sinks. All the while, Jesse held onto the wooden handle at the end of the rope while his butt bounced up and down on the water. When you're going that fast, water is as hard as a wood floor. You know the old saying: If a frog had wings, he wouldn't bump his ass. Well, wings are what Jesse needed because he kept smacking his ass like a hopping frog until he finally gave up and tossed the rope into the air. I spun the boat around to pick him up. My brothers leaned over and grabbed his arms.

"Don't touch me," he said. "Give me a minute."

Then I saw in the water what had happened. Bouncing his butt against the water had given him a natural enema and he'd shit his pants. That was the last time he ever tried to waterski, at least that I'm aware of. No way was he going to go out in a boat with Adelaide on the Fourth of July and let her know he couldn't get up on a pair of doubles.

That night, Jesse strutted around the Big Top in his combat boots and loose cotton sweatshirt, a warrior ready for battle, checking out his troops. When he thought enough guys and cars were there, we took off. Jesse drove his pink Olds with me in the front and Hank Palacios and a guy we called Scum Eddie in the back. Scum Eddie was a little bit crazy, but he could fight. Scum Eddie, Jesse, and me played this game when we were younger of taking turns hitting each other on the arm. Scum Eddie would rear back and slug hard. It would hurt but not like Jesse's shot, short and fast, straight from the shoulder. It was like a power came up from the earth through his body into his fist. That was a game I soon quit playing.

After we left town, the plan for a convoy broke up right away, with some cars speeding ahead and others pulling off to pick up friends or beer. In fact, we seemed the only car on the road as we passed dark wheat fields and approached Table Top Mountain. The flat mesa rose up out of the valley, just visible against the night sky. Two single taillights came into view ahead of us, then we saw they weren't from a car but two bikers in tandem out alone on the dark road, heading into the hills, with long hair and their hands high on the raised handlebars of their bikes. I don't know if they were riding Harleys or Indians, but they should have been on Indian-brand bikes because the fear and excitement jumping in my stomach made me think: this is how pioneers must've felt when they spotted lone Indian scouts on horseback, knowing up ahead waited a big war party and lots of trouble.

"I'm getting me a bike like that one of these days," Jesse said.

Parked motorcycles crammed the roadway when we pulled up to The Falls dance bar at the lake. I hurried inside because I had to piss like crazy from the beer I drank on the way up. Usually the drive to the lake was a six-pack ride, but this time we kept it down, knowing what was coming. When I walked back out, I saw Jesse on the balcony of The Falls with the county sheriff himself—a big galoot named Tiny Baxter—not just one of his deputies, showing how serious the law was about keeping things in line. They stood talking with a Hell's Angels guy in a sleeveless denim jacket. Jesse nodded his head and looked at the sheriff, as polite as he could be, no doubt agreeing that he and the Hell's Angels leader, who had a beer gut, would help keep everything under control that night.

When they finished, Jesse came up to me and I saw he was all worked up with his eyes electrified and his mouth twisting back and forth. "Those fuckers," he said. "Let's get this thing over with."

The mountain air smelled of pine mixed with pot and exhaust fumes from the Harleys roaring in and out of the lot across from The Falls. Bikers milled around, and not just Hell's Angels but also Devil's Disciples, who like the Angels wore jackets with their club names on the backs. The coolest and scariest to me were the bikers calling themselves Satan's

Slaves, with their gray frock coats, long hair, pierced ears, and faces streaked with war paint. Four or five of them revved up their choppers and lurched into a roaring race around the lake, their hair flying back like Indians', heading for the big biker encampment the sheriff set up for them in Willow Cove so they'd stay out of trouble. Everyone awaited the real bad-asses to show up, the Oakland Hell's Angels and their leader, who had the same name as me—Sonny—though some said he was already down at the cove. All these gangs had their feuds with each other, usually from the north and south, like the Angels from Berdoo and Oakland, but Jesse didn't care who was who, he just went looking for the guy with the potbelly he'd been talking to with the sheriff. Me and the other Madera guys followed him across the road into the parking lot, where a bunch of bikers stood around a bonfire they'd started.

Jesse said something to the head Angel, then dropped him with one blow to the temple. That clean shot showed how Jesse packed a wallop like a mule. I couldn't punch with that power. None of us could, except maybe Indian Lloyd. When Jesse hit him, the idiot thumped down fast and final-like; one minute he was this big, scary biker-man and the next he was a lump of dead meat on the ground—not really dead but looking that way.

Any other time, I might've started to laugh, but all of a sudden the night spun around and the ground tilted up until a black wall slammed into my face. They say you see stars when you're blindsided, and it's true. I rolled over and saw through spinning stars a bearded guy holding a biker chain that he'd whacked against the back of my neck. If he'd hit me in the skull I'd have been out. Instead, he sent stars shooting across my eyes. As I got to my knees I saw Jesse moving real slow as he cracked that guy across the jaw. Even the guy's beard moved slow as he pirouetted and sunk down to the ground. A bunch of the Madera guys jumped into it then, and those bikers swayed this way and that, but everything was in slow motion, a way of seeing I learned later comes from having a concussion.

I pulled out my knife, not to open the blade but to hold the closed knife in my hand to harden my fist, and I started swinging. No way was I going to go down again that night. I might get mad slow, but once mad you'd have to kill me to stop me. That chaining from behind made me furious. Way back when we were kids, we used to go out past the Santa Fe railroad tracks to where the road petered out into a dirt dip by the river, the same spot where we'd swing out into the river from a rope on a cottonwood and later formed what you might call a little club—probably called a gang now—that met up with some other clubs to fight. The first time some guys showed up with chains—log chains and motorcycle chains—Jesse said, "Put those away. We're going one on one. Anybody who doesn't like it will have to whip my ass."

Even with their chains, those bikers didn't have much know-how when it came to fistfighting. Maybe they were tougher when they weren't so fat-assed from sitting around smoking weed. We scattered them every which way, and soon enough we were back inside on the crowded dance floor, my fists so sore I could hardly close them. My neck throbbed. Jesse showed me a deep cut below his knuckle. He often got his hands hurt more than the rest of himself, and an old broken bone in his right one still gave him trouble. "The bastard opened his mouth just as I hit him," he said, mimicking the guy opening his mouth as he brought his fist up to his face in an uppercut. A front tooth had dug through his skin to the bone. He was trying to tie a handkerchief around his hand to stop the bleeding.

The music stopped and a deputy sheriff made an announcement that if the fighting didn't stop then the dance would. Everyone started hollering and the music started up again and so did the fights. Jesse knocked a biker over the falls. He hit him

with a beer can just as the lights from a passing car blinded him.
Some bikers even got to fighting each other, that's how crazy
they were. I was hot to get back into it with someone when I
saw Indian Lloyd. I was ready to break his ugly nose for breaking
mine, when he gave me a big grin. He and Jesse were now the
best of buddies, and he figured we were, too. Jesse saw me, put
his arm around the big Indian—he could hardly reach up high
enough—and said, "Now don't go beating on my friend Lloyd."
Then me, Jesse, and Lloyd found these bikers under the pine
trees, smoking, and we lit into them. The handkerchief flew off
Jesse's hand as he swung, Lloyd and I clocked one guy at the
same time, dropping him to his hands and knees, and I put a
hoof to his head.

That was the end of it. Back in The Falls, all the fighting
jacked up everyone, even the girls, who shook their asses like
crazy. Ray Camacho and the Teardrops picked up the mood
of the night and wailed on their guitars. I saw Adelaide on the
dance floor, and she gave me such a sweet smile I thought, *Oh,
my, it's coming.* Then I saw Jesse, and I knew I was totally wrong
about why he'd broken up with Adelaide. He was out there
dancing with Sonia Maycheck, her fiery red hair flying around
like in an electrical storm. I realized Jesse broke up with one rich
girl to go back to another. There he was, on the Fourth of July,
as happy as a toad in a summer rain, because we'd taken over
the lake and he was back with Sonia Maycheck, the doctor's
daughter, the love of his life.

LABOR DAY

An August heat wave scorched the valley. Yellow grass and dry
weeds along the roadsides crackled, so pale and brittle that a lit
cigarette tossed from a car was like to explode the country into

flames. Cornstalks drooped, cotton leaves wilted, and alfalfa fields turned black. Everyone walked around with their eyes cast down to the ground, away from where the sky was an open blast furnace. When I met someone in the field, we turned our backs to the sun and talked sideways.

I irrigated alfalfa at night, the days so blistering that even Dewey couldn't get the water to the end of the field—it just backed up, evaporating in the hot afternoons, as though running uphill. Since the only Sikh irrigator on the ranch was a ghost, Sam asked did I want to trade off every week with Mitch to irrigate at night when things cooled down. Then I would trade off with Jesse baling hay. We still had to work days, too, like cutting hay and loading tomato trucks. I catnapped when I could. I remember those days and nights as walking around with heaviness in my legs, a tiredness in my arms and head, but it was a good-feeling tiredness, like moving through a mellow dream.

It had to be nearing midnight, after I'd changed my water, when I saw Jesse's pickup creep down the road and park near the pond. I knew he was in the truck cab fucking Sonia Maycheck. That he wasn't working was okay because the hay in windrows was still too dry for him to start baling. The dew hadn't come in. Once the hay got a little moisture in it and the leaves wouldn't shatter all over the place, he'd take Sonia home and crank up the hay baler and work until the morning got too hot.

Jesse and Sonia went way back. She was in junior high when he started going out with her, so she was young, even younger than when Ana hooked up with me. Jesse himself started out with girls early, setting a pace for the rest of us. I knew I was never going to attract girls the way he did. When he started up with Sonia, I was way behind him in the pussy department, but of course I didn't let on. He was going out with Sonia by the time he got the peanut stuck up his nose and her father— Dr. Maycheck—had to take it out. We knew her as the doctor's daughter, though always a rebel, even as a little girl. She had a warm, earthy laugh and flaming red hair that didn't come out of a bottle in them days neither. I visioned her pussy hair fiery red, too.

When we were fifteen or so, Jesse told me—he wouldn't say this in front of a bunch of guys, just me—about making out with Sonia. "The first time I put my hand up under her dress her panties were already wet." His voice wasn't raunchy like when he was telling stories at the Big Top Drive In. There wasn't nothing disrespectful about what he said, he was just amazed. "That girl has the hottest cunt, the juiciest pussy I've ever known." It was like he was in awe. That's the only word I can think to use about how he was talking.

Sonia lived in a ritzy house with fancy palm trees out front. She crawled out her bedroom window to be with Jesse the same as Ana did to be with me. Sonia's daddy found out, though, and nailed her windows shut. I don't know why he bothered.

Her momma liked Jesse—her stepmomma, really. "He charmed her," Sonia told me once, "and that took a lot." Sonia didn't get along with her stepmomma. Fact is she hated her. She was mad at her daddy, too, for marrying her stepmother. She told me about it once when we were talking up at the lake. She and Jesse had just broke up again. They broke up more times than you can shake a stick at. Breaking up didn't bother Sonia the way it did other girls—she just did her thing, went out with other guys until she hooked up with Jesse again. I guess she knew he would come back to her eventually. I never went out with her when she and Jesse were split, but we had something—a special friendship, I guess you'd call it. It was like she could still be close to Jesse through me because he was my best friend.

We left the dance one night that summer and walked along the shore. I could see the lights from the cabins in the dark hills on the other side of the lake. Sonia said, "I know how people

talk about me—I hear about my wild side—but I just want
to get out of the house. Even when my dad nailed up all my
windows, I still got out. If that makes me wild, then I'm wild."

Girls talking about themselves like they were gossiping about
some other person gave me the willies. It was weird. Guys didn't
talk that way. At least not with each other. You start thinking
about yourself like you're somebody else and your mind quits
working right. Your words get all balled up. I mean, mine do,
not girls'—they're talking natural for them. The words pour out
of them; they never stop to think. To girls, thinking and talking
are the same thing.

I listened to myself saying something serious like I was an
adult: "You don't want your momma and daddy mad at you all
the time."

Sonia stopped to take off her shoes and walk barefoot on the
hard-packed sand by the lake. "She's not my mother. My mother
is dead. If I had my way I wouldn't ever be in the house with her."

It popped into my head to remind her, "If a frog had wings,
he wouldn't bump his ass."

Her face scrunched up. "I don't get the joke."

I tried explaining. "You have to play the hand you're dealt.
You can't go looking through the deck for the cards you want."

"Shit I can't," she said.

Here we'd been talking only five minutes and we were already
fussing at each other. I figured that's what led to her and Jesse
breaking up so much. But that's what you had to put up with—
her way of contradicting you—if you wanted the rest of her.
Ana could come back at you with the same words, but she didn't
sound ornery like Sonia.

"Someone's out in the lake," I said.

A few feet from shore a guy in his clothes floated in the
shallow water, splashing with his hands, dunking his head and
blowing bubbles underwater.

"It's my stupid brother," Sonia said. "Hey, Franklin, get out of that lake."

"I'm a bubble machine," Franklin said. "Look!" He inhaled and then blew into the water. His arms spread out as he floated on his stomach and his shirt ballooned on his back.

"That's pretty good," I said. "Who busted your eye?"

Franklin was a good swimmer, and like his sister he was on the swim team. He rarely got into fights, but he was drunked up enough that night to have had trouble. He sat up in the water. "Nobody," he said.

"He slid his car off the road," Sonia said. "I had to call Jesse to get it back to town for him."

"I thought you broke up with him."

"Who else was I going to call? Not my dad."

Franklin stretched his arms in front of him and slid into the lake. "Look, Sonny, I'm a motorboat." He floated on his stomach and blew to churn up bubbles, acting like he was ten years old and high from sniffing something, though he was sixteen.

I went along with him. "What kind?" I said. "Outboard or inboard?"

Franklin jerked his head up, staring at me. "Inboard. Don't be an ass, Sonny."

Sonia tugged on my arm. "Let's get back to the dance."

"It's like he's hopped up," I said.

She sounded pissed. "He can't drink. He shouldn't be drinking."

I knew their dead momma had been a lush. That's why it was hard to see how Sonia wasn't relieved to have her out of the picture the way I was to have my daddy out of my life. I felt bad that her stepmomma coming into Sonia's family hadn't made things better the way Dewey had ours. "You can't blame your daddy for getting married again," I said. "Your momma was dead."

"Something was going on before she died," Sonia said. "He didn't wait a month before he married her, and then she moved in and took over. I came home from school and found my stuff thrown out. She tossed out my forty-fives. The only one she missed was 'Sea of Love' because it was on the record player. She even threw away Franklin's old Lionel train set." She grabbed my hand. "Come on, let's not talk about this shit. Let's dance."

Inside The Falls she put her shoes back on and led me by the hand onto the dance floor, flashing that foxy smile of hers. Jesse gave me a V sign with his fingers from across the room, signaling an okay for me to be dancing with Sonia, though I knew he wouldn't like it if more happened between us, even if they were split up. Sonia pulled me into the crowd where the dancing was wildest. Her eyes looked greenish up close in the light of the dance floor. With her lips pursed, her eyes squinted, her sharp nose, and the light shining through the red tips of hair bouncing around her head, she looked foxier than ever. I could feel heat coming from her hand. That's how she was. She gave off heat.

Ray Camacho and the Teardrops were rocking. *"Hey, little girl in the high school sweater."* That's the song that got stuck onto Sonia. She came to mind whenever I heard it, and now the band was singing it. *"Gee, but I'd like to know you better."* Jesse used to sing that when he got to thinking about her, too. *"A-wearin' that crazy skin-tight skirt and that crazy Ivy League shirt."* One time before our team ran onto the football field for a game on Friday night, we were all clumped together in the end zone when Jesse started that song to get us revved up. I jumped in. *"Hey, little girl in the black silk stockin's."* On the sideline, Sonia was one of six Letter Girls in a tiny flared skirt and a high plumed hat with a white strap around her chin, holding the letter A in front of her chest and kicking up her bare legs so that the tassels on her white boots shimmied in the stadium lights. *"Lookin' just like a juicy plum."* Then Danny Yamaguchi, a halfback on our team, began singing next to me, and other guys joined in—Hank Palacios, Wilbur Flowers, the whole bunch. *"Gee, but you got my heart rockin'."* I remembered how my brain seized up, feeling almost ready to explode, when I'd heard from another girl how Sonia liked to do "around the world" on Jesse. *"I'm hopin' that you'll tell me yes."* We ran onto the field, the Madera Coyotes ready to tear apart the Tulare Redskins, though I think, if I remember right, we lost. *"You're the girl that I love best."*

After I again changed my water in the alfalfa field at around one in the morning, Jesse was still in the pickup with Sonia. I watched the moon come up over the Sierras—a mountain range I couldn't see but knew to be there because of how the moon popped into view higher than the valley horizon. It was a half-moon, almost three-quarters, silvery but less pale than in early summer. Moonlight brightened the ditch water creeping over the ground like slow-moving mercury as it twisted around the alfalfa stalks, giving the air a sweet, musty smell. You could almost hear the water crackle through the hay stubble. I liked irrigating at night when it was quiet and peaceful this way, and I liked it much better than when I traded off with Jesse and climbed onto the Jeep pulling the rackety hay baler. Waiting to bale hay wasn't so bad, though. I'd stretch out in the hay field and lay my hand on top of the windrow so that when the dew came in, the wetness would wake me.

Off in the distance I saw the window light of Mitch's cabin near the pond. He was probably reading, which is what he did when he wasn't drinking, chasing tail, or working. But even when he was working I sometimes found him on a ditch bank or under a tree with a book while he was waiting to change his cotton or corn water. He was going to college in the fall, and he was back with the girl he'd busted up with at the beginning of the summer, so he was happy. Jesse was back with Sonia. Ana, as it turned out, was going steady with a guy from the Bay Area, who drove down to see her. I supposed she was happy, too. Adelaide had crapped out on me once she learned that she wasn't really pregnant as she thought. What hurt in that deal wasn't so much Jesse pushing her off on me—I can't blame him for that—but her really wishing she was with Jesse all the time she was with me, who was nothing but second pickings to her. I wanted nothing to do with her after that and was glad to be rid of her.

Up in the sky, the man in the moon had only a half-face, like someone had whacked his head off at an angle. The moon's slashed face tipped with a scary tilt to it, like it might tumble out of the sky with all the stars streaming behind it. Then the earth would go black. But the moon hung up there, a crazy, cocked half-head staring down at me, all alone in the alfalfa field. I imagined my head like that half-moon, a fractured skull with no body. That my head would some day sure as hell look that way—a cracked skull with no flesh—gave me the creeps.

I wished I could understand what I was doing out there. I don't mean what I was doing in the field of alfalfa stubble—I was irrigating hay to make it grow, I knew that—but what the hay and myself were even doing out there on an August night in the San Joaquin Valley under a tilted moon. It was something I couldn't figure. Why wasn't I someone else? It stumped me why I wasn't one of Duane's cows in the feedlot or the wet gopher that Dewey had pulled from a ditch by the tail and whacked in the head with the sharp point of his pocketknife, then laughed that wheezy laugh of his while the gopher wiggled around from its tail pinched between Dewey's fingers, flinging blood all over the place. I could've been, I suppose, a gopher or a cow, just like Sonia could've been a fox, not a girl. Or not born at all. Any of us. Or like my momma told me when she was drunk how she could've strangled me when I was born.

When I thought about it, I might've been killed by now in other ways—from how we drove drunk on mountain roads, switching seats, or getting whacked in the head with a biker chain, or almost getting chopped up by a hay swather. Last summer when I was cutting hay all by myself far from other farmhands, I climbed down to get the swather unjambed, and the sickle blade slipped free and cut my fingers to the bone. Like as not I would've passed out and bled to death out there in the field if Jesse hadn't happened by in the pickup. It was just an accident he came along. An accident after an accident. Any other day in the summer it wouldn't have happened. He looked at my bloody hand and took off his T-shirt to wrap it.

"I think I'm going to lose it," I said.

"You big baby," he said. "You ain't going to lose nothing."

Jesse raced like Billy Vukovich from the ranch to Dearborn Hospital and did not so much as pause at a stop sign all the way to town. I kept feeling weaker and weaker, my whole body going light, and Jesse talked louder and louder to keep me awake. With the gas pedal jammed to the floorboard, the old pickup screeched and rattled like it was about to shatter. A cop pulled behind us at the edge of town, but Jesse let him chase us all the way to the hospital, and only when we stopped and got out of the truck with me hanging on Jesse's shoulder did the cop catch on. The doctor bent my fingers straight and gave me shots right into the cut flesh, then stitches both inside and outside the wounds. I don't think Ana's momma could've done a better job. I've still got my fingers, and I also have the scars to remind me how Jesse saved my hand, and maybe my life.

He tried to do the same thing this summer when we come upon another accident, two actually, though the first he couldn't do nothing about.

After we tangled with those dumb-ass bikers, my knuckles swelled up so sore the next morning I couldn't hardly hold the steering wheel of the tractor. My ribs ached and the back of my neck throbbed. I smelled dried blood in my nose. Those

bikers registered more blows than I thought. Jesse looked pretty
bruised, too, not just his hands but his ribs and jaw. Late Sunday
afternoon, we set all the ranch water for the night and took off
with Mitch for Millerton Lake, where a bunch of guys and gals
lay around drinking beer near Friant Dam. Some waterskied.
Not Jesse, of course, though he did climb into a Chris-Craft
when we coasted along shore to clip watercress for Mitch's
momma. On the drive home, the car ahead of us started to slow,
then we saw other cars and motorcycles pulled to the side of
the road where swirling dust rose up from an accident. A Hell's
Angel lay crumpled next to his sprawled motorcycle. I knew he
was dead, the way his body lay twisted with a weird stillness.

We learned how two squads of Hell's Angels left Bass Lake
after their weekend powwow, one behind the other. A SoCal
leader from Berdoo dropped a muffler and was making a U-turn
to pick it up when someone from the Oakland crew up north
swung out and sideswiped him. It looked like an accident, but
no one thought it was.

On a Sunday evening three weeks later, we were again driving
from the lake on 145, heading for Madera, straight into a
bloody sundown, when we came up on another accident. Cars
were parked every which way off and on the two-lane road,
and people were running to where a Chevy Impala convertible
had flipped over in the yellow weeds sloping off the roadside
into a ditch. Jesse, Mitch, and I ran down and saw a girl in a
white blouse and khaki shorts sprawled on her back with her
legs pinned under the flipped car. She was unconscious, the car
crushing her thighs.

"It's Linda," Jesse said. It was Linda Antonelli, all right, on the
way home from the lake with a bunch of girls, probably laughing
and having a good time until the next minute she lay in the dirt,
her face scraped and bloodied, her legs pinned under the door-
edge of the upside-down car.

"Sonny, Mitch, get over there." Jesse pointed to the front of the Chevy. He yelled for other guys to line up alongside him and grab the car. He wanted us to lift it off Linda. "Okay, on three," he said. "Make sure you have a good grip. Let's lift. One, two—"

"No, no." A pudgy man I didn't recognize, wearing a sports coat, slacks, and penny loafers, skidded down the road bank and pushed Jesse aside. "Get away from the car. Wait till the ambulance comes."

Jesse shouted at him, "We've got to get this car off her!"

"You can't move her!" the chubby man shouted back.

By this time a bunch of other adults crowded in and agreed. "You kids get back."

"We're moving the car, not her!" Jesse shouted at them.

"You'll crush her more," a woman said.

"You can't lift that car," someone else said.

"Get away from her. Get away. It'll fall back on her."

The adults scattered us away from the car, yelling and pushing at us. Jesse saw there was nothing he could do, the adults had their way, and he stood there with frustration all over his face, staring down at Linda with his hands hanging helpless by his sides, his arm muscles twitching, while down the road we heard the wail of a cop siren coming our way.

Linda's funeral was sad, with her girlfriends and even a lot of guys crying. Jesse wasn't asked to be a pallbearer, which hurt his feelings, I know, because he thought he should've been. He didn't say nothing, though. The funeral was in Merced—my first time in a Catholic church—and when the coffin came up the center aisle, I felt terrible for Linda. Dying young is bad enough, but being dead forever is awful to think about.

I saw the yellow light click off in the window of Mitch's cabin. Where the lightbulb had been shining through the window, another light, like a silver column, glided past the

cabin. I thought of the Sikh's ghost and remembered Nellie
telling me he'd once seen his guardian angel, who appeared to
him in a silver column of light. Mitch's guardian angel hanging
around the cabin would make more sense than the Sikh. Then
I saw nothing but the black shack in the moonlight and told
myself the window light snapping off had played tricks with
my eyes. Still, I was kind of spooked. I thought about Linda,
dead before her life really started, as they said in church, and I
wondered which would be better: being a ghost and knowing
yourself dead or just being dead without knowing it. Either way
was pretty scary.

Jesse's pickup had disappeared from the pond, to take Sonia
home, I figured. Now I saw it creeping back up the road, the
headlights turning and coming toward where I was irrigating.
I worked at the end of the field, building up a levee with my
shovel, until I saw Jesse's pickup park by the pump. He was
waiting for me. I walked toward the head ditch, splashing
through the shallow water between the levees. I kicked up the
water with my rubber boots to see the drops flash in and out of
the moonlight, like fireflies sparking the night for a moment,
then fizzing into darkness.

Jesse bent down to get a drink at the pump. He'd taken out
the plug from the iron discharge pipe leading into the white
concrete standpipe. Water shot out parallel to the ground in a
powerful stream, and Jesse gulped it up like a man nearly dead
of thirst, then straightened with a satisfied sigh, sounding a faint
"Aaaaah." He wiped the back of his hand across his mouth. He
had to talk loud to make himself heard over the whine of the big
pump. "You want some?"

I nodded and bent over the spurting stream. It was great
water, cold and clean, fresh from the ground. "This is the best
water on the ranch," I said after drinking.

Jesse screwed the plug into the sweating iron pipe, cutting

off the flow. The pump whined. "I like it from the pump at the Cottonwood Creek piece."

We each had our favorite-tasting water on the ranch, and some days, especially during the heat wave, just the thought of a drink from one of the pumps made my head go light. All these pumps on the Etcheverry ranches, whining day and night, spewing out water from the deep, chilly ground, made the land hum. Nellie said the valley was going to cave in some day from all this water being pumped out, which made us laugh.

"The water's plumb out in this field," I told Jesse. "I have to shut down this pump and change the headgates in South America."

"I'll give you a hand," he said. "It's going to be a while before I can start baling, if at all. The dew ain't coming in."

"That hay's got to get baled no matter what." Another day or two in this heat and the hay would be as dry as straw. The tomatoes in the field also ripened faster than they could get picked.

I cut off the pump switch and screwed down the oil. The pump began its reverse whine, growing fainter until the shaft stopped spinning. The night's quietness made me and Jesse not say anything for a while. We sat on the cool pump pipe and looked out over the dark alfalfa field. I got to thinking what Linda would give to be sitting there with us, doing nothing else but sitting there, feeling the cool metal pipe against her butt.

Jesse must've been thinking something similar because he said out of the blue, "We should've pulled that car off Linda. We could've saved her."

I wanted to help him quit eating away at himself. He'd kept bringing her up since the accident. "There was nothing we could do," I said. "Even if they'd let us get it off, she probably would've died anyway."

"I think we could've saved her."

"Forget it, man. You done what you could."

He kind of shook his head and then took out a fresh tin of snoose, slit the top free with his thumbnail, and offered me the first dip. I dug out a sizable bit.

"Hey, fuckhead," he said, "save a little for somebody else."

That took our minds off things while we sat there, letting the snuff do its work and getting us to feel better. I thought about him in the pickup with Sonia and saw my chance to climb into his thoughts. Now that summer was ending, I wondered if he was making plans.

"Are you going to run off with Sonia?"

He thought a little bit before he said, "I don't know."

"If you don't know, who the fuck does?"

"I'm not thinking in that direction right now."

"What direction might you be thinking?"

"I have to get that hay baled."

I tried to edge him back on track. "Sam wants us to settle down."

Jesse was quick to answer. "That's easy for him to say. He's got it all."

"His daddy before him, too," I added.

"He started with nothing."

"Mitch's daddy? That ain't true."

"I'm talking about Sam's daddy, you lunkhead."

Right up until he died, Sam's daddy used to drive out to the ranch from town, where he'd moved with a new wife. I said to Jesse, "I miss that old fart coming around the ranch."

I told Jesse how it wasn't Sam but his daddy—Old Man Etcheverry himself—who'd originally hired me. At the time I was working for a guy on the West Side when I ran into the Old Man—that's what we called him—while he was talking with some farmhands about his hay not drying right to be hogged for the feedlot. I put in my two cents about how I thought it should be raked so it would dry right. Old Man Etcheverry asked me, "Who do you work for?" I told him and then, "Not anymore," he said.

"Sam ain't been the same since the Old Man died," Jesse said.

"I'm thinking it's more Sam's wife that's getting to him. He's got her to deal with."

"Ana told me they're putting her momma into a sanatorium up in Santa Cruz. They done it before."

"She'll come back the same," I said. "At least our mommas quit drinking."

"Yours did," Jesse said.

He kept looking out over the alfalfa field like something was on his mind.

"This is quite the spread, ain't it?" I said.

"Fuckin'-A," Jesse said. "It was even better when the Old Man ran sheep and cattle."

"There's still cows in the feedlot."

"Those are Duane's cows. I'm talking about when they had cattle and horses and sheep in open pasture."

I knew what Jesse liked about the ranch was the open land, maybe not pasture and livestock anymore but open-ground crops like cotton and alfalfa. I did, too. The Etcheverrys had some forty acres of vineyard and an apricot orchard at the spread where the Old Man used to live—what they called the Home Place—but Jesse and I didn't have much to do with the grapes, except in the fall when we drove tractor to scrape the vineyard rows for raisin trays or sometimes drove the gondolas when the pickers were in the wine grapes. Both of us would just as soon forget the days as kids when we picked grapes, turned raisins, and rolled trays. Vineyards and orchards bored us. We liked working in open fields.

We didn't say nothing about Mitch getting all of this land someday, but we knew he would. He worked right alongside us—in summertime anyway. We figured he didn't have to be out here the way we did, though he told me once, "I have to work somewhere if I want any dough." Sam wasn't going to give him money he didn't earn. Mitch usually worked off the ranch—one summer for a well-drilling outfit, another time bucking hay—but this summer Sam needed him in the tomatoes.

"Alfalfa, corn, cotton, milo maize, now tomatoes," I said, thinking about Sam, "all these tractors, swathers, balers, harrowbeds, trucks, cars, a nice house, a swimming pond—I mean, this fucker's got it all."

What I said triggered something in Jesse's voice. He looked out across the ranch, and without finishing the sentence he just said, "Man, some day…"

His thinking that way got me remembering eating homemade ice cream at the Old Man's place. Morris Epstein, who owned Money Back Moe's in town, was one of the Old Man's best friends, and people said in the old days Money Back Moe would drive his horse and wagon all the way from town on Sunday to eat ice cream with Old Man Etcheverry. "You remember that peach ice cream the Old Man used to make?" I asked Jesse.

"Don't get me started," Jesse said. "Let's get that water changed."

The next week, Jesse and I worked days again while Mitch irrigated at night. Because the corn had dented early in the heat, I was on the harvester, hogging it into silage for cows. That's where this field corn went, either into cow feed or Wampum corn chips for people. When I was caught up with the corn, I went back to work in the Tomato Piece, waking in the darkness before dawn to start flagging the crop duster with a six-cell flashlight so he could spray sulfur on the tomatoes to keep them from mildewing. At first light, I went over to the ranch's airstrip, where Jesse helped me refill the hopper of the biplane, and

Lonnie Simmons leaned over the side of his airplane and puked, no doubt hungover or still drunk, one.

Lonnie flew the biplane down so close to crops that the tires were stained green. Yellow sulfur dust, smelling like rotten eggs, covered Jesse's face and hair as he poured a sack of it into the hopper. When I started laughing at him, he said, "Look at your own self."

The heat wave broke, but the tomatoes were rotting in the field. Sam Etcheverry lost his shirt on that little experiment. The first picking went okay—the braceros loaded buckets of tomatoes about to turn pink, which the shippers sprayed with some chemical to keep them from ripening too fast while traveling east in refrigerated freight cars—but trouble commenced with the second picking and got worse from then on. Not enough braceros were available to keep up with the ripening tomatoes, and the price wasn't worth a damn. Sam grumbled the way all ranchers gripe about lousy prices for crops, but in the end those tomatoes didn't make him a bum nickel, I don't believe. It cost more to irrigate, spray, pick, swamp, and haul them than what he got on the market.

By the last picking in August, we were trucking overripe tomatoes to the cannery for ketchup, but even then some loads got rejected. I drove a rejected truckload under the cottonwood trees near the blacksmith shop, where Jesse, Mitch, and I sorted through to try to save what we could. We threw the rotten ones off the truck into the dirt. *Splat! Splat! Splat!* The ground looked like a bloody massacre. Those tomatoes let loose an acid stink. Cottonwood pollen flew through the air and mixed with the dust and the buzzing blowflies on the tomatoes we'd sorted, ready to go back to the cannery and into ketchup bottles. Years later, when I saw on TV the helicopters evacuating people out of Vietnam, I thought of us desperately working in the wind and dust under those trees. I know the mind makes funny connections, and I'm not saying it was the same kind of disaster, I'm just saying how strange it was to have that day pop up so vivid while watching people scrambling into helicopters on TV years later.

Sam was a good sport about the tomato mess and kept taking his home movies, even when we were under the cottonwoods sorting out the rottens. I was in the field swamping once and saw him filming a picker coming down a row with three buckets of ripe tomatoes, one in each hand and another bucket balanced on his head. Those braceros were tough. When a jackrabbit jumped up in the vines, the picker shouted something in español, and braceros ran from all directions to circle the rabbit until they caught him, another one for the pot that night.

After we trucked away the last of the tomatoes, Sam asked me to film him. He made a hangman's noose from a big rope, put it around his neck, and acted like he was hanging from the limb of a sycamore tree, with his tongue hanging out like a dead goose's. I looked through the viewfinder and pushed the gizmo on top of the sixteen-millimeter. The camera made a whirring sound. Then Sam held himself up on the rope with his hands while I filmed his feet kicking around in the air. All I could see in the viewfinder were his shoes swinging crazily above the ground, like he'd really hanged himself. It was pretty funny. Sam never raised tomatoes again, but that field always got called the Tomato Piece no matter what crop was on it.

We had a lot of cotton, corn, and hay still to harvest, along with the raisins and wine grapes, but with those tomatoes out of the way I felt summer about finished. I looked forward to that good feeling in the fall with the crops all picked and the fields fallow again. With Labor Day coming on, Sam planned a barbecue for Mitch's send-off to college. Duane killed a steer a few weeks beforehand so it had time to hang in the locker and gain some age on the beef. I sat on the wooden fence rail that

morning and I was stunned—I have to admit it—by the way
the cow dropped so quick in the corral after Duane shot it in
the head with a .22 rifle not much bigger than a Red Ryder BB
Gun. Duane pointed the rifle close to the cow's skull, between its
eyes, and pulled the trigger. *Pop!* went the little .22. The steer's
legs flew out like the ground was jerked from under its hooves.
The cow was dead before it hit the dirt.

Mitch wanted the brains as appetizers for his party, and the
guy from the locker who'd come to butcher the steer struggled
with a hacksaw to cut a wedge into the skull to scrape out the
brains. He looked up from the sawing, his dusty face waxy with
sweat. "How do you want the steaks cut?" he asked.

"Thick T-bones," Mitch said.

If Duane had his way we'd be eating thin, overcooked, chewy
steaks, the way cowboys liked them. Mitch's daddy had paid
Duane for the steer, though, so the steaks would be like he
wanted them: thick, charred on the outside but bloody inside.

The weekend before the barbecue, I was at the Big Top
shooting the bull with some guys when Sonia came up and
pulled me aside to say, "Jesse and I broke up. I want you to take
me to the dance on Saturday."

Jesus H. Christ, I thought, *here we go again.*

"You don't need me to take you to the dance," I said. "You got
plenty of people to go to the dance with. I'll see you there."

Her fingers kind of brushed my bare forearm with a feathery
touch the way a girl can do, and I felt heat from her fingertips.
"I want to go with you. It's the end of the summer."

Now, Jesse and Sonia had busted up enough times and I'd
danced with her enough times that I could've said, Sure, why not?
She went out with bunches of guys when she and Jesse were split.
An end-of-the summer breakup was no surprise, but this time I
was leery. "You and Jesse will probably be back together before
the week's out. Anyway, I don't think I'm going to the dance."

Her back arched, her eyes grew big and round, and her tongue flicked across her lips. "Yes, you are," she said. "You're going with me." And damned if I didn't. I picked her up, drove her to the lake, and drove her home. We even made out a little bit in the car outside her house, the way friends would do. "You're a sweetheart," she said, and pressed her puffy lips against my mouth.

I pulled back and said, "Sonia, do you think you're pregnant?"

A streetlamp shined into the car enough for me to see her eyes spark. "My aching ass, what the hell is that question about?"

"I need to know," I said.

"No, I do not *think* I am pregnant, and I *know* I am not pregnant. I have to go."

"Don't get your butt in an uproar." I wasn't afraid to talk to her this way. I didn't care if she got mad at me, but I had a lot to lose if she was just using me to get back at Jesse for breaking up with her, or if I got suckered into something the way Adelaide did me.

The porch light of her house was shining when we drove up, and now a light flashed on behind the patterned drapes covering the bay window. "You have to understand something," she said. "Jesse and I are through." In the past, Sonia acted like she didn't give two hoots when they broke up, but this time she sounded choked up. I felt my own chest tighten. Through all of Sonia's feistiness and toughness, a look of pain lingered around her eyes, and those curvy lips of hers quivered. Being a doctor's daughter loaded with dough didn't keep her from hurting. And compared to me and my stepdaddy, she'd gotten a raw deal with her stepmomma. She kissed me again, so quick and hard our teeth clacked. She slid away to open the door. "You don't have to get out. I'll call you."

Sonia was on my mind when a bunch of us guys on the ranch took off frog hunting for Mitch's upcoming party. We met in Sam's yard by the toolshed when it started turning dark. Swarms

of night bugs flew around the outside lightbulb on the shed.
While waiting for Jesse to show up, we downed a six-pack. The
high-pitched whine of the house's water pump cut out, and in
the silence I could hear bugs getting zapped in the fly-catcher
hanging under the eave of the shed. After half an hour, Jesse still
didn't show. Mitch said, "Fuck him. Let's go."

After pairing off—Sam and Dewey walked together on one
side of the canal with me and Mitch on the other bank—we
rubbed ourselves with stinky 6-12 insect repellent and walked
through buzzing mosquitoes. Mitch shined a flashlight into the
dark canal where the edge of the water met the bank. I carried
a long-handled gig. The night air smelled of DDT from the
last spraying—though the mosquito abatement boys say it's not
supposed to smell, it does—with a hint of kerosene.

Bullfrogs in the canal raised a racket. Clouds of mosquitoes
rose from the wet weeds like they'd never been sprayed. In
the beam of the flashlight, Mitch caught the bulging eyes of a
frog, its ugly black-green head poking through the surface of
the water, its throat pumping as it croaked. I eased the four-
pronged spear toward the frog's throat, then jabbed. Water
splashed, blocking my view for a second, until I raised the long
handle of the gig with an enormous bullfrog dangling at the
end, stringy with green moss, its punctured throat secure on the
barbed prongs. I jerked the big frog off the gig, tossed it into a
dampened gunnysack, and tied the top with twine.

Mitch and I traded off, taking turns with the flashlight
and the gig all the way up the canal to the pond. We left one
gunnysack, heavy with frogs, in the tules, and drank a couple
more beers at his cabin. Mitch kept the double-barrel shotgun
propped against the wall by his bed from when we had that
run-in with the Mexicans in the bar after he did his magic show.

Ready for more frogs, we rode in the pickup to the canal
between North America and a neighboring ranch. We didn't

usually hunt this canal, but Mitch had called the rancher for
permission to cross onto his land to a ditch thick with croaking
frogs. From the high canal bank, off in the distance, I saw the
pink top of Jesse's Oldsmobile across the dirt road, peeking
through the high weeds down in the slough. "Well, looky there,"
I told Mitch.

"What?" he said. He couldn't see Jesse's car until I pointed out
the top. It was pretty well hidden down in the weedy slough. "So
that's where he is," Mitch said. "Stood us up for some tail."

My first thought was that he and Sonia broke up because he'd
hooked onto some new snatch that made him so crazed he was
willing to skip a night of frogging to get into her pants. "Let's
flatten him," I said.

I could see Mitch grin in the darkness. He was no doubt
remembering the night Jesse had flattened his tires when he was
making out by Cottonwood Creek. We'd all done it to others
and had it done to ourselves. We left the gigs, flashlight, and
gunnysacks on the levee and made our way on foot toward the
slough, with me coming up to the driver's side. It hit me that I was
likely to see inside the car with her pants off not some new babe
but Sonia herself, after she'd somehow made a fuss to get Jesse to
give up a frog hunt for her. My stomach felt gigged like a fat frog.

I looked through the side window, rolled up to keep out the
mosquitoes, and saw Jesse's bare foot hooked into the steering
wheel. Sure enough, he was bare-assed, stretched out in the
front seat, facedown on top of whoever he was humping, her
knees hooked up by his ribs as she lay underneath him, her
face looking right at me over his shoulder, though I didn't
think she could actually see me. Her eyelids drooped and her
mouth gasped with squeaking sounds. Jesse was putting the
wood to Ana.

I backed away from the car and hurried around to where
Mitch squatted down to unscrew the valve-stem from the tire.

He was surely thinking I was doing the same thing on the other side. I grabbed him by the arm to get him away from seeing his sister.

"I think Jesse saw me," I whispered. "Let's get out of here."

A panicked look crossed Mitch's face. He'd been slugged by Jesse before—the time he got hit in the throat by accident— and though if we scampered away after flattening the tires Jesse would laugh off the joke in the coming days, if he caught us now he would come out swinging. We ran down the slough and back up to the canal where we'd left the sacks and gigs. Mitch looked back, but Jesse's car didn't move and no lights came on.

"Who was in there with him?" Mitch asked.

"I couldn't see," I said.

Back at the house, we met Sam, Dewey, and the other guys under the eucalyptus trees. We cracked open the beers left cooling in a big washtub of ice. Sam turned on the yard light. I lifted the heavy gunnysack so it would sit upright and untied the twine. Bulging eyes looked up from the dark mass of wet frogs. We all got to work. I pinned an ice pick through a frog's neck into a two-by-four, cut around its waist with my pocketknife, and with pliers pulled down until the skin slipped off the frog's legs like a pair of pants. The curvy white legs glistened under the yard light.

The back screen door of the house opened and Ana's momma waved a lit cigarette in her hand and yelled out in her raspy voice, "Is Ana out there? Sam, do you know where Ana is?"

"Jesus," Sam said and stood up to go into the house. "Just a minute, boys. Finish this frog for me, will you, Sonny?"

I jerked the blackish green skin off the frog's white legs, down over the plump thighs and tapered calves. "Fuck," I said out loud. "Fuck, fuck, fuck."

"What's eating you?" Mitch said.

"Nothing," I said.

We were about finished with the frogs, but I was in no mood to go home. "Let's go knock off some of those rats."

That also seemed like a good idea to Mitch, and he went into the house for a bolt-action .22 rifle and a box of bullets. I sure as hell wouldn't leave a gun like that in the house with Ana's momma, but the house was full of shotguns and rifles. "You can shoot first, if you want," Mitch said.

We walked behind the barn to the dark shed stored with milo maize. Our moving out of the yard light into the darkness must have triggered my mind, and I saw again Ana's naked legs inside the shadowy car, her knees bent by Jesse's sides and her mouth moving like someone being saved at a wild prayer meeting. She didn't have that look of peaceful concentration like when she was with me. I put the picture out of my mind. I wasn't going to let it bother me. "Shine the light up top," I said, and took the rifle from Mitch.

A rat scurried over the mound of milo maize stacked near to the ceiling of the shed. Sam grew about three acres of the stuff behind the pond, keeping enough in the shed for chicken feed after selling off the rest. I don't know why he bothered with it. It just bred rats. As soon as I fired the .22, the dark milo maize looked like a pot starting to boil, and the bubbling shadows were swarming rats. Mitch flashed the beam of light around the shed, but I didn't need no light. I fired into the tumbling mass of rats again and again, jerking the bolt open to eject a shell and slamming it closed to feed a fresh cartridge into the chamber.

"Jesus," Mitch said, seeing me shoot again and again like I'd gone nuts, "what's got into you?"

"Nothing," I said. "I hate rats."

Next night, I was still in a foul mood and sat in the Ranchers' Round-Up downing glasses of rum and Coke. I got to talking with some guys at the bar while watching the annual preseason

football game between the pros and the college all-stars. It must
have been a rerun because I thought that game had been played
earlier. Trying to puzzle it out got me kind of confused, but my
mind slipped into a better place than it was until I saw in the
bar mirror two of those Mexicans who'd threatened us earlier in
the summer. The older guy who'd just gotten out of prison and
the tall, skinny kid in a white T-shirt sat at the end of the bar,
drinking mugs of beer and eating pickled pigs' feet from a jar
that Hazel kept on the counter.

I waited until the kid went to the bathroom, his taps clicking
across the floor, and when he came out I pushed him through
the back door of the bar into the night.

"What the fuck are you doing?" he said.

"Now's your chance, pal," I told him. "You're the big talkers
wanting to get back at us. Go to it."

By then, Jesse would've hit the guy, but I wanted it clear what
he was in for, even though he said, "You're talking crazy, man."

One of the mysteries of life is how word spreads through the
walls of a bar, but soon guys spilled out the door around us. I
saw the older cholo, who was still probably on parole and not
wanting trouble, get pushed back by a winery worker I knew.

"Stay out of this. This is between these two," he said.

The older Mexican looked at me with flat, dead eyes, two
black dots with whites round them the color of smudged piano
keys. At that moment, on the edge of a fight, I'm thinking, *That's
how prison kills a man's eyes.*

The tall, skinny kid in the T-shirt wore tight pegged jeans
cinched at the waist with a thin black belt. I could see the edges
of toe taps on his shiny Bates shoes, built-up with leather soles
an inch thick and probably heeltaps, though I couldn't see those.
His long hair swept onto his forehead in a pointy curl. You could
tell he worked on that curl. "You think you're fucking cute, don't
you?" I said.

The kid's lips wormed into a lazy smile. Lanky guys are hard to fight. They can get the angles on you. Their fists slash like slingblades. This one had a hooked nose and sparkly eyes. His T-shirt showed off smooth brown arms, without the hard muscles of black dudes, like Jesse's buddy Wilbur Flowers, who had eye-popping bulging arms. Mexicans weren't built that way. Their muscles didn't show, but nobody was tougher than a tough Mexican. Baby Gallegos looked soft—cuddly, the girls said—but he knocked out everybody he fought in the Punch Bowl. The best wrestler on our team was Hank Palacios and his arms were as smooth as a girl's.

The kid in front of me stood loose as a goose, with a cocked hip and dangling hands, his shoulders relaxed, his head tilted and his lips in a smile so slight you hardly noticed it, and I thought: *This cholo is going to kick my ass.*

Before he had a chance to swing, I dropped to one knee, grabbed his legs in a wrestling takedown, and twisted him facedown into the dirt. I hooked one elbow behind his back and slammed my forearm hard against his head. I had him down now and could have whacked him with my fist but I just laid on top and mashed his face into the hard-packed dirt until blood spurted from his nose. I felt a rush of relief, as much from outsmarting the kid and not trying to fistfight him as from getting control over him. Then I whacked him with my fist. The little fucker had scared me. I hit him again in the head and the face. Hands smothered my next shot and pulled me to my feet. Hazel shoved my chest and shouted at me, "What's the matter with you, Sonny? You gone crazy?"

Her angry look shocked me. She didn't understand, and I told her, "They threatened us, Hazel."

She then gave me a look of disgust that stopped my tongue cold. "Don't be a twerp," she said. "You get home right now." She gently took the kid by the arm, helping him up. "You come inside. We'll get you cleaned up."

She whirled her back to me and walked inside with the tall, skinny cholo. I could not fucking believe what I was seeing. And she'd called me a twerp. When the back door of the bar closed behind her, I shouted, "Who are you calling names, you ugly, fat dago?"

"Can it, Sonny." The winery worker put his hand on my shoulder. "Come on, I'll follow you home."

The next morning, I found myself in my own bed with hot spikes stuck through my brain. That's how it felt anyway. My eyes ached, my dry throat stung. Worse were all the jangled thoughts tumbling around in my mind and the shame burning me up, not for jumping the cholo but for the disgusted look on Hazel's face that kept swimming into view, and for what I'd said to her, even though she hadn't heard.

"I am going to quit drinking," I said to myself out loud. "This ain't no fucking good."

A song from the jukebox last night pounded against my skull: *"I'm a-walking in the rain. Tears are fallin' and I feel the pain."* I couldn't get the jangling song out of my head. Then I felt furious, at Hazel. Where the hell did she get off for meddling in something that was none of her business, and then for acting like I was the only one at fault? It wasn't fair. She ruined the good, tired, bruised, relaxed feeling that comes the morning after a fight, like when we tangled with the bikers at Bass Lake. I felt beat up. My skull throbbed. *I am going to quit drinking,* I told myself again, but this time, at least, I wasn't talking out loud.

When I shaved, I kept my eyes glanced away from my face in the mirror. I couldn't stand the thought of looking at myself.

I drove to work nicked with razor cuts, and who was the first person I had to bump into but cowpoke Duane on his fucking horse. "Jap Corner is buzzing," he said.

I was filling up my truck at the gas tank. Jesse pulled in behind me. "Shut the hell up, Duane," I said.

"Buzzing, I tell you."

Jesse joined us and said, "I heard how you took him down."

"I fucked up," I said.

"The hell you did," Jesse said. "He didn't take you down. You took him down. Not everybody could do that."

Those few little words changed my mood like I can't tell you. Everybody else was beating up on me, including yours truly. Sure as shit Jesse would've punched the kid as they stepped outside, but even he noticed that he wouldn't have thought to take him down the way I did, nor even knew how to do it. Jesse did try out for wrestling one time, but he got so frustrated during practice at the way Hank Palacios tied him up that when he wiggled free he took a swing at Hank and the coach told him to get the hell off the mat and not to come back. He came to our wrestling meets in the gym to cheer me on. Out on the mat I could hear him yelling through the roars the pep girls roused in the crowd. Nobody had a voice like Jesse's. Now I felt he was cheering me on again for doing something special, and I felt grateful to him more than I think I ever had. If he wanted to plug Ana, I thought, and she was abiding, well, then, more power to him.

I didn't say nothing to him about Ana, and he didn't say nothing to me—it was up to him to talk when he was ready—and I kept my mouth shut the same way about Sonia. She did call me, like she said she would, and we went out to the drive-in movie, where we got pretty hot making out, but she grabbed my wrist and stopped me when I reached up under her skirt—her panties *were* wet—and she said, "Not here, Sonny." If Jesse's words had made me feel good, hers sent me swinging through the stars. *Not here.* I knew I was home with her. She said she was coming to Mitch's going-away barbecue because he had invited her.

"You'll see Jesse there," I said.

"I'll see you, too," she said.

On the day of the barbecue we set up redwood picnic tables under the eucalyptus trees in Mitch's yard, stringing them into one long table. We fired up the barbecue pit with grape stumps, letting them burn down to coals. I sat on a milking stool in the barn, churning some peach ice cream, when Hazel's black Lincoln pulled into the yard and I felt embarrassed all over again. She drove in with her old farmer boyfriend, carrying a gigantic dish of lasagna covered with tinfoil. I walked out of the barn with the intention of telling her I was sorry about the other night, but before I had a chance she smiled at me and sang out in that husky, musical voice of hers, "How ya doin', Sonny?" like nothing ever happened. I guess she'd seen enough fights in her life that if she got worked up over every one she couldn't stay in business. But that smile and nice voice of hers was why her joint stayed packed. She ran the best bar in the valley because she didn't carry a grudge.

The yard grew crammed with cars and trucks. Duane showed up with a bucket of fresh-cut bull nuts, pink and slick. Duane's wife, Thelma, went into the kitchen to help Ana's momma cook them, dredging them with flour and sautéing them in wine, along with the brains. Man, they were good. Ana had already helped her momma cook up the frog legs we'd caught the other night, and platters went up and down the table and were emptied before Sam and Mitch had the steaks cooked. All the tasty smells floating around—mixing with the spicy scent of the eucalyptus leaves hanging above us—made me heady. Red beans, potato salad, roasted peppers, and green salad with Bermuda onions filled my plate. I kept my word to myself and let everyone else tank up on the jugs of wine, sticking just to beer, but even before we'd finished off the lasagna and T-bones and were digging into the ice cream, I was pretty looped, even if it was only with beer.

Ana's momma came out of the house and took some Polaroids of us and passed them down the table. "Didn't Geoffrey want to come today?" she asked about the guy who drove from the Bay Area during the summer to date Ana.

"He wasn't invited," Ana said. She and Jesse sat at opposite ends of the long table, acting like they hardly knew each other.

"Mitch, didn't you invite Geoffrey?" It seemed that Ana's momma really had a thing for this guy Geoffrey.

"I invited him," Mitch said.

Ana looked down at her plate. "He couldn't make it," she muttered.

Jesse gnawed on the T of a steak bone, holding it in his hands to get the last shreds of the red meat, which is sweetest, as the saying goes, closest to the bone. Jesse saw me watching him gnaw on the bone and asked, like he was reading my mind, "Why is it so true that the meat is always sweetest next to the bone?"

"You want another steak?" Mitch asked. "You don't have to devour the whole bone."

"I got room for two more," Jesse said. "That's why I didn't eat yesterday."

"Oh, no," Duane said. He tipped his big Resistol back from his forehead. "You got to eat a lot the day before a big meal. You always want to stretch your stomach so you can eat more the next day."

"You guys are so full of it," Sonia said. Her voice was as gravelly as Ana's momma's, even though she didn't smoke. "No wonder everyone says the guys on this ranch are sure dumb."

Sonia sat across from me, paying little attention to Jesse, and every once in a while, under the table so no one could see, she stuck her bare foot up under the cuff of my Levi's and stroked my shin with her bare toes. Even with all the beer I drank I had a hard-on that wouldn't quit, trapped against the rough metal buttons of my fly. Sonia had her hair down, so it flared around the sides of her face and caught the sunlight when she stood up to take some dishes into the house, leaving her sandals under the table. She wore a green top that flopped down to the crease between her boobs. White cotton pants showed off her naked legs when the sun shined through them, the cloth was so thin, and I could see that she wasn't wearing underpants because when she turned around no lines or ridges cut around her ass, moving free under those loose cottony pants.

Looking at her made me remember how just a couple years ago girls in the suburbs—even fifteen-year-olds—wore girdles when they went out. If Jesse and I were lucky to date or hook up with one of those girls after a party, it was hell to get your hand down into those rubbery things, and if you did, you like to sprain your wrist if her hips jerked. Those days are over, thank God.

Thinking of rubber panty girdles got me to realizing that I didn't have a rubber. I looked around and saw Hank Palacios over by the horseshoe pits, where Duane and other guys were pitching with some girls, who were allowed to stand closer to the pegs when they threw. I figured Hank always had a condom on him, but when I asked, he said he didn't. "You have something lined up?" he asked. A horseshoe clanged against a metal peg.

"I'm hoping. Where can I get one now?"

"Ah, man," Hank said, "go straight."

"Watch out," Duane shouted. "Clear the decks. Sonia's gonna throw."

Back at the tables, Sam played "When It's Nighttime in Nevada" on his big two-row harmonica. That's the state where Ana's momma had grown up. She'd come back from the alkie ward in Santa Cruz and was hanging in there, drinking only lemonade. Sam played "Rambling Rose," a song she liked. She smiled at the song like it wasn't easy for her to smile but she was trying. When Sam played "Red River Valley," he made that thing sound like two harmonicas playing together. He had some little blues harps on the table for others who wanted to play, and Dewey took one and blared out "Freight Train," wailing like a locomotive huffing and moaning down the tracks. A breeze could have blowed me down the road like a tumbleweed, I was so weak with surprise. I'd never heard Dewey play a harmonica. My momma sat at the table, too, and said, "I never heard him play before neither." Dewey laughed the wheezy laugh of his, his glinting eyes almost shut.

Sam was so talented with the harmonica that if he didn't know a song someone called out, he could pick up the tune if you hummed it or sang it for him, the way he did when Sonia sang "Under the Boardwalk" in that sexy voice of hers. Besides being a letter girl, she'd wanted to be the lead singer with the high school dance band but got beat out. She stared across the alfalfa field now, looking at no one, as she sang. Sam played along perfectly, like he knew the song all his life, with his eyes closed and his hand flapping against the harmonica so that it yodeled. A brandy bottle and a drained Tabasco bottle filled with toothpicks made the rounds of the table. I took a toothpick but stuck to beer.

Hazel and her farmer friend were the first to leave, Hazel saying, "I have to check on the bar," but most of the rest of us sat around listening to the harmonicas, jabbering and singing while the sun went down. Across the canal and the alfalfa field, the last of the sun flashed, the way it does just before it sputters out. Then the sky went from rose to bluish pink to ashy gray. When it was night, we migrated into the barn and turned on a record player. I danced with Duane's wife, Thelma, and some of the other gals before Ana put on a forty-five of "This Magic Moment" and then I danced with Sonia. Ana was dancing, too, but Jesse was gone.

"Let's get out of here," I told Sonia at the end of the song.

We walked from the barn, under the trees to my Valiant. A wind had picked up. Eucalyptus leaves rattled above us. I pulled Sonia against me and kissed her, without thinking or caring who might see, although it was pretty dark there under the trees. It was the first time I'd kissed her while standing up, and it was a shock to feel the full length of her body pressed against me from her lips to her thighs, not a girl's body, I thought, but full and easeful like a woman's. On the dark side of the barn, vertical strips of light shined between the wall planks. Laughter and whoops came from inside the barn. Patsy Cline sang "I Fall to Pieces."

Sonia didn't let me kiss her very long. She pushed my chest— it seemed like she was always pushing me away—though she smiled in a way that wasn't pushing. "I like that song," she said. "My stepmother hates it."

"Are we going to go or what?" I asked. I noticed I was woozier than I'd thought, what with the steady sipping of beer all day long.

"We're going," she said.

I drove down the dirt road past the pond and around North America by the slough, where I'd seen Jesse parked with Ana, almost expecting to see his car again, though we'd left Ana back at the barn dancing with Duane. I kept going, not wanting to park where Mitch or Jesse or anybody else would come driving up. I turned between South America and Cottonwood Creek into a narrow dirt strip between the creek levee and the cotton rows. The Valiant jolted and bottomed out with a clang under the floorboard, and I thought that I should've brought the ranch pickup. The tires spun in the dirt and I'm thinking, holy shit, we're stuck, but the car bolted forward and creeped next to the high bank of Cottonwood Creek. Weeds scratched the side of my door. Tall bamboo shoots pressed against the window on

Sonia's side, closing it in with a crisscrossed grid of weird, spiky leaves.

"Hey," she said, "what's with this jungly stuff? Where the hell are we going?"

I stopped the car, tuned off the ignition, and switched off the headlights. "We're here," I said. She seemed relaxed once we stopped. I knew she'd parked on the ranch with Jesse, but not in this particular spot. I wanted our own place.

"Leave that song on for a minute," she said. The radio had cut out when I turned off the engine.

"I don't want to run down the battery," I said. "Then we won't get out."

"Just for a second."

I turned the key and we listened to the last part of the song, *"...God speed your love to me."* I turned off the key, and the dark and quiet closed down on us more intense than when we first stopped. Listening to that song so careful in the quietness tuned my ears to how the music in the barn left a dull roar in my head, sounding like surf at the ocean. Through the bug smears across the windshield, my eyes adjusted to a few scattered stars, then more and more until the Milky Way, so bright in late summer, swept across the sky like fireworks. Bullfrogs croaked to each other in Cottonwood Creek. A mosquito hummed inside the car. I could smell the creek.

I put my arm around Sonia's shoulders and she cuddled up to me. We started kissing. I'd been hot and hard for so long I thought I was going to explode. I moved my hand up under her green top and felt her firm boobs and hard little nipples through her bra. She raised her arms over her head and helped me take her top off. I fiddled one-handed with her bra hook, but it wasn't like Ana's stiff double-hooked straps that just snapped up and off. It was light and lacy, hardly a bra at all, and with a funny hook. She reached behind her back and undid it herself.

When I ran my fingers down her smooth skin to the waistband
of her white cotton pants, she arched her hips up so I could slide
them down her legs, the same bare legs I remember flashing
under the lights of the football stadium as she danced with the
other letter girls.

She tugged on the end of my belt. "Take these off," she said.
"I don't want to break my nails."

I obeyed. I unbuckled the belt, twisted around, lifted up
my knees, and finally got my Levi's off in that cramped space.
I slipped my Jockeys down my legs and my cock sprang free,
stiff and swaying like a drunken sailor called to attention. Sonia
curled her hand around it. "Do you like to be sucked?" she
asked.

I thought I was going to shoot all over the car, I was so
turned on. I could feel that tickly spark running up through
me. I saw a disaster coming. Why didn't I jack off earlier, the
way you're supposed to with whores? But, of course, I wasn't
with a whore, that's why. I was with Sonia Maycheck, and we
were both totally naked, which was a fact so incredible to me
at the time that I heard voices in my confused brain telling
me in a jumble: *Sonia Maycheck. Her and me. Here. Naked.
Now. With. Me.* I felt a clang in my skull like I'd been whacked
upside the head with a crowbar. For a moment, I thought I saw
Jesse's face looking in at me through the door window behind
Sonia's head, the way I'd stared in at him and Ana. I jerked to
sit up straight behind the steering wheel. Sonia pulled away
from me, her face startled. I leaned toward the window. No
one was there. Stalks of dark bamboo swayed back and forth.
My eardrums roared.

"I can't do this, Sonia," I told her.

Her face hardened into the tough expression she regularly
showed when she made up her mind she was going to do
something. She licked her curvy lips. "Yes, you can," she said.

But I couldn't. I felt myself wilt in her hand. I threw my head back against the seat. "I can't."

I felt her fingers give my limp prick a little flick. "I guess you can't," she agreed. She tossed her head back against the seat exactly like me, and then giggled, which didn't strike me as the totally fair thing to do under the circumstances. "That's all right," she said in this happy, musical voice. "It's fine. It doesn't matter to me. I don't care."

I felt my face heat up at what I knew wasn't a compliment. Sonia sat naked, a shadowy outline in the faint starlight, her eyelids closed, her white chest and dark nipples rising and falling as she breathed. I couldn't see the exact color of the hair in the fork of her legs, but to my shock, when I'd put my hand on it, it was long and smooth as soft corn silk. I realized that I was about to lose the most fantastic girl I'd ever been with in my entire life. Give this up and there would be no going back. *You never make up any piece of ass you pass up,* Jesse told me once. If there's a truer saying in life, I don't know it.

"This has never happened to me before," I said.

Sonia's eyes gave me that squint. "Me neither," she said. She rested her head on the seat back and closed her eyes again. "You think I'm trying to trick you, don't you?"

I hadn't known I'd been thinking such a thing at all until she said it. I didn't let on, though. Now I really was suspicious. "How do you mean?"

"When you asked me before if I was pregnant," she said, "you were wondering. And then you were wondering if I was only out to make Jesse jealous. Now you're wondering if I'm going to dump you and go back to him, or if I'm just doing this on the rebound."

"You're saying these things," I said, "not me."

"You're thinking them. You don't trust me."

Her being so blunt made me feel bad for thinking what she

claimed. "Maybe it would help if you told me why you broke up with Jesse."

"It didn't happen that way," she said. "Jesse broke up with me. We planned to get married this fall. At least that's what I thought. I told my dad we wanted a real wedding, and he said, 'Don't even think about it because you're not getting married.' I told him that I certainly was going to get married, even if I had to run away, so he might as well give us a real wedding, and he said, 'No, you're not, Sonia. You're not marrying that Okie kid.'"

I thought I knew what happened next, so I didn't even say it as a question. "And after that, Jesse wouldn't run off with you."

"No, that's not what happened either. I didn't tell Jesse what my father said. So he didn't know. I didn't have a chance to tell him. All I know is that I was wanting to marry Jesse and he wanted to marry me, and we were going to get the hell out of this fucked-up valley, but the next time we got together he said he was breaking up with me. We had split so many times before that he could just say it wasn't working, like all the other times, but I found out the reason was Ana Etcheverry. He's boffing Ana. He dumped me for her."

I let her talk like she was giving me fresh information. "You sure couldn't tell it by looking at them today."

"They're doing it on the QT, but everyone knows. Ana's momma isn't stupid."

"I don't think Mitch knows."

"He would if he got his nose out of his books."

"You've been down this road lots of times," I said.

"Not this way," Sonia said. "I told my father I was marrying him—I put my ass on the line for Jesse—and he left me high and dry. I never want to be with that prick again. I want to be with you."

All the time Sonia was talking we sat side by side, her naked shoulder brushing mine, but she otherwise didn't touch me.

She simply talked, but by the time she finished I was turned on again. That gave me a lesson in the power of words I like to never forget. I put my arm around her shoulder and pulled her close. "I trust you," I said.

"You have to," she said. "We've known each other a long time, Sonny."

"I'm sorry you had to have this happen." I wasn't just saying those words. I meant what I said. I didn't care whether Jesse and her would get back together. I was with her now. That's all that mattered to me. In the long run whatever made her happiest was all right by me, but now I was the happy one. "But if it had to happen," I told her, "I'm glad I'm the one you're with now."

She put her hand on the side of my face the way women do in the movies. "You're nice," she said.

I smelled the heat our bodies gave off hugging and kissing each other naked the way we were, mixed up with her hair smelling like cloves and maybe gardenias. Our tongues were like slick snakes going in and out of our mouths, licking and kissing, and our hands were wild touching each other. I thought we might go so far crazy we'd never come back to our right minds. "Get that redhead worked up," Jesse once said, "and she'll give you quite a ride," but Sonia's the one who rode me. She knelt on the seat, facing me, and lifted her knee, swinging her leg over me like she was mounting a horse on its left side the way you're supposed to. She settled down onto me, guiding me with her hand. She was sitting on top, straddling me, her face close to mine, so I could see her eyes but not their color, though the whites were almost scary bright. "I love you," she whispered. "I love you, Sonny."

Before I knew it I was crying, but not so you could hear. The tears popped hot from my eyes on their own account, letting me know how girls must feel when their chests swell up, their throats tighten, and everything gushes out in a way they can't help, and I couldn't either. Not since I was a little kid when my momma beat me with a belt, telling me that unlike my brother or stepdaddy I wouldn't be worth nothing, did I taste my own salty tears, smeared down my cheeks and mouth. I ran my hands down Sonia's naked backbone to her hips and they spread against my palms, starting to rock. "I love you, too," I said. Never again was I ever to be so happy.

III

JESSE'S GHOST

Sonia and I got married at Carmel-by-the-Sea in a wedding chapel near the ocean, a year after Jesse ran off with Ana. Dewey and Momma drove to our wedding, as did Sonia's daddy and stepmomma. I guess Sonia's dad knew she was old enough to do what she wanted by then. Though her marrying me didn't gladden him, there was nothing he could do about it. We were happy, Sonia and me, for a while, in our way.

I stayed working on Sam's ranch until the cold winter morning he walked out to the barn, where I was replacing spindles on the mechanical cotton picker, getting ready for the next season, and he told me, "I've got to sell the ranch for inheritance taxes. I don't want to, but that's what I have to do."

Mitch's momma was dead. He found her when he came home from college for Christmas vacation, all twisted in sheets on the floor of her bedroom, where she'd chugged gin till her lungs overdosed and she suffocated. When I visited the mortuary chapel in the afternoon before the Rosary, I saw her laid out in a coffin. Somebody told me she looked peaceful—that's what they always say—but I thought she looked different: not sober, not drunk, not peaceful, but stern, with a new, waxy face.

Sam hauled a little portable record player into the chapel and played over and over a scratchy thirty-three record of "Rambling Rose" for his wife, like she was alive and could hear it. He sat alone crying next to the casket, and I smelled the booze on him. He stayed drunk a lot after that day, almost like he picked up where his wife left off, but I recalled that time he got looped when we traveled up to see the Giants play, and I figure his drinking probably went far back but wasn't so noticeable because all the attention focused on the missus until she died. I recollect how after the game, when we came out of the all-you-can-eat restaurant in San Jose, Sam was tipsy. He stood grinning by the car door and recited an old jokey saying: "Don't stand in front of the target, Mother. Father's loaded tonight."

Old Antiguo died, too. He disappeared like a feather blown off the earth. He was sick a long time, and Sam used to go out to his cabin and rub his back to make him feel better. Then the old man's nephew Nellie caught pneumonia and died alone in his cabin a few weeks before Sam walked out to the barn to tell me he was fixing to sell the ranch. Sam arranged for Nellie to get a military funeral. A gray-haired vet in a VFW cap read the ritual and called Nellie his "comrade," a word surprising to me since I associated it with Commies. A bugle played taps on a tape recorder. Two vets folded the American flag from Nellie's coffin into a tight triangle and gave it to Sam, who was the chief mourner. "On behalf of a grateful nation," the VFW chaplain told Sam, "I present to you this flag for safekeeping." The vet stepped back a pace and snapped a salute.

It was in January, I remember, because on the day of Nellie's funeral Cottonwood Creek swelled up with rainwater and flooded the ranch. On the horizon, the creek bank stretched like a gray shadow in the mist with a silver spot marking the break where escaping water spread across the field. That morning I drove a D9 Cat into the rushing water to try to shore up the levee where it broke and I buried the Cat in mud. I looked out over the ranch fields covered with a gray sheet of floodwater.

I remembered years earlier, just before Christmas, when another winter flood soaked the ranch. I'd gone to hunt jackrabbits in the rain and returned to my pickup to find it stuck in the floodwater. I fired up a Farmall tractor to pull out the truck with a chain, but the tractor got stuck, too, its big tires spinning. A week later the floodwater dried back, the ranch turned to a mass of mud, but I was able to get the pickup unstuck and drove it with my brother, who was foreman then, to check on the migrant workers living in cabins at the Camp Ranch. I drove slow on flooded roads with the water leaking up through the floorboard.

A bunch of migrants who'd been picking cotton lived in the cabins—all men. They'd been stranded there since the flood started. Gray tule fog shrouded the camp. A weathered Okie, who reminded me of Dewey in some ways, spotted the five soggy rabbit carcasses in the truck bed, laying there for days since I'd shot them. The man's eyes lightened up under his hat.

"Can we have them rabbits?" he asked.

I was going to throw them away. "You bet," I said, and he scooped out the stiff jackrabbits, their fur all matted from sitting in the rain and the fog, and cooked them for the cotton pickers for their Christmas supper.

"Times have sure changed since those days," Mitch said after I told him that story.

"Ain't that the truth," I said.

Mitch had driven down from San Francisco to see me again in February, nearly four months after his last visit, some four months after Lynette left me. He'd mailed me a typed copy of the magazine article he'd written about Jesse, but I didn't read it. When he called to check on what I thought, I told him I didn't think anything because I did not read the story.

"I know you have a lot on your mind," he said. "I heard about Lynette leaving."

"I imagine you have," I said.

"Listen," Mitch said on the phone, "I'll come see you and we can go over some things."

"Tell you what," I said, "why don't you come and we'll take a drive to the old ranch."

I thought that idea would put him off, reminding him how it felt to remember things you don't want to, but he said, "We can do that." Then he asked me, "Would you be interested in me buying you lunch at the Basque Hotel?"

I thought about the shrimp potato salad I hadn't eaten in years. "The talking part's over," I told him.

Mitch picked me up mid-morning in his silver Camry. He wanted to drive up through Oakhurst to Bass Lake. The sky was clear blue. The lake water was rising but still waited for the snow runoff from the mountains. The Falls had burned down years ago, leaving nothing of the bar except the cracked concrete dance floor and the balcony with the iron railing, now rusted and bent, that Jesse had knocked guys over. Winter rains had sent some water rushing down the chute of the falls. An overgrowth of chaparral and willows clotted the hillside where the rest of the lodge once stood. Across the road, pines and buckbrush nestled up to a crumbling stone wall where we'd tangled with the bikers. I didn't mind thinking about that night, the fighting part of it anyway, on the summer we took over the lake.

"Those bikers weren't so tough as they thought," I said to Mitch, "were they?"

"I wasn't there," Mitch said.

"What are you talking about? You were in it as much as I was. We drove up together—you, me, Jesse, and Hank."

"It wasn't me."

I saw him in a shadowy part of my mind, sitting next to Hank Palacios in the backseat of Jesse's Oldsmobile when we came up behind those two lone Hell's Angels on the road to Table Top Mountain.

"Well, I figure I wasn't there neither," I told Mitch, "but I know I was. My knuckles were so busted up next morning I couldn't steer the tractor."

"It was someone else," Mitch said, "not me. I had a date in Selma that night."

I grabbed the bent iron railing of the balcony overlooking the lake to catch my balance from my back seizing up on me. I'd rolled out of bed after waking at three-thirty a.m., as usual, from pain shooting up my spine and through my shoulder into my neck, a normal morning for me.

"Shitfire," I said. "Let's get out of here."

"What's with you?" Mitch asked. "You look like death warmed over."

"Don't sweat it. I'm honking along."

We drove into the valley through patches of fog. "Do you want to drive to the ranch first," Mitch asked, "or eat first?"

"Same difference," I said.

At the Basque Hotel, heavy white plates and soup bowls ran down two sides of the long boarders' table when the bell rang at twelve-thirty and we trooped from the bar, filling up the chairs, everyone talking loud, three or four women and about forty men. After the garlic soup and lettuce salad, I waited for the shrimp potato salad, but it didn't come. When I asked a waitress about it, she said, "Not today."

"Why's that?"

"That's the way it is."

I saw people sitting at the little tables eating shrimp potato salad. "They've got some."

"They ordered off the menu. Go sit over there if you want it, or come back Wednesday or Sunday. That's when it's on the boarders' table."

"I'll pay extra," I said. "Can I have a little taste?"

She smiled at me. "You can have a kick in the ass," she said.

"Ain't nothing the same no more," I said to Mitch.

He laughed. "It's the same."

After lunch, Mitch and I drove north toward the ranch through a heavy fog along Highway 99 that used to scare me when I was a kid because back then no median guard divided the highway, only oleander bushes with poisonous pink and white flowers. Missing bushes left ugly gaps, showing where out-of-control cars had plowed through at high speed.

We turned off Avenue 11 into the ranch. Fog made the eucalyptus around Mitch's family house look ghostly. Water dripped from the leaves and splattered onto the windshield. The carport behind the house sagged on the crimped metal poles Mitch's momma had banged her car into. Old Antiguo's cabin was gone. We drove down the dirt road into the ranch, past rows and rows of leafless grapevines. The pond was gone. Mitch's cabin was gone. After Sam sold the ranch, Caterpillar tractors crashed into barns and knocked down trees. The big tractors even dredged out Cottonwood Creek to make it run in straight lines rather than meandering through the ranch. Grapevines, with their bare, spindly stalks after winter pruning, covered the fields where the pond and cabin had vanished.

"He sold this place for a song," Mitch said about his daddy. "He got screwed."

When Sam sold and moved into town, his wife was dead, his daughter had run off with Jesse, his son was away at school, the ranch was going under, land prices hit rock bottom, and he was drinking. I don't know how much money he had after paying off his debts. Mitch didn't say nothing about his daddy squandering the rest of the money before he died, but I'd heard that Sam left Mitch and Ana practically zilch.

"With all your education," I told him, "you're better off without the headaches of ranching, especially these days."

"That has nothing to do with it. He never asked what I wanted."

I didn't understand what he was getting at. It was his daddy's ranch. Sam still should've left him some dough, though I think Mitch wasn't all that surprised to make his own way. What hurt, I gathered, was losing this ranch without his being able to do anything about it. Maybe he felt like Jesse after Linda had her car accident, thinking he could've saved it.

"It looks sad," I said about the ranch.

Saddest of all was the Tomato Piece, recently covered with grapevines that now had been pulled out, piled into clumps, and burned when prices crashed. The field stretched bare and black in the fog. The feedlot corrals, where Duane kept his cattle, had been torn out, leaving behind only a long, rusting metal roof and concrete slabs along the conveyor belt as a storage shed for broken-down tractors, disks, old trucks, and piles of grape posts.

"This place used to be humming," Mitch said.

"You said the right word," I told him. "This ranch hummed. Excepting those tomatoes, we made your daddy some money, with us getting up to two-plus bales of cotton and twelve tons of hay to the acre. Humming is the right word."

"No point in talking about it. It'll probably hum again someday. People would just say we're being nostalgic, idealizing the good old days as better than now."

"Fuck those people," I said. "Just drive them out here. Let them look for their own selves."

I thought how I once knew every acre of this ranch. I worked it, sweated it, cussed it, but now I felt like a stranger.

Caterpillars had leveled Nellie's cabin and the haunted black-smith shop, leaving bare dirt. I wondered where the Sikh's ghost wandered off to. Where was Nellie's ghost? Tractors had pushed down the old hay barn and the house where I'd lived with Dewey and Momma. The pecan tree next to the house got ripped down, too.

"I was sorry to hear about your mother," Mitch said.

"I was ready for it," I said. "After Dewey croaked, nothing surprised me. I thought Dewey was too tough to die."

Like me now, Dewey got clobbered with diabetes, only worse than me. Doctors chopped off his feet, then cut off his legs at the knees, then at the hips. After the second operation, I took little Trisha to see her granddaddy. She was six years old at the time. Dewey swiveled out of bed on his new artificial legs. Laughing in that wheezy way of his, he joked, "Now I'm as short as Trisha." We were in the hospital when he was dying. Dewey lay under the sheet without any legs, his eyes closed, hardly breathing, when of a sudden he sat bolt upright in bed and sucked in his last breath. The doctor said, "I've never seen anything like that."

After Mitch's daddy sold the ranch, Sonia and I rented a house in town and I took the job at the winery, working the graveyard shift from ten-thirty at night to seven-thirty in the morning, until I bid my way up to where I ran the grape press during crush season. Even when I started out I was earning half again more than Sam paid me, and I kept making more. At that time, I might not have hooked up with Jesse again except for the National Guard. We both joined and did six months of basic training at Fort Ord, with the army letting us out ten days early so we wouldn't be eligible for veterans' benefits later on. For the next five years, Jesse and I served in the guard together at weekend drills, once-a-month meetings in town, and two weeks during the summer at Camp Roberts, except for the summer they sent us to Hawaii for jungle warfare training to ready us for Vietnam, although we never got sent. No guards went over there. They had enough draftees, like my cousin, to get killed.

"I wouldn't think Jesse could get along in the army," Mitch said. "I'd expect him to be in the brig after punching out a drill sergeant for yelling at him."

"He didn't welcome those screaming sergeants," I said, "but he was a soldier. He did fine, same as he did on our high school football team. Being with his buddies made him happy."

"He liked the camaraderie?" Mitch added, kind of as a question he knew the answer to.

"He liked his comrades, all right," I said, thinking of the word at Nellie's funeral. "I mean he liked you until he didn't like you."

The war games in summer camp made us kids again, me and Jesse, like back when we used to roam the ditch banks carrying water pistols filled with gasoline fired up to napalm ants and crawdads and frogs and snakes, which Jesse hated. For all his toughness, Jesse was scared shitless of snakes and spiders. Once at Camp Roberts, I caught a tarantula on the firing range and made it my pet. Taking some thread from my army sewing kit, I tied it around the spider's hairy leg and pinned it to the chest pocket of my fatigue, short-threading it so it couldn't climb up and bite my neck. It hung there like a medal.

We'd just finished on the firing range and had live ammo in our pockets when I walked up the trail at Jesse, and he started backing away, screaming at me. "Get the fuck out of here with that spider."

I snapped it off my shirt and dangled the wiggly tarantula on its string. "What's the matter, big man? How's a little spider scare you?"

He kept backing up, his face like a cadaver's. I made a motion like I was going to throw it at him. "Get away from me," he said. "You better hold on to that spider. You better sleep with it because when you let go I'm going to kill you."

"How can you be so scared of a little spider?"

Jesse unslung his M1 rifle off his shoulder, shoved a live round into the chamber, and pointed the muzzle at my nose. "You take one more step," he said, "and I'll blow your head off."

I didn't think long on that one. "Come on, spider," I said, "we're leaving."

"Jesse loved to scare me when we were kids," I told Mitch. "He went out of his way to play tricks to see what you were made of. I remember when we come into town with our folks on Saturday to buy our groceries for the week, stuff you couldn't find at the Little Oklahoma stores—canned goods and big rolls of bologna—and us kids were allowed to go to the movies. We went to the Rex Theater because it was ten cents cheaper than the Madera Theater, and you could sit there as long as you wanted, watching the same double feature over again from the matinee into the evening. I once walked home late at night after this spooky zombie movie—scared of the shadows around me— and was about to crawl into the sheets when someone under the bed grabs my leg and goes 'Arrgghhh!' like a zombie ghost in the movie. I about pissed my pants. Jesse had run ahead of me, snuck into my house, and waited for me under my bed."

"That's why he liked the way Duane and those cowboys went so far to trick each other," Mitch said. "He could take it when you turned the tables on him. You could joke him back. Like that time we were letting the air out of his tires, he would've laughed it off later."

"Maybe if we'd done it," I said, "but we didn't." I didn't want to say anything, even now, about running off because of me seeing Ana naked in the car with Jesse, though I don't know what difference it would've made to Mitch at this point. I kept talking. "I remember during football season when we put wintergreen in his jockstrap and he had to ask the coach to excuse him from practice. He laughed it off. But he didn't laugh off my spider."

We started having good times again, me and Jesse, but always without our wives, which was fine because Sonia carried bad feelings about Jesse, while I had no interest in seeing Ana. After he married Ana in Reno, Jesse left Sam's ranch and took charge of his own dad's business—the Floyd Septic Tank Company. Jesse was a honey pumper. "Ain't no better business in the world than pumping honey," Jesse told me, "except maybe the restaurant business. People always got to do one or the other."

When he was a kid, Jesse had helped his daddy after school and on weekends, pumping honey and digging septics by hand. That's how he gained his muscles before doing ranch work. Ninety percent of the septics in those days were dug in place, cemented, with a concrete lid pushed on top. Jesse dug the holes with a shovel and mixed the sand and rock in a half-yard mixer, all by hand. Sometimes he finagled me into helping him. I would be down in a septic, hosing the walls, with shit splattering over me for twenty bucks a week and all the Pepsi I could drink. That was pretty good in those days.

"He did everything full throttle," I told Mitch. "He didn't hold back. You didn't have to wake his ass up to go to work. Just like on the ranch, he worked from sunup to sundown."

I helped Jesse again after I started work at the winery because I had weekends free. The first week at the winery I was loading trucks and the union steward told me, "You better slow up. You're finishing too quick. You're making the other men feel bad."

"Well, then, fire their asses," I said.

"You have to understand. Some guys have bad backs. Some have problems at home. We all have to work together here."

I learned how the union works and stood with everyone else on the picket line. After a tiff with his daddy, Jesse and I talked about going into business together hauling hay. We drove harrowbeds together for a Russian farmer one summer, and

Jesse designed a newspaper ad calling himself "The Harrowbed King of the San Joaquin," but he dropped that plan. "You can't get ahead with seasonal work," he said. "People are on the john every day."

Jesse made the septic business successful in a way his daddy never could. He hooted, "I'm just a shit-hauling guy!" He talked about expanding into Clovis and Fresno and up into the mountains. His daddy had started up his own business—you had to say that for him. He wasn't out there chopping cotton for somebody else. He also moved his family into a brick house in town, but he drank heavy. He and Jesse's momma always had a bottle going, and I figure he was just as glad to have Jesse run the show so he could drink. Jesse's daddy looked a lot like Hank Williams—not the one on TV now but the real Hank Williams. He was rawboned, lanky, and tough. He wore khaki pants, Wellington boots, and a hat like Hank's—not a cowboy hat but a snappy felt fedora. Jesse's pop was a wheeler-dealer, all right, but nowhere near as big as he thought he was. While Jesse's brother kicked Jesse around as a kid, his daddy knocked the crap out of them both.

"His daddy used to call him Goose Squat Jesse," I told Mitch. "He was mean that way. Not many people know that, but when I used to rib Jesse, that's what I called him—Goose Squat. Nothing so nasty as that. Course when I did it he could blow it off because he was grown and didn't have to prove himself no more."

The same with the fighting. After Jesse ran the septic business, he didn't fight for survival, like when he was a kid getting picked on and needing to prove himself, or in high school when he fought for recognition, with survival attached. Anymore he didn't go looking for fights, but he wouldn't back down when they came looking for him. Guys all over the valley wanted to fight him for no reason at all, just because he was Jesse Floyd. It reached the point, I think, where he felt he couldn't back down or he would've tarnished something. But it wasn't play anymore. It was just business.

One Saturday night, we sat at the Ritz bar on Yosemite Avenue after I'd helped him all day putting in a septic. A guitar band played some Bob Wills songs that our folks had liked, and we nursed our drinks and smoked Marlboro Reds with the filters attached, not torn off the way the cowboys did. Three guys at a table taunted Jesse across the room. You could hardly hear what they said because of the wailing music, but from the way they laughed and waved around their cigarettes we got the message. Jesse now sported seventeen- or eighteen-inch arms without an ounce of fat on him. I don't think Muhammad Ali could've taken a street fight with him. He swiveled off the bar stool and walked over to the table without so much as glancing at me, not asking for help or expecting it, like always, and began to talk to one of the guys, who started to raise up, and soon all three of those guys were sprawled down flat on the floor. Out. Jesse knocked the crap out of them before they could even come up off their chairs. Cold, brutal, businesslike. I wished Dewey could've seen that one.

"One night," I told Mitch, "Jesse said to me, 'Let's go to Fresno. I'm going to get in the last fucking fight of my life.' We drove to a pool hall, where some guy had been mouthing off about how scared Jesse was to fight him, when Jesse said to me, 'Now why the fuck do I want to go kick the shit out of some poor son of a bitch in Fresno? I've got honey to pump and a driver to hire. Let's go home.'"

"He was getting more serious," Mitch said.

"Businesswise," I said, "but not otherwise."

I didn't help Jesse after he hired full-time workers. He had a plan. His old man never owned but one truck, or one-plus if you count his original small 1950s Ford, driven in a pinch by a sometimes helper. Jesse acquired four trucks and was looking for others. He didn't buy on credit neither. He paid his bills right away with cash-money, oftentimes from a big wad he kept folded in the front pocket of his Levi's. He didn't want to be bound with payments or to stockpile money to buy a house, at least not for a while. He lived with Ana in a rundown white-board house he rented for sixty a month outside of town with tall sycamores and mostly dirt around it. He parked his trucks in the back near the barn he worked out of and kept his tools and equipment in. All his money went into his rigs and his first twenty-acre piece of land with alfalfa that he leased out soon after buying it. Once he got another twenty acres he said he was going to farm it himself on the side. He was driving a five-year-old pickup while Ana was still driving the same car he had in high school. He just kept repairing it to keep it going. I figure he made Ana see how his way of doing things would pay off later.

"There were days," I told Mitch, "in a pinch, when he had more honey to pump and not enough time to get back to his station with his full truck, and he could always think of some royal asshole with a swimming pool, koi pond, Chevrolet Camaro, or trailer full of porta-potties where he could dump his load and get out of there. But he never dropped it on someone undeserving."

"I don't believe all those stories," Mitch said, "but I do know his valve jammed once and he drove through town splashing raw sewage down Yosemite Avenue."

"He was going to be unstoppable," I said. "His brother went on to become a millionaire twice over building shopping malls, and Jesse always outdone his brother."

Some people think Jesse married Ana for her money, but they got another think coming. Sonia had money, too, but neither of their fathers was going to help us. Jesse knew he had to work for everything he got. He wanted money, sure, he wanted to be noticed, he wanted to be accepted and liked, coming from the family he did, though deep down I think he feared he wouldn't be good enough. He liked Sonia's swimming pool and he liked Ana's ranch pond, but he knew they weren't going to be handed to him, and he didn't expect them to be. He liked having Ana attached to him, I believe, for everything she stood for, but I also think—on a day-to-day basis—he just felt more comfortable with Ana than with Sonia. I remember what Ana's daddy had told me when I asked to marry her, how she was spoiled and I couldn't provide for her needs, but that was more true of Sonia than Ana, and I think Jesse knew it. Ana didn't have pretensions. She was a country girl. She knew her place. At least that's what I thought back then, but Mitch didn't think so.

"Ana wasn't happy," Mitch said, "depriving herself until Jesse made it. She wasn't used to struggling that way. He married the wrong woman."

"Are you saying Sonia was the right woman?"

"No, and not for you either."

The fog lightened up as Mitch turned out of the ranch and headed toward town, passing Alpha Grocery, all boarded up. I told him, "I thought I was in hog heaven when I married Sonia."

Right after our wedding, I was still working on the ranch when we drained the pond to clean out the overgrown cattails and oversized carp. The Russian farmer Jesse and I had driven harrowbeds for came to the pond for the carp. Nobody else wanted them. It was a Sunday afternoon. Sonia was with myself and the Russian. As the pond drained down, we waded into the muddy water, black as dirty crankcase oil, swarming with fat carp, some almost two or three feet long, their silver backs slithering above the surface of the shallow water. The Russian was a real religious milk-drinking Molokan and wore a tunic over his shirt. He stood in the muddy water with a sharp butcher knife. Sonia and I held those strong, squirming fish while the

Russian cut their throats. Blood had to drip while he said a
prayer to purify them. After he drove off with the fish stuffed in
burlap sacks in the back of his pickup, it turned twilight and the
pond emptied down to its bottom of thick, greasy mud. Sonia
and I took off our wet clothes and squirmed around naked in
the mud, her screaming and me coming and her coming, too.

Jesse and I still didn't get together with our wives, which was
no big deal because we had separate jobs, separate friends, and
we were seeing less of each other except for a drink now and
then. Jesse and Ana had a baby boy, and me and Sonia had a girl.
"You'd think," Jesse joked one night when we were at a bar, "that
after the baby was born those doctors would take a little pity on
a guy and sew up that slit an inch or so. Next time Ana has a
baby, I'm going to make sure it's done."

I wish that was the only problem I had with Sonia after our
kid was born. Things slid south between us after that. I thought
I learned what Jesse must've known about her before I did. She
was bound to look down on me when she saw the situation she
found herself in. One night we were having a fight and she said,
"This is what I get for marrying a fucking wino loser." Course,
Sonia could put the drinks away, too. Maybe not like me, but
in her wild days back in high school she especially liked to belt
them back.

My working the graveyard shift at the winery didn't help.
It was a party out there. At one point, after I'd bid up to the
warehouse, I had keys to the brandy room, the champagne
room, every room. Me being stuck in the nightshift didn't spark
our sex life neither, me and Sonia's, and it grew worse during
crush season, when I worked around the clock on the scaffolds,
pumping down bennies to make it through the long hours. Bit
by bit things changed with Sonia, first with her not in the mood,
or mad at me so she slept on the couch on my nights off, and
after the baby came it got to where it was like fucking a board,

that is, if we did fuck. *My twat is my castle* was her position—*I can bar the door whenever I want.* That's what I got for marrying a doctor's daughter.

I took to hanging out at Skeeko's or the Ritz or the Kerman bars on weekends, often with Hank Palacios's brother, who also worked the nightshift. That crazy son of a bitch had Polaroids he took of blindfolded women tied to bedposts. I didn't want to think about the weird shit he tried with those dames, though I did try his weed. I had some wild times with a black chick I liked a lot, but even when things got wildest she warned me, "Don't touch my hair." One night, in a Kerman bar, Hank said I was pouring the coals to a broad on the pool table, but I don't remember a thing of it. Maybe the bastard was lying, but either way, I can't remember. What the hell good is that? I quit the wacky tabacky but it still kept happening. I could drive home from a bar and not remember a thing. Once I drove all the way to Bakersfield without remembering. I know what they say about blackouts: you can be an alcoholic and not have blackouts, but if you have blackouts you're an alcoholic.

I got scared. I didn't like what was happening, and after our baby was born I liked it less. At the time, I was flirting with a married gal at the winery, but it was slow going, only smooching at first, then playing with her titties and ass through her clothes, without touching skin—that's all she'd let me do—and I thought, *Hell, this is as bad as at home.* But I kept talking. On red bennies you can talk the balls off a brass billy goat. Or you think you can. We finally got naked, but she no sooner let me start banging her than she came up and said, "I'm marrying your boss, Sonny. I'm leaving the winery."

I wasn't the only one out there shocked. My floor boss had it made in the shade with a top job, a nice home, kids, wife, swimming pool—the whole shebang. We got along—me and my boss—from the time I was on the scaffold and stood up to him. I was changing some cross screws on a panel when he told me to do something else, and I said I was going to finish this job first, and he said, "I'm your boss," and I said, "I don't care if you're Jesus H. Christ. I've got to keep these berries moving."

After that, he respected me, and even liked me, I think. We both came from farmhand families. Our folks knew each other. I was only a worker at the winery, but he was high on the totem pole. Then he blew everything over a piece of ass. He was one of those guys who's so smart he's stupid. He lost his job, his home, his wife, his kids. "All for a gut with hair around it," Hank Palacios's brother said. People are killed every day, stabbed, shot, put in prison, all for a piece of ass. It takes over your mind. I seen it happen before, but this time I swiveled a hundred and eighty degrees and took a look at myself.

I tried to get back on track with Sonia, but we'd let things slide too far. We'd drifted along, me catting around and her taking care of Darlene and going to 4Cs to study accounting, hardly talking to each other. If we ate together, she kept her eyes directed toward her plate, away from me, not so much bringing the food up to her lips but lunging her mouth downward with quick jerks like the food might jump off the fork if she didn't lurch at it quick. She'd quit sleeping with me altogether. I brought up our shattered sex life, thinking if we could get back together in bed we could get together in other ways and turn this thing around.

"This has been going on for months, Sonia," I said.

She ate without looking at me. "Is that a fact?" she said.

I kept it up after supper. Sonia put our daughter to bed, but Darlene wouldn't go to sleep until I sang her a Hank Williams song she liked, "I'm So Lonesome I Could Cry." It was a Monday night, and Sonia wanted to watch *Laugh-In*. She put on a white cotton robe over her nightie and curled her legs under her on the couch, bending them at the knees like a vise. She tucked the skirt of her robe over her knees so she was encased like a cocoon. She lit a cigarette. The TV flickered. I stood by the coffee table.

"How would you like to be pulled off those cigarettes?" I said, talking to be heard above the loud TV. "How would that make you feel?"

"Okay," she snapped, her voice so sharp I felt my head flinch. "Come on." She flung the robe away from her knees and rolled her back onto the couch. She hooked her hands under her knees to pull them up to her chest, her nightie sliding down her bare legs. She lay on her back, her naked thighs forking into a V down to her rust-colored hair, matted like a rat's nest. I stood there, not believing what I was seeing. "Come on, fuck me," she said. "You want it so bad, big boy?"

How I felt in that moment was dead—not mad, not sad— just dead. All I could bring myself to say was "No," sounding so lame it made my chest go weak. The emptiness in my chest swelled with regret not just for what was happening to me but to Sonia, too, my wife and the mother of my daughter. Her grief-twisted face reminded me of Momma's when drunk out of her mind. I grabbed my blue-jean jacket from the hook by the door to head for the bar.

"Go on, you coward," she yelled at me. "Go fuck Jesse. That's all you wanted with me anyway."

I saw myself in my mind whirling around in a rage and slugging her—she'd never said anything like that to me before, and I was already thinking of Jesse when she'd called me "big boy," similar to how I remember taunting him with the spider at Camp Roberts—but I didn't do it. I didn't hit her. I didn't say nothing. I climbed into my pickup and screeched rubber, heading for the bar.

That was it. That night in Skeeko's I got into the fight with the guys who dragged me across the parking lot and broke both my wrists. I got no sympathy from Sonia. We'd as much as quit caring for each other. We hung together for Darlene, though we both knew without saying that the end was near. My mind locked onto one desire, to get those three guys who broke my arms.

One afternoon, I was doing wrist curls with dumbbells, seething with rage, thinking of those guys, when Sonia walked into the room, looking smart in a pair of tan slacks. "I'm leaving you," she said.

I answered her fast. "Don't let the screen door bang you in the ass."

"I'm not joking around," she said. "I want a divorce."

"Where do I sign?" I said.

Sonia moved to her own apartment on the other side of town, while I stayed in the house we were renting, shuttling our daughter back and forth. I started feeling the emptiness of the house, missing Sonia and Darlene, and of a sudden I recognized I didn't want a divorce. All alone in that empty house gave me fresh eyes. I didn't want to live the way we had, but I wanted us together, to do it right this time, to have a second chance. Just like now with Lynette, I didn't want to divorce her neither, which is why I didn't smart-mouth Lynette when she said she was leaving, because I knew I would miss her, like I missed Sonia. Surprising thing is she gave me some hope, Sonia did, for reconciliation, or at least I thought she did. Being apart seemed to make things different for her, too. We talked on the phone. She was nice when we met so I could see Darlene. Drinking alone in the house, I sang along with a record: *"Maybe if I pray every night, she'll come back to me."* Now I just think Sonia was leading me along, trying not to rock the boat until she could get her divorce.

"I don't know when I learned at what point Jesse got involved," I told Mitch as we drove through Madera in his Camry, past the big water tower with the arrow-pierced heart painted on it: ⌣ to show where we were, dead-center in the valley, the heart of California. I told Mitch, "After Sonia moved out, I was drinking coffee with Jesse one afternoon at the counter of the Fruit Basket, and I got to thinking if it wasn't for Sonia maybe me and him would be partners in business together, and I wouldn't be where I was then. I told him about Sonia leaving me, and while we talked, he sucked on one Marlboro after another, real nervous, but he didn't say what was on his mind, except he told me he was under a lot of stress, holding down two jobs, day and night."

"You and Sonia were split," Mitch said, "when Jesse was with her."

"I'm trying to tell you I didn't know when it started between him and her—how long it'd been going on. Maybe all that time I was blaming myself for what was happening with my marriage, she was running around with him and I was too stupid to know it. Here I was wanting my life settled down into something regular like what I thought Ana offered, and Jesse, who had what I wanted, was maybe bored and wanting Sonia's wildness, or at least how he remembered it. The cocksucker wanted it all."

"Sonia's point of view is what I'm talking about," Mitch said. "In her mind, you and she were split, the divorce was coming down the pike. She'd started proceedings. Jesse was about to leave Ana and marry her, and they were going to run the business together. She would keep the books and schedule the jobs."

"Maybe that's what Sonia thought," I said. "Maybe, too, all the time she was with me she was wishing to be with Jesse."

Driving east out of town toward the foothills, Mitch picked up speed through shreds of fog, past raw, puddled fields. Across the muddy flats, killdeers skittered on quick feet like waterbugs on a pond, squeaking, *killdee, killdee, killdee*. We headed toward the Coarsegold hills and my house.

I told Mitch, "One night I was drinking at the T-room in Parkwood Village, where Jesse tended bar, filling in for a friend. He didn't need to tend bar, but I think it gave him an excuse to be out at night away from Ana. He was burning the candle at both ends, digging septics and pumping honey during the day and bartending at night, and then, maybe, lighting another candle after the bar closed at two. I sat at the far corner of the bar, minding my own business, snakelike, Dewey-like, not listening to anything but hearing everything. Jesse was washing beer glasses. With one hand he pumped a glass up and down over the brush rod in the soapy water and then plunged it up and down in the tub of clean rinse water. He was telling some of his buddies at the bar, 'Oh boy, Ana almost caught me last night. I was out with some guy's wife and didn't get home till five-thirty. I kicked off my shoes and sneaked into the bedroom so as not to wake Ana. I unbuckled my belt and was sliding down my pants when Ana woke and said, "What are you doing, Jesse?" I pulled my pants right back up and buckled my belt. "I got a septic to put in," I said. "I was just leaving." I went into town and drank coffee at the Fruit Basket until it was really time to go to work.'"

The guys at the bar whooped it up over that story. Now in the car Mitch laughed, too, even though the joke was on his sister. "I see he stayed quick-witted," Mitch said. "And then you knew he was talking about you."

"No, I thought he *could* be talking about me. Maybe I wasn't the last to learn about him and Sonia, but I was close to it. I was out of work with my broke wrists and started sleuthing around. I saw Jesse's car parked in front of a motel on the old 99 strip. I waited until I saw him and Sonia come out. It was like a double whammy, a double betrayal. Here was Jesse, who was like my brother, and my wife—"

"Your former wife," Mitch said.

"We weren't divorced, I'm telling you. Anyway, it doesn't matter. She'd told me she'd never see Jesse again after he dumped her, and I believed her. That belief kept me blind. After I saw them come out of the motel, I bought the .38 pistol from a guy I knew, who used to be a cop. Inside my house when I held that cold pistol in my hand, felt its heft, I thought, *This is ridiculous.* I thought we could move past this. I thought Sonia could have her fling, but things would be okay if she gave it up and we kept our family together. That was my thought when I next saw her and told her I knew about her and Jesse."

Sonia didn't show any surprise when I told her. "I thought you knew," she said.

"Oh, sure, that makes a lot of sense. That's why you been sneaking around."

"Ana's pregnant. Jesse doesn't want her to know until after the baby comes."

I realized then that she—Sonia—was the one being duped. "He's stringing you along," I said. "After his baby's born, he'll dump you."

"He's not happy with Ana," she said. "Their marriage is on the rocks," but I could see she wasn't sure.

"That's just what you're trying to make yourself think."

"Ana's a homebody," Sonia said. "She doesn't like how he has to work long hours, always having to make phone calls or do books or repair equipment."

"Or run around with you."

"No, Sonny, that just started." She hadn't seen Jesse for years, she told me, until they chanced to meet when he was digging a neighbor's septic and got to talking about their marriages.

"We can make this thing work, Sonia—you, me, and Darlene."

"It hasn't worked. The sooner we face facts the better off we'll be—and Darlene, too. We made a mistake, Sonny. I made a mistake."

To look back on this swampy mess now makes me seem idiotic, but in the middle of a swamp things aren't so clear. Jesse's nervousness at the Fruit Basket when he sucked hard on those cigarettes, I believe, wasn't just because of him worrying about me finding out about him and Sonia, but also, and mostly, he wasn't sure about leaving Ana and their little boy and another on the way. Until a guy does something, you can't know he's really going to do it even if he says he is. If I could hold out long enough, I believed, she and Jesse would start clashing, his kid would be born, and he'd drop her, just like he did so many times before. Jesse's the last person I wanted Sonia to end up with— that's true—but I believed if he left her, or she left him, what happened between them wouldn't matter anymore, and things would come out right. Sonia would come back to me. We could be together again.

Sonia told me on the phone that she'd found an apartment in Fresno and was moving out of Madera. I drove an El Camino pickup at the time and offered to help her move, which I did, leaving Darlene with Sonia's stepmomma. We had lunch that day, and afterward drove back to Madera to load the rest of her stuff, finishing up around eight that night. I felt things looking up. We seemed to be getting along. We'd worked together all day, had lunch, and talked about a bookkeeping job she was looking to get. Not that tension wasn't there, but less than before.

"I brought up the reconciliation again," I told Mitch, "and promised Sonia I would do anything to keep her, Darlene, and myself together. I tried to convince her that Jesse was just bluffing about leaving Ana to marry her. She said she'd talk to Jesse about it. She looked to be weakening about the whole deal. Not weakening, maybe, but recognizing that Jesse's reason for not telling Ana was really an excuse."

"Sonia thought Jesse was going to marry her before," Mitch said, "and then he left her in the lurch."

"That's not how it happened that summer," I told him. "Jesse never told her the true story of why he broke up with her that summer, not till they started up again. She didn't know, and I didn't know until that night after helping her move. When her daddy found out she planned on getting married, he called Jesse over to the house. Both her parents—her dad and stepmother— were there. Her daddy told Jesse he wasn't good enough."

"That's what Sonia told you?"

"That's how the cow eats the cabbage. Those are her exact words."

Mitch drove past the Indian casino and turned up the road to my house. "Knowing Jesse, I can't figure why he didn't stand up to Sonia's folks and run off with her."

"Not if he believed what Sonia's daddy told him, he wouldn't."

"He ran off with Ana."

"That was later."

What I didn't tell Mitch was this: Sonia and I were in her new apartment, after she told me what happened that summer, when the phone rang and she went into the kitchen. "I can't talk now," she was saying. "He's here." The change in her tone of voice, more gentle and whispery than when she was talking to me, sent the blood roaring into my head. All the hurt and hatred and rage—whatever you want to call it—rushed through me.

I walked into the kitchen and said, "I've had it with your lying. Don't even try to tell me you're being straight with me."

She cupped her hand over the mouthpiece of the phone. "What the hell are you talking about? I haven't lied to you. I don't have anything to lie about."

"Saying you're going to talk to him. Stringing me on this way."

"You think I'm going to talk about this on the phone? You better go until you calm down. I told you I was going to talk to him. I meant what I said."

Those words stopped me. My mind felt blocked up. What I saw in her eyes, full of disgust at me, was there was no way out of this spot. Maybe if I'd left an hour earlier, maybe if Jesse hadn't called, maybe if I'd bit my tongue, maybe…but now things had gone too far.

"Give me that phone," I said.

She held the phone tight to her chest. "Get out of here, Sonny, or I'll call the cops."

"Go ahead and call them. Tell them some lies, too."

"Lying? Who's the liar, Sonny? Your whole life is a lie."

I grabbed at the phone, but she held on to it. "You're the liar," I said, "stringing me on, lying to keep me calm till you can run off with him. You two aren't stomping on me no more."

Something snapped in her eyes then and they filled not with fright but rage. "You're not telling me what the fuck I can or can't do."

"He's not going to have you," I said.

"Have me? Have me?" She was screaming at me. "He can have me whenever he wants."

I pulled the phone out of her hands and pushed her against the counter. I put the phone to my ear, knowing Jesse was on the other side, not knowing what I was going to say till I heard his voice, slow and steady, "Sonia, are you there? I'm coming over."

In my mind I saw his face when he threatened to shoot me at Camp Roberts with the M1 pointed at my head. "Jesse," I said, "this is Sonny. You keep away, you hear?"

His voice stayed calm. "Settle down, Sonny. Put Sonia on the phone. I need to talk to her."

"You're not talking to her. You're not doing nothing with her."

He spoke again, sounding much like me in the past when I tried to settle him down. "Let it go, Sonny. It's over with you two. She's left you."

"Not for you," I said. "You ain't having her."

"That's not for you to say."

"I'm saying it, and you better listen 'cause I'm not saying it again."

"Forget it, Sonny." Then he said without moving his voice out of neutral, "You know you were always second choice."

Sonia bounced off the sink counter and was pulling the phone away from me, screaming, "Stop it you two! Jesse, hang up! Sonny, get the fuck out of here!"

And that's when I told her, "We'll see who's first and second choice."

She couldn't get the phone away from me, but she pushed the plunger down to cut off the line. When I saw her eyes so hard and her face so full of hate, I knew there was no going back, not ever. I tore out of there in the El Camino and drove back to my house. It was around nine o'clock. I fished out the pistol from the drawer where I kept it hidden beneath my underwear. I popped open a quart of Coors and stared at the pistol on the kitchen table. The phone rang. It was Sonia, worried about how I'd screeched rubber driving off, scared I was going to get Darlene, trying to calm me down, saying she would talk to Jesse.

I told her, "He makes any more trouble for us, Sonia, and I'll shoot him." Hearing my own voice was like having a steam valve release pressure built up in me. I sensed how saying those words meant I didn't really want to do it. I wouldn't have said nothing to her if I did.

"Stay put," she said. "Give me time. I'm going to talk to him."

We hung up and I sucked on the beer. Then it hit me. Everything was different to what I thought it was. The situation grew real clear. Sure, she was going to talk to Jesse all right about reconciliation with me, but only as a way to threaten him to shit or get off the pot. I was just a pawn in her game with him. I chugged the beer, loaded the pistol, grabbed a double six-pack of yellow bellies, and headed back onto Highway 99, downing beer all the way to Fresno.

I rang the doorbell. No one answered. I looked in the window. All the lights were off. I drove up and down the dark, unfamiliar streets, then back to her apartment and rang the bell again, but she still wasn't back. It was after eleven. I parked the pickup a half-block away on a side street. On the radio the Ice Man was singing "For Your Precious Love." I switched off the radio, thinking of how I'd done the same thing to save the battery in the bamboo along Cottonwood Creek. I opened another beer and waited for her.

"I can't talk anymore about this," I told Mitch.

We sat inside my kitchen, and I offered him a beer. I didn't feel like drinking.

"Don't you have to feed the dogs?" Mitch asked.

"They're done eating," I said. "They're planted in the backyard." When Buddy and Lily weakened to the point of not eating, I'd thought about shooting them, but I couldn't do it. I took them to the vet and then buried them together in the same hole, side by side the way they'd been all their lives.

"Sorry to hear," Mitch said. "I know how you felt about them."

"I guess I'm learning how to accept it. They were good friends."

"Tell you what," Mitch said, "let me read you what I wrote, and you can tell me if I got it right."

"If that's what you want to do, go ahead."

"It's not that long. I'll start at the beginning."

Excepting for Jesse and the other people who were dead, Mitch changed the names in the story. He read about Jesse and me growing up together as best friends, our fights, our girlfriends, our days on the ranch and in the National Guard. He told about the time at Bass Lake when Jesse warned me of a big galoot threatening to kick my ass and then he told that guy I was saying the same thing about him, all so he could step in and take on the guy himself, claiming to protect me.

I found myself listening to Mitch read his story like it wasn't about me but someone like me, and other guys like me, just as Sonia and Ana, with different names, were like other girls I'd known. I kept listening, almost relieved in some strange way from what I was hearing, having it be about other people, like a play under lights in a school auditorium, different from the hot, jumbled-up dream pressing against the walls of my skull.

Then Mitch reached the bad part. His writing grew real clear. He described how after I left Sonia and drove back to my house to get the pistol, Jesse showed up at her apartment with a friend named Richard, who worked for him pumping honey. The three of them went to a bar for some beers. Sonia told Jesse I'd threatened to shoot him, but he laughed it off.

"That's enough," I told Mitch. "I know the rest."

"Where were you going after you shot Jesse?" Mitch asked.

"Back to Madera. I was thinking I had to fetch Darlene. I knew they'd be after me. I was going to load her and some of my stuff into the pickup and head out of there. I didn't know where. I was going to run for it the same way Dewey did after cutting that guy. I wasn't thinking right."

I'd drunk seven, maybe eight cans while waiting in the pickup, not counting what I'd downed beforehand. I raced north on 99 with the gas pedal slammed to the floorboard, the speedometer needle buried and quivering at a hundred and ten, the blurry highway nearly empty with some cars pulled off to the side for drowsy drivers to catch a few winks like they did in those years. Red taillights flashed in front of me and I swerved to miss them, then I overcorrected. The pickup went airborne and careened across the median through white-flowering oleander bushes that slapped against the windshield. I skidded

into the southbound lane of oncoming traffic, busting through
the wire fence on the southwest side of the highway, just
missing a parked car, then rolling several times down the road
bank into the grapevines.

A truck driver pulled over, helped me into his cab, and drove
me to Dearborn Hospital, where the highway patrol and the
police showed up. My spine was fractured again, my face a
cut-up mess. I was charged with first-degree homicide.

Like I'd told Mitch earlier, the trial seemed a made-up play,
separate from what really happened, a little like the words he
wrote but in a different language. My lawyer found witnesses
to testify against Jesse. It was like Jesse got put on trial, not me.
I probably wouldn't have had a decent lawyer to turn things
around that way if Sonia's daddy hadn't paid for him. They
didn't come to the trial—Sonia's folks—but they'd taken my side
against her from the time we split, maybe for Darlene's sake.
They didn't want her with Jesse neither.

An important witness for me was a prisoner in the county
jail who was let out to testify that he'd seen Jesse open a sharp
pocketknife in a bar and wave it around in a threatening manner.
This testimony, my lawyer said, was "necessary and material to
the defense of Mr. Childers" because it showed how Jesse not
only had a "violent, aggressive, and dangerous character" and
frequently provoked fights, but he also carried a knife, so that
"Mr. Childers was justified in his fear and apprehension of him
to have a gun to defend himself, and said evidence is relevant to
Mr. Childers's state of mind at the time of said homicide."

A charge of assault with a deadly weapon against Sonia and
that guy Richard also hung over me, but the judge ordered
the jury to find from the evidence whether on that night I had
a "substantially reduced mental capacity due to intoxication,
mental illness, or any other cause," because if my "mental
capacity was so diminished," and the jury had reasonable doubt

about whether I formed a "specific intent" to shoot Sonia or Richard, then the jury couldn't find me guilty.

All I can say is there was a lot of morality in those days. A judge back then would ask why a person would do such and such a thing, like kill a man for running around with his wife. What was the killer's state of mind? There was immorality, too, just like now, but there was also more morality. The jury dismissed the charge of assault against Sonia and Richard and found me guilty of displaying and using a deadly weapon. I sure enough was drunk, or I otherwise wouldn't have shot at them. For shooting Jesse, I was convicted of voluntary manslaughter.

My supposed state of mind, I think, was why I got sent to Folsom State Prison, with its unit for psychological evaluation. I wasn't insane, but I felt insane, locked in a bad dream I couldn't wake up from, like I'd told the police, and couldn't remember whole either, just fragments of it.

I learned how to survive in prison by being ready to die for a penny on the floor. I wouldn't back off. That's how I got left alone. Whether I was really crazy enough to die for a penny on the floor wasn't the point. Other inmates and guards couldn't be sure. That was the message I had to get across.

No one can know how it is in prison without doing it. Johnny Cash hadn't done time, I realized the moment I heard him sing "Folsom Prison Blues." He was just singing a song. The inmates whooping and cheering on the record after he sang the line—*"I shot a man in Reno just to watch him die"*—was dubbed in later. No inmates cheered in real life.

I served nearly five years, counting the time in jail between the murder and the trial. Murder is the right word. No matter what the judge or jury said, I knew I had murdered Jesse. I just couldn't believe it.

"You look upset," Mitch told me after he'd finished reading to me.

"Why shouldn't I?" I said. I'd come a long way, I knew, from those prison days when my face maintained a state of NR—no reaction. "I believe you would, too, if you were me. I'd rather you didn't print this story. I guess you have a right to tell what you want, but you shouldn't have put in that part about the pine needle."

"The pine needle?" Mitch said. "Of all the stuff I reported you're upset about that?"

I knew I wasn't thinking right. I'd told him not to tell Lynette about the rich girl and me out in the woods, and I guess he hadn't—not directly anyway. Who knew whether Lynette would read the story, and what did it matter, now that we were split? Funny how something like that pricked me, first the pine needle years ago, and then the memory of it. In prison I saw it happen more than once, how guys felt shame for some little thing. An inmate once started crying for remembering how he'd hurt his kid brother's feelings years earlier, but he didn't give two shits for the guy he'd stabbed thirteen times.

"Have you talked to Lynette?" I asked Mitch.

"I have," he said. "She told me the story about the pine needle herself. She said you'd told her."

"If people keep saying that I said or did something, when in my memory it's like I wasn't even there, I think my mind is going to snap."

I didn't recollect telling Lynette that story, though I must've because I told her everything, or almost everything, when we hooked up and she as much as saved my life. I remember we moved into a nice neighborhood, a lot fancier than where Sonia grew up across town in the house with palm trees, a place that didn't look too swanky to me anymore. Lynette was leery about living in the new tract, but that's where I wanted to be. I'd done my time and wanted to start over.

One day not long after we married and moved in with her daughter, who was then fourteen, I waved to a high-hat neighbor lady and said, "Howdy, ma'am. How're you doing today?" and she gave me this my-shit-don't-stink look and said, "You're the new people here, aren't you? I want you to know that my family and I don't like to be disturbed." I don't think she knew who I was, I mean, in relation to Jesse. It was that kind of neighborhood, though: you didn't make your neighbor's acquaintance, and they didn't want to make yours. Not mine anyway.

Lynette and I soon plowed into what Father Dan called "temporary turbulence," inevitable in a marriage, he said, but able to be overcome. He gave me a call and drove down from Sacramento to visit. It was Saturday and Lynette was working the weekend shift at the hospital. Father Dan wore black pants and black shoes, but instead of his priest's collar he sported a dull plaid shirt that I came to learn priests consider pretty wild when they're trying to dress casual.

Father Dan was blunt—that's what I liked about him from the time I met him in prison. He looked tired, as usual, when I told him how my life was going good until Lynette and I started having these scraps, much of it my fault for drinking and catting around, and he said, "Love your wife, Sonny."

"You have to understand," I told him, "it's not just a one-sided deal in this household."

"I don't care how many sides it has," Father Dan said. "I'm talking about you. Love your wife. No 'buts.' You're not the only husband who needs to be told. One counseling session is all I'd need to tell other husbands what I'm telling you."

"But you don't know Lynette."

"I don't want to know her," Father Dan said. "I don't need to know her. Love your wife." Then he asked me, "Sonny, do you know the difference between loving and fucking?"

"No," I said, probably too quick, like it was a joke question someone would ask you in a bar.

"My sweet aching ass," Father Dan said. "No conditions, Sonny. It's willing the good of the one you love." He gave me some Bible passages to study, and after he left I read in Ephesians the same thing he told me about husbands needing to love their wives the same way Christ loved the church: God didn't calculate conditions for loving us, he just did. I'd be shit flat out of luck if he looked for reasons to love me.

I also read how the wife is the weaker vessel. That idea, I knew, was sure to go over real big with Lynette. Advice from priests, Father Dan included, was that way: they would say something that blew away the fog, like this thing about love, but the next bit they added, like wives being weaker vessels, would be off the wall, maybe not screwy if we lived in olden times, but nutty now.

We managed to maneuver ourselves back on track, Lynette and me, and though I followed Father Dan's advice best I could, it was Lynette's love, I think, that did the real work. She's the one who found the house in the mountains and said we had to move out of the valley, out of the fog, away from the uppity neighborhood and people who kept me thinking about Jesse. She turned me serious about church. The more I got into it the more sense it made about how grace can save your life, if you ready yourself. Then Trisha's birth really changed me. No way my new daughter, I swore, was going to grow up with a carousing and drunk daddy the way Darlene did.

Now, fifteen years later, I'd let them—Trisha and Lynette—slip away just like Sonia and Darlene. I felt like a jackrabbit I'd seen on the ranch when I was out hunting in the rain once. A soaked jackrabbit ran directly at me, bounding almost like a dog through the spreading floodwater, shallow enough for the rabbit, though losing strength, to get purchase on the ground underneath so it could leap and lurch toward me. The rabbit was three-quarters across the field and looked able to make it to clear ground when all of a sudden it turned around and started running back in the wrong direction into the deeper gray flood from where it came until I lost sight of it.

"I really fucked up with Lynette," I told Mitch.

My back was killing me in the kitchen chair. We went into the living room, where I sat in my comfortable chair. Mitch kicked back on the couch with his beer. I didn't turn on the lights. Mitch sat in the shadows. "You can unfuck it," he said.

I hadn't talked to Lynette in a month. When she left she said she was entirely to blame, but I knew it was me, just sitting around the house, molding over, not looking to work, not doing what I said I'd do, not doing anything but drinking and lying about it. Any man would look good compared to me. "I imagine she's settled in pretty well by now," I said.

"She's not with anybody," Mitch said, "at least when I saw her. Just her and Trisha. She told me Trisha missed you."

The deliberate way Mitch spoke made me think he was delivering a message from Lynette. "When she left," I said, "she was going off with a guy at the hospital."

"Not anymore," Mitch said. "I talked to her. I think she would reconcile."

I felt a lift in my chest that I tried to let settle down. I hadn't even let myself dream that Lynette and I would reconcile after she walked out. I think I reached a point where I learned to live without dreams. My life was dream enough. I was back at work, getting along. I didn't call Lynette or snoop after her the way I'd done with Sonia, not wanting to make that mistake all over again. I just let her be. Now Mitch's words, the warm way he said them along with what he said, gave me reason to hope.

"I miss Lynette, too," I told Mitch, "her and Trisha both. No one's here to smart-mouth me now that Trisha's gone." I knew I was sounding a little giddy, but I couldn't help it. "From the time she was a little kid Trisha had a sharp tongue."

"From her mother, no doubt," Mitch said.

"I remember one time this old boy from the winery was visiting us—Trisha was about six—and he was telling me how he went about receiving government checks as an enrolled Indian. I said I'd like some of that money to come my way, seeing as how my grandma on my daddy's side—my real dad, not Dewey—was full-blood, and Trisha, who's listening to us, asks this old boy, 'Are you an Indian?' and he puts his nose up in the air and says, 'I am one hundred percent Native American,' and Trisha says, 'You look like a Mexican to me.'" I saw Mitch's nose twitch, but he didn't laugh, and I said, "Kids don't lie."

Mitch drained his beer and said, "I have to get going. I would give Lynette a ring, if I were you."

When he stood up, I asked him, "Did you talk to Sonia and Ana, too?" Sonia, like Ana, fled the valley after remarrying, but to the opposite end of the state, up north. Neither came back to the valley.

"I did," Mitch said. "Sonia still carries a torch for Jesse. Ana's very bitter."

"I can see how Ana would be that way."

"Not about Jesse," Mitch said. "She's bitter about you. She had her baby the month after the shooting, and she named him after Jesse. What does that tell you?"

If I heard the reverse—that Sonia was still angry about me killing the man she thought was going to leave his wife and marry her—that would be one thing. "Jesse was cheating on Ana," I said. "He was planning to leave her."

"Ana's bitter about everything," Mitch said, "except Jesse. That's why I don't see her much. She feels justice wasn't done."

I sensed the old turmoil coming back from the days when I left prison but hadn't felt released. Back then I felt like a rat let out of one cage and locked into another, and now I felt the same way. No way could I find peace no matter what I tried.

I remember one night a few months after serving my term, I was at Farnesi's, nursing a drink at the bar, when Mitch walked into the restaurant, the first time I'd bumped into him since shooting Jesse. Mitch was still married then and came to dinner with his wife. I went up to his table and asked to see him outside. He gave his wife this wary look but followed me into the dark parking lot, where the roar of the highway traffic forced me to repeat myself.

"What did you say?" Mitch stood tense among the parked cars outside the restaurant, still not knowing what was up.

I stepped closer, facing him with my arms straight down by my sides and said, "Okay, do what you have to do."

"What the hell are you talking about?" Mitch said. He didn't step back.

"I killed your brother-in-law. Go ahead, do what you have to do."

Mitch's shoulders untensed and slumped. "Sonny, you did your time," he said. "I'm not going to do anything."

I started to sob, my arms still stiff, tears running down my face.

Father Dan said I had to tell Jesse's friends, one by one, I was sorry, and though I wasn't expecting it, one by one, they told me they were sorry, too, but held nothing against me. I didn't talk to Ana or Sonia, but I did seek out a lot of other people who'd loved Jesse. "If you hadn't done it," one said, "someone else would've." Another told me, "Jesse had no business doing what a married man shouldn't." Even Mitch back then said, "Live by the sword, die by the sword." Maybe they were hiding other feelings, but one by one they made me feel forgiven, except for one woman friend of Ana's, who said, "You're a loser, Sonny. Always were."

She was the only one who spoke mean that way, though, and like I said, I didn't talk to Ana or Sonia themselves. I did track

down the highway patrolman who'd come to the hospital with
the other cops to arrest me. I knew him from high school, when
he was in the class behind me. After getting out on parole, I
waited in my pickup across the street while I watched him giving
someone a ticket. When he finished and pulled his cruiser up
to me, I saw in his face that he didn't know what I was going to
do. He hadn't seen me since that night in the hospital when he'd
arrested me. As far as he knew, I was out of prison and meaning
to shoot him. That night at the hospital he hadn't bullied or
bad-mouthed me like I was scum the way some cops would do.
"I just want to thank you," I told him, "for treating me like a
person that night." Afterward, when we sat together in the high
school gym at a wrestling match, he told me that when I was
talking to him that day he'd pulled out his .357 Magnum and
held it pointed and ready inside the door of his patrol car.

Now in the dark living room, I asked, "Mitch, what are your
thoughts now? Do you have hard feelings toward me?" I was still
thinking of what he said about Sonia and Ana.

Mitch didn't pause enough to blink. "Not a one," he said.

I felt my throat tightening up. "If there was any way I could
change things, I would."

"I know you would, but that's all behind now. That doesn't
mean I don't feel bad for Jesse, even if he brought it on himself.
Lots of people feel sorry about him."

"I'm sorry, too," I said, feeling something screwed up as soon
as I said it. Something seemed terribly wrong until I realized
what it was and I told Mitch, "Hell, why's everybody feel so
sorry for Jesse? I'd rather be him than me."

That night, after Mitch left, I had a dream, brighter and
sharper than the ghostly dreams of past years, the only dream,
in fact, where one thing clearly followed another. I saw Jesse in
the Catholic church in Madera. That was the odd part, because
the only time I was in a Madera church with him—a Protestant

church—was back in high school when a friend of ours married
a girl from another town he'd gotten pregnant at our New Year's
Eve party. In my dream I walked up the aisle and saw Jesse
leaning against the sidewall under a stained-glass window with
his arms folded across his chest, looking relaxed and easy with
himself in the way of a resting cat. I awaited the lifting of his
chin that guys in the high school hallways liked to get from him
to show that he knew them, an exchange between guys like a
signal between members of a secret society. In my dream, Jesse
noticed me and smiled in a way that made me realize that he
sent out the affection that everyone like Sonia and Ana, even me
and Mitch, kept returning to him now. I was glad to see him,
but he also was glad to see me. In my dream, we were glad to see
each other.

Spring came. April, the sweetest month, my favorite month,
marked the year's beginning for me ever since I was a kid, with
the hills green as a felt pool table after the winter rains, the
fields ready for planting, and the long, wild grass taking my
mind back to what the valley must have looked like when elk
and grizzlies roamed here and the sky was so thick with ducks
and geese they looked like clouds. After several dry years, we
finally had a pretty good snowpack in the mountains, and I
was on the road, managing farmers' allotments for the Madera
Irrigation District, riding the ditch banks I'd stolen water from
as a field hand but now protected. I was getting along on my
own with Hamburger Helper and cans of Campbell's soup,
which were a treat when I was a kid. Since I wasn't drinking at
night, just watching the Food Channel until I fell asleep, I was
up fresh before dawn. Getting up in the dark made me think
how Sam used to gripe about Daylight Savings Time making
the mornings even darker for us ranch workers. "If those city
people want another hour of daylight," Sam used to say, "why
don't they get up an hour earlier?" With my travel mug full of

steaming coffee, the farm news on the pickup radio, and Table
Mountain, as we now call it, in the rearview mirror, I drove into
the valley before the burning red crescent of the sun broke over
the Sierras behind me.

Mitch was right about Lynette. I didn't call her, but I saw her
at church, where we talked. Either the thing with the guy at the
hospital hadn't lasted or hadn't really started, one, but she'd said
right from the get-go her reason for leaving wasn't someone else,
so it was enough when she said she wasn't seeing anyone and
would consider getting back together.

"Trisha misses you," she said. "I miss you, too."

"How do I know you won't leave again?" I said.

"You don't," she said.

On Easter Sunday, in the church pew ahead of me, Lynette
wore an outfit that hugged her thighs, lavender-colored like
a dyed Easter egg ready for peeling. I thought of the tender
whiteness underneath the lavender shell.

"We have to move step by step here," Lynette said. "I think
we should get some counseling."

I wanted to say I'd rather have a root canal. Instead, I told her,
"What if I don't want to do that?"

"I'd still try to work things out," she said, "though I think
counseling would help us."

"I'll do it," I said.

I don't know how much Mitch might've told Lynette about
how I was living, but when I went back to work it wasn't with
the hope of enticing her. I was doing what Father Dan had told
me when I struggled with my guilt for killing Jesse. "No matter
how many times a man sinks, there's a chance for redemption,"
Father Dan told me, direct like always, "but you have to do
something, Sonny. You can't just pray and think about things or
you'll be spinning your wheels. You can't just do time." That's
when he told me to quit running in my mind the scene of Jesse

coming through the door reaching for me. "Damn it," Father Dan said. "Do something."

Without expecting Lynette's help, I did do something. What mattered to me in return was that Lynette didn't lay threats on me like, "If you quit working…If you start drinking…If you don't see a shrink…" She said she'd consider coming back, period.

After Mass, I drove by myself over to Arbor Vitae Cemetery and parked the car facing the city of tombstones, flooded in sunlight. I knew where Dewey and Momma were buried. Nellie and Old Antiguo were buried on the other side of town in Calvary Cemetery, where Sam and Mrs. Etcheverry slept in aboveground crypts. I had no idea where they'd planted Jesse. Over a tombstone in the distance rose a weird column of silvery light. I thought of the ghosts Nellie had seen. I stared through the dusty windshield at the silver light and remembered that night when I sat in the pickup watching Jesse return from the bar, get out of his septic truck, and walk up the sidewalk toward the dark apartment with Sonia shoulder to shoulder next to him. I always knew I was second pickings. He didn't have to say it.

I rang the doorbell. When Jesse's friend Richard opened the door, I pushed the muzzle of the .38 into his stomach. I heard Jesse holler from the kitchen, "Who is it?"

"I don't know," Richard yelled back.

Through the kitchen doorway came Jesse, walking toward me fast. I swung the pistol and shot twice at him but missed. Jesse charged me and I fired two more shots. He groaned and dropped to the floor on his hands and knees. I turned and shot at Richard, who ran into the bathroom and slammed the door. I fired twice at the door, and the metallic hammer snapped on an empty chamber.

I swiveled open the cylinder and fumbled out the extra cartridges I'd stuffed into the front pocket of my jeans, dropping some bullets while reloading, my hands were shaking so bad. Jesse lurched to his feet and grabbed an end table next to the couch, knocking a lamp and magazines to the floor. With the round table in front of him like a shield, he backed into the bedroom and banged the door shut. The lock clicked. I was shoving the last cartridge into the chamber when Sonia ran out of the kitchen and tried to stop me. She grabbed and scratched at my hands, yelling, "Sonny, no!"

I knocked her away and shouted, "I can kill you, too!" I pushed her hard against the wall, her legs flew out, and her butt dropped to the floor. With her back against the wall, she lifted her hands to her face and covered her eyes.

I raised my foot and kicked my heel hard against the bedroom door just above the doorknob. Wood splintered, the door flew open, and Jesse lunged through the doorway, coming at me, raising his arm, as I backed up, firing the pistol. Jesse fell to the floor on his chest. His hips twisted as he tried to bring his legs up to swing onto his knees. I bent over and shot him in the bone behind his ear. I then pointed the pistol toward Sonia and fired two shots that slammed into the wall behind her.

The column of light had disappeared from the tombstone. I stared through the windshield and started to cry. At Mass that morning, I'd prayed for Jesse, and I promised to remember him every Sunday during prayers for the dead, like I'd done many times before. Did he have a chance? I'm wondering if in that moment of dying did Jesse have a chance to repent and say, "Lord, I want to accept you as my savior." Was there time? I'd loved him so much. In that hour of need, in that last moment, was there still hope and a chance?

The police report said I shot Jesse four times—in the leg, the shoulder, the throat, and the head. The way he lay stretched out in the hall with his feet at the bedroom door showed how he'd come out of the bedroom toward the gun. His chest lay pressed flat on the floor with his hips corkscrewed, one leg on top of the other, knees bent, his head turned. The side of his face rested on his left hand. His sightless eyes gazed at the wall. His right arm was cocked toward his head, his hand doubled into a fist. He was twenty-seven, same age as me.

ACKNOWLEDGMENTS

Many people helped with the making of this book. For their memories, stories, or informational details, my heartfelt thanks go to Ray April, Ralph Clement, Sonny Clement, Jonathan Deschere, Sheryl Daggett, Ronn Dominici, Chris Fenner, Kay Frauenholtz, Coann Garvey, George Jones, Roy Jones, Marie Hardin, Willie Hibdon, Leon Lancaster, Fred Massetti, Don Nelson, Steve Sagouspé, Bill Sterling, Tina Unti, Short Watson, Jerry Weinberger, Allen Wier, and Carol Wilkins. I'm also indebted to James N. Gregory's splendid history, *American Exodus: The Dust Bowl Migration and Okie Culture in California*.

I'm deeply grateful to those who read this story in manuscript and offered helpful responses and valuable editing: Mark Bergon, Roser Caminals-Heath, Barbara Frick, Leonard Gardner, Bill Heath, David Means, Zeese Papanikolas, Amira Pierce, Paul Russell, Jim Unti, Ann Vernon, and Jack Vernon.

For the transition from manuscript to print, the equanimity and loyalty of my literary agent, Tracy Brown, proved invaluable, as did the publishing vision of Malcolm Margolin, the inspiration of Gayle Wattawa, and the enthusiastic cooperation of Lillian Fleer, Lisa K. Manwill, Natalie Mulford, Susan Pi, Lorraine Rath, Julian Segal, and the entire team at Heyday.

This novel would not have been written were it not for the effort of two friends whose shared interest in this story goes back to our high school days: Frank April tirelessly searched out people with information, urging me on when I was ready to quit, and Joe Claassen influenced my writing of the novel at every phase, from its inception, through its drafts, to its final publication.

My deepest debt, as always, is to Holly St. John Bergon, whose good judgment oversaw everything.

ABOUT THE AUTHOR

Frank Bergon was born in Ely, Nevada, and grew up on a ranch in Madera County in California's San Joaquin Valley. He is the author of the novels *Wild Game, The Temptations of St. Ed & Brother S,* and *Shoshone Mike,* and the editor of *The Wilderness Reader* and the Penguin Classics *The Journals of Lewis and Clark.*

HEYDAY
into California

About Heyday

Heyday is an independent, nonprofit publisher and unique cultural institution. We promote widespread awareness and celebration of California's many cultures, landscapes, and boundary-breaking ideas. Through our well-crafted books, public events, and innovative outreach programs we are building a vibrant community of readers, writers, and thinkers.

Thank You

It takes the collective effort of many to create a thriving literary culture. We are thankful to all the thoughtful people we have the privilege to engage with. Cheers to our writers, artists, editors, storytellers, designers, printers, bookstores, critics, cultural organizations, readers, and book lovers everywhere!

We are especially grateful for the generous funding we've received for our publications and programs during the past year from foundations and hundreds of individual donors. Major supporters include:

Anonymous; James Baechle; Bay Tree Fund; B.C.W. Trust III; S. D. Bechtel, Jr. Foundation; Barbara Jean and Fred Berensmeier; Berkeley Civic Arts Program and Civic Arts Commission; Joan Berman; Peter and Mimi Buckley; Lewis and Sheana Butler; California Council for the Humanities; California Indian Heritage Center Foundation; California State Library; California Wildlife Foundation/California Oak Foundation; Keith Campbell Foundation; Candelaria Foundation; John and Nancy Cassidy Family Foundation, through Silicon Valley Community Foundation; The Christensen Fund; Compton Foundation; Lawrence Crooks; Nik Dehejia; George and Kathleen Diskant; Donald and Janice Elliott, in honor of David Elliott, through Silicon Valley Community Foundation; Federated Indians of Graton Rancheria; Mark and Tracy Ferron; Furthur Foundation; The Fred Gellert Family Foundation; Wallace Alexander Gerbode Foundation; Wanda Lee Graves and Stephen Duscha; Walter & Elise Haas Fund; Coke and James Hallowell; Carla Hills; Sandra and Chuck Hobson; James Irvine Foundation; JiJi Foundation; Marty and Pamela Krasney; Guy Lampard and Suzanne Badenhoop; LEF Foundation; Judy McAfee; Michael McCone; Joyce Milligan; Moore Family Foundation; National Endowment for the Arts; National Park Service; Theresa Park; Pease Family Fund, in honor of Bruce Kelley; The Philanthropic Collaborative; PhotoWings;

Resources Legacy Fund; Alan Rosenus; Rosie the Riveter/WWII Home Front NHP; The San Francisco Foundation; San Manuel Band of Mission Indians; Savory Thymes; Hans Schoepflin; Contee and Maggie Seely; Stanley Smith Horticultural Trust; William Somerville; Stone Soup Fresno; James B. Swinerton; Swinerton Family Fund; Thendara Foundation; Tides Foundation; TomKat Charitable Trust; Lisa Van Cleef and Mark Gunson; Whole Systems Foundation; John Wiley & Sons; Peter Booth Wiley and Valerie Barth; Dean Witter Foundation; and Yocha Dehe Wintun Nation.

Board of Directors

Getting Involved

To learn more about our publications, events, membership club, and other ways you can participate, please visit www.heydaybooks.com.